World's Best Loved Classics

Heidi

Johanna Spyri

Book Essentials Promotions, Inc.
New York • Indianapolis • Boca Raton

HEIDI
World's Best Loved Classics

Cover Art by MJ Studios
Jim Seward

ISBN: 1-56960-210-7

World's Best Loved Classics are published by
Book Essentials Promotions, Inc.

Published in the United States of America

PRINTED IN THE UNITED STATES OF AMERICA

0 9 8 7 6 5 4 3 2 1

Contents

Part One

Heidi's Years of Learning and Travel

Part Two

Heidi Makes Use of What She Has Learned

PART ONE

Heidi's Years of Learning and Travel

Chapter 1

The Alm-Uncle

From the pleasantly situated old town of Maienfeld a footpath leads up through shady green meadows to the foot of the mountains, which, as they gaze down on the valley, present a solemn and majestic picture. Anyone who follows it will soon catch the keen fragrance of grassy pasture lands, for the footpath goes up straight and steep to the Alps.

One bright, sunny June morning, a tall, sturdy-looking girl, evidently a native of the mountains, was climbing this narrow path. She led by the hand a little maiden, whose cheeks glowed as if a ruddy flame were under her dark-brown skin. And what wonder? In spite of the hot June sun, the child was bundled up as if for protection against the sharpest cold. She could not have been five years old, but it was impossible to tell anything about her natural figure, for she wore two or three dresses, one over the other, and a big red cotton scarf round her neck; her feet were lost in heavy hobnailed shoes, and the little thing was quite formless as she made her hot and laborious way up the mountain.

At the end of an hour of steady climbing the two girls came to the group of houses that lies halfway up the Alm Mountain and is called Dörfli, or the Little Village. Here they were greeted from almost every cottage, and by everyone in the street, for the older of the two girls had reached her home. Nevertheless, she made no pause but hurried on, answering all questions and greetings as she went. At the very end of the hamlet, as she was passing the last of the scattered cottages, a voice from the doorway cried, "Wait a moment, Dete, I'll go with you, if you are bound up the mountain."

The girl addressed stopped; immediately the child withdrew her hand and sat down on the ground.

"Are you tired, Heidi?" asked her companion.

"No, I am hot," replied the little girl.

"We are almost there," said her companion encouragingly. "You must put out all the strength you have for a little while longer; it won't take us more than an hour."

Just then a large, pleasant-looking woman came out of the cottage and joined them. The little girl jumped to her feet and followed the two women, who had instantly fallen into a lively conversation regarding all the inhabitants of the village and of the neighborhood.

"But really, Dete, where are you taking the child?" asked the new-comer. "It is your sister's little girl, isn't it—the orphan?"

"Yes, it is," replied the other. "I am taking her up to her grandfather; she will have to stay there."

"What! the little girl is going to live with the Alm-Uncle? You must have lost your senses, Dete! How can you think of doing such a thing? The old man will send you back with such a scheme as that."

"He can't do it; he's her grandfather, and it is time for him to look out for her; I have had her till now, and I must tell you, Barbel, that I could not think of letting her hinder me from taking such a place as I have just had offered me. Her grandfather must do his part now.

"That's very well, if he were like other men," urged Barbel with some indignation. "But you know what he is. What will he do with a child—especially with such a young one? He won't hear of such a thing—But where are you going?"

"To Frankfurt," said Dete. "I have an extra good place there. The family was down at the Baths last summer; I had charge of their rooms, and they wanted then to take me back with them. I couldn't manage it; but they are here again this year, and still want me to go with them, and I am going; you may be sure of that."

"I'm glad I'm not in the child's place!" cried Barbel with a shrug of the shoulders. "Nobody knows what ails the old man up there. He will have nothing to do with a living soul; from one end of the year to the other he never sets foot in a church; and if once in a twelvemonth he comes down with his thick staff, everyone keeps out of his way and is afraid of him. With his heavy gray eyebrows and his tremendous beard he looks like a heathen and a savage, and people are glad enough not to meet him alone."

"Nevertheless," said Dete stubbornly, "he's her grandfather, and it's his business to look after the child; he won't do her any harm; if he does, he will have to answer for it."

"I should like to know," said Barbel inquisitively, "I should really like to know what the old man has on his conscience that makes him look so fierce and live all alone up there on the Alm and keep almost hidden from sight. People tell all sorts of stories about him; of course you must know something about it, Dete; your sister must have told you; hasn't she?"

"Of course she has, but I hold my tongue; if he should hear of it, I should suffer!"

But Barbel had long desired to know the real cause of the Alm-Uncle's strange behavior, and why it was that he looked so gloomy and lived by himself on the mountain, and why people always spoke of him in a low voice, as if they were afraid to be against him and yet would not say anything in his favor.

Barbel also was ignorant of the reason that all the people in the village called him the Alm-Uncle, for of course he could not be the actual uncle of all the inhabitants; but as everyone called him so, she did the same and never spoke of the old man as anything else than Ohi, which in the speech of that region means uncle.

Barbel had only recently married into the village; before that her home had been down in the valley at Prättigau, and she was not familiar with all the happenings and all the curious characters of the village and the surrounding region through a long series of years.

Her good friend Dete, on the other hand, was a native of the village and had lived there till within a year. Then her mother had died and she had gone down to Ragatz, where the Baths are, and had found a fine position as chambermaid in a great hotel. She had come from Ragatz that very morning with the little girl, having had the chance to ride as far as Maienfeld on a hay wagon which an acquaintance of hers was driving home.

Barbel thought that this was a good chance to find out something, and she was bound not to let it slip. She seized Dete's arm familiarly and said, "But one can learn the real truth from you instead of the gossip which is talked; I am sure you know the whole story. Come now, just tell me what is the matter with the old man; has he always been so feared? Has he always been such a hermit?"

"I can't tell whether he has always been so or not; I am twenty-six now, and he is certainly seventy, and of course I never saw him when he was young; you might know that. If I were certain that he would never again be seen in all Prättigau, I might tell you all sorts of things about him; my mother was from Domleschg, and so was he."

"There now, Dete, what do you mean?" exclaimed Barbel, a little offended. "You need not be so severe on our gossip in Prättigau; and, besides, I can keep a secret or two if need be. Now tell me; you shan't regret it."

"Well, then, I will; but mind you hold your tongue," said Dete warningly. Before she began she glanced round to see if the little girl were so close at their heels as to hear every word that was said. The child was not to be seen; she must have ceased following them some distance back, but in their lively conversation they had not noticed it. Dete stood still and gazed all round. There were several turns in the foot-path; nevertheless they could see almost all the way down to the village. Not a soul was in sight.

"I see her!" exclaimed Barbel. "There she is! Don't you see her?" and she pointed with her finger to a place quite distant from the path. "She is climbing up the cliffs with the goatherd Peter and his goats. Why is he so late today with his animals? But it is just as well, for he can look after the child, and you will be all the better able to talk with me."

"Peter needn't trouble himself to look after her," remarked Dete. "She is not dull for a child of five years; she keeps her eyes open and sees what is going on. I have already noticed that, and it's a good thing for her that she does. The old man has nothing to leave her but his two goats and his mountain hut."

"And did he once have more?" asked Barbel.

"He? Well, I should say that he did once have more," replied Dete warmly. "He used to have the finest farm in Domleschg. He was the eldest son and had only one brother, who was quiet and well behaved. But the elder would do nothing but play the fine gentleman and travel about the country, mixing with bad people that nobody knew about. He drank and gambled away the whole property; and so it happened that his father and mother died, one first and then the other, from sheer grief; and his brother, who was also reduced to beggary, went away out of humiliation, nobody knew where; and the uncle himself, as he had nothing left but a bad name, also disappeared—at first no one knew whither, then it was reported that he had gone with the soldiers to Naples, and after that nothing more was heard of him for twelve or fifteen years. Then he suddenly appeared again in Domleschg with a half-grown boy and tried to find a home for him among his relations. But every door was closed to him, and no one wanted to know anything more about him. This made him very bitter; he said he would never set foot in Domleschg again, and he came here to Dörfli and lived with the boy. His wife was probably a Grison woman whom he had come across down below and lost soon after their marriage. He must have had some money still, for he let the boy Tobias learn the carpenter's trade; and he was a steady fellow and well thought of by all the people in Dörfli. But nobody had confidence in the old man, and it was said that he had deserted from Naples, that he had got into trouble, that he had killed somebody, not in war of course, but in some quarrel. But we recognize the relationship, for my mother's grandmother was his grandmother's first cousin. So we called him uncle, and as we are related to almost all the people in Dörfli, on father's side, they all call him uncle, and since he went up on the Alm he has been known as the Alm-Uncle."

"But what became of Tobias?" asked Barbel eagerly.

"Wait and I'll tell you. I can't tell everything in one breath!" exclaimed Dete. "Tobias was serving his time in Mels, and as soon as he finished he came home to Dörfli and married my sister Adelheid, for they had always been fond of each other, and after their marriage they lived very happily together. But it didn't last long. Two years after, while Tobias was working on a new house, a beam fell on him and killed him. Adelheid's fright and grief when her husband was brought home so disfigured threw her into a violent fever, from which she did not recover. She never was very strong, and was often in such a condition that it was almost impossible to tell whether she was asleep or awake. Only two weeks after Tobias's death Adelheid, too, was buried. Then the sad fate of the two was in everybody's mouth far and wide, and it was hinted and openly declared that it was a judgment the uncle deserved for his wicked life. It was said so to his face; even the pastor warned him seriously to repent, but he only grew more and more cross and hard and no longer spoke to anyone, and everyone avoided him.

"Suddenly it was reported that the uncle had gone up on the Alm and no longer came down at all; since then he has stayed there and lives apart from God and man.

"Mother and I took Adelheid's little child; she was a year old. Last summer mother died, and as I wanted to work down at the Baths, I took Heidi to board with old Ursel up in Pfäfferserdorf. I was able to stay at the Baths all winter. I found plenty of work, because I could sew and mend; and early in the spring the lady I served last year came back from Frankfurt, and she is going to take me home with her. Day after tomorrow morning we start. It is a good place, I can tell you."

"And now are you going to give the child to the old man up there? I'm surprised that you should think of such a thing, Dete," said Barbel reproachfully.

"What do you mean?" retorted Dete. "I have done my duty by the child. What else could I do with her now? I don't think I could take a child scarcely five years old to Frankfurt. But where are you going, anyway, Barbel? We are halfway up the Alm now."

"I have already reached the place where I was going. I want to speak to old goatherd Peter's wife. She does spinning for me in winter. So good-bye, Dete; good luck to you!"

Dete shook her companion's hand and stood still while Barbel went into the little, dark-brown mountain hut standing a few steps from the path in a hollow, where it was somewhat sheltered from the winds. It was a good thing that it was in a little hollow, for it looked so tumble-down and decayed that it would have been a dangerous dwelling when the mighty storm winds swept across the mountain, making everything in the hut, doors and windows, rattle, and all the worm-eaten rafters tremble and creak. On such days, if the hut had been up on the Alm, it would certainly have been blown down into the valley.

Here dwelt the young goatherd Peter, the eleven-year-old boy who every morning went down to Dörfli to get the goats and drive them up on the Alm, to feed till evening on the short, nourishing herbs. Then Peter would hurry down again with the light-footed animals, give a shrill whistle through his fingers as soon as he reached Dörfli, and all the owners would immediately come and get their goats. Little boys and girls came for the most part, for the creatures were peaceful and harmless. All through the summer this was the only time in the day when Peter associated with his fellow beings; the rest of the time he lived alone with his goats.

To be sure, he had his mother and blind grandmother at home; but he had to go away very early in the morning, and come back from Dörfli late in the evening; so, in order to play with the children as long as possible, he spent only enough time at home to swallow his bread and milk.

His father, who had also been called Peter the goatherd, because he had followed the same calling in his earlier days, had met with an accident some years before while cutting down trees. His mother, whose real name was Brigitte, was called by everyone, to distinguish her, "goatherd Peter's wife," and the blind grandmother was known by old and young, far and wide, simply by the name of "grandmother."

Dete waited a full ten minutes, looking round in every direction for a glimpse of the children with the goats; but as they were nowhere in sight, she climbed a little higher, where she could have a better view of the Alm down to the foot. Here she peered first this way and then that, showing signs of increasing impatience both in her face and in her movements.

Meanwhile the children were coming along by a roundabout way. Peter knew many spots where there were all sorts of good shrubs and bushes for his goats to nibble; so he frequently wandered from the path with his flock. At first the child in her heavy garb climbed after them with great difficulty, panting with heat and discomfort and straining every nerve. She said not a word, but gazed first at Peter, who jumped about without any difficulty in his bare feet and light trousers, then at the goats with their small, slender legs climbing still more easily over bushes and stones and steep rocks.

Suddenly the child sat down on the ground and in great haste pulled off her shoes and stockings; then she stood up again, took off her thick, red scarf, unfastened her Sunday frock, quickly took that off, and began to unhook her everyday dress. This she wore under the other, to save her aunt Dete the trouble of carrying it. Quick as lightning came off also the everyday frock and there the child stood in her light underclothes with delight, stretching her bare arms out of the short sleeves of her underwaist. Then she laid them all in a neat little pile, and, by Peter's side, jumped and climbed after the goats as easily as any in the whole company.

Peter had not noticed what the child was doing while she remained behind. But when she came running after him in this new costume a grin began to spread over his face, and when he looked back and saw the little pile of clothes lying on the ground, the grin grew still broader and his mouth reached almost from ear to ear; but he said nothing.

The child, feeling so free and light, began to talk with Peter, and he had all sorts of questions to answer, for she wanted to know how many goats he had, where he was going with them, and what he would do when he reached there.

Finally the children with the goats approached the hut and came in sight of Aunt Dete. She had hardly caught a glimpse of the group climbing up the mountainside when she screamed out, "Heidi, what have you been doing? What is the matter with you? Where is your best dress and the other one and your scarf? I bought you brand-new shoes on the mountain, and I made you new stockings, and they are all gone! all gone! Heidi, what have you done with them? Where have you put them all?"

The child calmly pointed down the mountain and said, "There!"

The aunt followed the direction of her finger. To be sure, there lay something, and on the top of it was a red speck; that was surely the scarf.

"You careless girl!" cried the aunt in great excitement. "What were you thinking about? Why did you take everything off? What did you mean?"

"I didn't need them," said the child, without looking in the least sorry for what she had done.

"Oh, you careless, senseless Heidi! don't you know anything?" the aunt went on, lamenting and scolding. "It will take half an hour for anyone to go down there again! Come, Peter, run back for me and get the things! Come, be quick, and don't stand there staring at me as if you were nailed to the ground."

"I am late already," said Peter slowly, and with both hands in his pockets stood still just where he was when he heard the aunt's angry reproaches.

"If you stand there staring like that, you will not get far, I'm thinking," called out Aunt Dete. "Come here! You must have something nice. Do you see this?"

She held up a new penny, which glistened before his eyes. Suddenly he started, and with tremendous leaps went the shortest way down the Alm, and soon reached the little pile of clothes. He picked them up and brought them back so quickly that the aunt could not help praising him, and gave him his money without delay. Peter put it deep down in his pocket, and his face lighted up with a broad grin, for such a treasure did not very often fall to his share.

"You may carry the things on up to the uncle's, as long as you're going that way," continued Aunt Dete, while she set about climbing the steep cliff which rose high behind Peter's hut. The boy willingly undertook the task and followed the others with his bundle in his left hand, and swinging his stick in his right. Heidi and the goats skipped and jumped along merrily by his side. Thus in about three quarters of an hour the procession reached the height where, on a projecting cliff, stood the old uncle's hut, exposed to every wind, but also open to every ray of sunlight and with a wide view of the valley below. Behind the hut stood three ancient fir trees with long, thick, untrimmed branches. Farther back, the mountain with its old gray rocks rose higher still, now displaying lovely, fertile pastures, now a tangle of great stones and bushes, and finally, above them all, bare, steep cliffs.

The uncle had made himself a seat outside the hut on the side that overlooked the valley. Here he sat with his pipe in his mouth, his hands resting on his knees, calmly watching the children, Aunt Dete, and the goats as they came climbing up the mountain. Aunt Dete had been gradually left behind, and Heidi was the first to reach the hut. She went straight to the old man, held out her hand to him, and said, "How do you do, grandfather?"

"Well, well, what does this mean?" asked the old man roughly, barely touching the child's hand and giving her a long, searching look from under his bushy eyebrows. Heidi gazed back at him in return without once winking her eyes, for she had never seen anyone like her grandfather, with his long beard, and heavy gray eyebrows meeting in the middle of his forehead like a thicket. In the meanwhile Aunt Dete arrived with Peter, who stood still for a time looking on to see what would happen.

"I wish you good morning, uncle," said Dete, stepping up to him. "I have brought Tobias and Adelheid's child to you. You will hardly know her, for you haven't seen her since she was a year old."

"Well, what can the child do here with me?" asked the old man curtly. "And you there," he called out to Peter, "you can go along with your goats. You are none too early. Take mine too!"

Peter obeyed without delay and disappeared, for the uncle had made it plain that he was not wanted.

"She must stay with you, uncle," said Dete in reply to his question. "I am sure I have done my duty by her these four years, and now it is your turn to do what you can for her."

"Indeed?" said the old man; and his eyes flashed at Dete. "Suppose the child begins to fret and whine for you, as is usually the case with the unreasonable little things, what shall I do with her?"

"That is your business," retorted Dete. "I am sure no one told me what to do with the little one when it was given into my hands, only a year old, and I already had enough to do to take care of myself and mother. Now I must look out for myself, and you are next of kin to the child. If you can't have her, do what you please with her; you will have to answer for her, if she comes to any harm. You don't want to have anything more laid to your charge."

Dete's conscience was not quite easy; she became excited and said more than she had intended. The uncle rose at her last words; he gave her such a look that she took several steps backward; then he stretched out his arm and said sternly, "Get you gone down where you came from, and don't show yourself here again very soon!"

Dete did not need to be told twice.

"Good-bye, then; and good-bye to you, too, Heidi," she said quickly, and hurried down the mountain to Dörfli as fast as she could go, for her great agitation forced her onward, as if she were a powerful steam engine. In Dörfli many more asked her about Heidi; they all knew Dete well and whose child Heidi was, and all that had taken place. When from every door and window came the question, "Where is the child? Dete, where have you left the child?" she called back with more and more irritation, "Up with the Alm-Uncle! Up with the Alm-Uncle, I tell you!"

She was disgusted because the women everywhere exclaimed,

"How could you do so!" and "The poor little soul!" and "Such a little helpless thing left up there!" and then again and again, "The poor little soul!"

Dete pushed on as fast as she could, and was glad when she was out of their hearing; she did not feel quite easy about the matter, for the dying mother had given the child to her. But she quieted her misgivings by saying to herself that it would not be long before she could do something again for the child, since she would be earning a good deal of money; so she felt very glad that she would soon be in a fine situation, and far away from all the people who would speak to her about the matter.

Chapter 2

At the Grandfather's

After Dete had disappeared, the uncle sat down again on the bench and blew great clouds of smoke from his pipe, while he kept his eyes fixed on the ground without saying a word. Meanwhile Heidi was content to look about her. She discovered the goats' shed built near the hut and peeped into it. It was empty.

The child continued hunting about and came to the fir trees behind the hut. The wind was blowing hard, and it whistled and roared through the branches, high up in the tops. Heidi stood still and listened. When it stopped somewhat she went round to the other side of the hut and came back to her grandfather. When she found him in the same place where she had left him, she placed herself in front of him, put her hands behind her, and gazed at him. Her grandfather looked up.

"What do you want to do?" he asked, as the child continued standing in front of him without moving.

"I want to see what you have in the hut," said Heidi.

"Come along, then!" and the grandfather rose and started to go into the hut.

"Bring your bundle of clothes," he said as he entered.

"I shan't want them anymore," replied Heidi.

The old man turned round and looked sharply at the child, whose black eyes shone in expectation of what might be inside the hut.

"She's not lacking in brains," he said half to himself. "Why won't you need them anymore?" he asked aloud.

"I'd rather go like the goats, with their swift little legs."

"So you shall, but bring the things along," commanded the grandfather. "They can be put into the cupboard."

Heidi obeyed. The old man opened the door, and Heidi followed him into a good-sized room, which occupied the whole hut. In it were a table and a chair; in one corner was the grandfather's bed, in another the fireplace where hung the large kettle; on the other side, in the wall, was a large door, which the grandfather opened; it was the cupboard. There hung his clothes, and on one shelf lay his shirts, stockings, and linen; on another were plates, cups, and glasses, and on the topmost a loaf of bread, smoked meat, and cheese. Everything the Alm-Uncle owned and needed for his living was kept in this closet. As soon as he had opened the door, Heidi came running with her bundle and pushed it in, as far back of her grandfather's clothes as possible, that it might not be easy to find again. Then she looked carefully round the room and said, "Where shall I sleep, grandfather?"

"Wherever you like," he replied.

This was quite to Heidi's mind. She looked into every nook and corner to see where would be the best place for her to sleep. In the corner by her grandfather's bed stood a little ladder, which led to the hayloft. Heidi climbed this. There lay a fresh, fragrant heap of hay, and through a round window one could look far down into the valley below.

"This is where I will sleep," Heidi called down. "It is lovely! Just come and see how lovely it is up here, grandfather!"

"I know all about it," sounded from below.

"I am going to make a bed," called out the child again as she ran busily to and fro in the loft. "But you must come up here and bring a sheet, for the bed must have a sheet for me to sleep on."

"Well, well," said the grandfather below; and after a few moments he went to the cupboard and rummaged about; then he drew out from under his shirts a long, coarse piece of cloth, which might serve for a sheet. He came up the ladder and found that a very neat little bed had been made in the hayloft; the hay was piled up higher at one end to form the pillow, and the bed was placed in such a way that one could look from it straight out through the round open window.

"That is made very nicely," said the grandfather. "Next comes the sheet; but wait a moment,"—and he took up a good armful of hay and made the bed as thick again, in order that the hard floor might not be felt through it. "There, now put it on."

Heidi quickly took hold of the sheet, but was unable to lift it, it was so heavy; however, this made it all the better because the sharp wisps of hay could not push through the firm cloth. Then the two together spread the sheet over the hay, and where it was too broad or too long Heidi quickly tucked it under. Now it appeared quite trim and neat, and Heidi stood looking at it thoughtfully.

"We have forgotten one thing, grandfather," she said.

"What is that?" he asked.

"The coverlet; when we go to bed we creep in between the sheet and the coverlet."

"Is that so? But if I haven't any?" asked the old man.

"Oh, then it's no matter," said Heidi soothingly. "We can take more hay for a coverlet"; and she was about to run to the haymow again, but her grandfather prevented her.

"Wait a moment," he said, and went down the ladder to his own bed. Then he came back and laid a large, heavy linen bag on the floor.

"Isn't that better than hay?" he asked.

Heidi pulled at the bag with all her might and main, trying to unfold it, but her little hands could not manage the heavy thing. Her grandfather helped, and when it was finally spread out on the bed, it all looked very neat and comfortable, and Heidi, looking at her new resting place admiringly, said, "That is a splendid coverlet, and the whole bed is lovely! How I wish it were night so that I could lie down in it!"

"I think we might have something to eat first," said the grandfather. "What do you say?"

In her eagerness over the bed, Heidi had forgotten everything else; but now that eating was suggested to her, a great feeling of hunger rose within her, for she had taken nothing all day, except a piece of bread and a cup of weak coffee early in the morning, and afterward she had made the long journey. So Heidi heartily agreed, saying, "Yes, I think so, too."

"Well, let us go down, since we are agreed," said the old man and followed close upon the child's steps. He went to the fireplace, pushed the large kettle aside and drew forward the little one that hung on the chain, sat down on the three-legged wooden stool with the round seat and kindled a bright fire. Almost immediately the kettle began to boil, and the old man held over the fire a large piece of cheese on the end of a long iron fork. He moved it this way and that, until it was golden yellow on all sides. Heidi looked on with eager attention. Suddenly a new idea came to her mind; she jumped up and ran to the cupboard, and kept going back and forth. When the grandfather brought the toasted cheese to the table, it was already nicely laid with the round loaf of bread, two plates, and two knives, for Heidi had noticed everything in the cupboard, and knew all that would be needed for the meal.

"That is right, to think of doing something yourself," said the grandfather, laying the cheese on the bread and putting the teapot on the table. "But there is something still lacking."

Heidi saw how invitingly the steam came out of the pot, and ran quickly back to the cupboard. But there was only one little bowl there. Heidi was not long puzzled; behind it stood two glasses; the child immediately came back with the bowl and glasses and placed them on the table.

"Very good. You know how to help yourself; but where are you going to sit?"

The grandfather himself was sitting in the only chair. Heidi shot like an arrow to the fireplace, brought back the little three-legged stool and sat down on it.

"Well, you have a seat, sure enough, only it is rather low," said the grandfather. "But in my chair also you would be too short to reach the table; still you must have something anyway, so come!"

Saying which he rose, filled the little bowl with milk, placed it on the chair, and pushed it close to the three-legged stool, so that Heidi had a table in front of her. The grandfather laid a large slice of bread and a piece of the golden cheese on the chair and said, "Now eat!"

He seated himself on the corner of the table and began his dinner. Heidi grasped her bowl and drank and drank without stopping, for all the thirst of her long journey came back to her. Then she drew a long breath and set down the bowl.

"Do you like the milk?" asked the grandfather.

"I never tasted such good milk before," answered Heidi.

"Then you must have some more"; and the grandfather filled the bowl again to the brim and placed it before the child, who looked quite content as she began to eat her bread, after it had been spread with the toasted cheese soft as butter. The combination tasted very good, with frequent drinks of milk.

When the meal was over, the grandfather went out to the goat shed to put it in order, and Heidi watched him closely as he first swept it clean with a broom and then laid down fresh straw for the animals to sleep on. Then he went to his little shop, cut some round sticks, shaped a board, made some holes in it, put the round sticks into them, and suddenly it was a stool like his own, only much higher. Heidi was speechless with amazement as she saw his work.

"What is this, Heidi?" asked the grandfather.

"It is a stool for me, because it is so high; you made it all at once," said the child, still deeply astonished.

"She knows what she sees; her eyes are in the right place," remarked the grandfather to himself as he went round the hut driving a nail here and there; then he repaired something about the door, and went from place to place with hammer, nails, and pieces of wood, mending and clearing away wherever it was needed. Heidi followed him step by step and watched him with the closest attention, and everything he did interested her very much.

Evening was coming on. It was beginning to blow harder in the old fir trees, for a mighty wind had sprung up and was whistling and moaning through their thick tops. It sounded so beautiful in Heidi's ears and heart that she was quite delighted, and skipped and jumped under the firs as if she were feeling the greatest pleasure of her life. The grandfather stood in the doorway and watched the child.

A shrill whistle sounded. Heidi stopped her jumping, and the grandfather stepped outside. Down from above came goat after goat, leaping like a hunting train, and Peter in the midst of them. With a shout of joy Heidi rushed in among the flock and greeted her old friends of the morning one after the other.

When they reached the hut, they all stood still, and two lovely slender goats—one white, the other brown—came out from the others to the grandfather and licked his hands, in which he held some salt to welcome them. This he did each evening. Peter disappeared with his flock. Heidi gently stroked first one goat and then the other and ran round them to stroke them on the other side; she was perfectly delighted with the little creatures.

"Are they ours, grandfather? Are they both ours? Will they go into the shed? Will they stay with us always?" asked Heidi, one question following the other in her delight.

When the goats had finished licking their salt, the old man said, "Go and bring out your little bowl and the bread."

Heidi obeyed, and came back at once. The grandfather milked the goat and filled the bowl and cut off a piece of bread, saying, "Now eat your supper and then go up to bed! Your aunt Dete left a bundle for you; your nightgowns and other things are in it. You will find it downstairs in the closet if you need it. I must attend to the goats now; so sleep well!"

"Good night, grandfather! Good night—what are their names, grandfather? What are their names?" cried the child, running after the old man and the goats as they disappeared into the shed.

"The white one is named Schwänli* and the brown one Bärli,"† answered the grandfather.

"Good night, Schwänli! Good night, Bärli!" called Heidi at the top of her voice. Then Heidi sat down on the bench and ate her bread and drank her milk; but the strong wind almost blew her off her seat; so she finished hastily, then went in and climbed up to her bed, in which she immediately fell asleep and slept as soundly and well as if she had

* *Schwäli = little swan*

† *Bärli = little bear*

been in the loveliest bed of some royal princess.

Not long after, even before it was entirely dark, the grandfather also went to bed; for he was always up with the sun, and it came climbing over the mountain very early in the summertime. In the night the wind blew with such force that its blasts made the whole hut tremble, and every rafter creaked. It howled and groaned down the chimney like voices in distress, and outside in the fir trees it raged with such fury that now and then a bough was broken off.

In the middle of the night the grandfather rose and said half aloud to himself, "She may be afraid."

He climbed the ladder and went to Heidi's bedside. The moon outside shone brightly in the sky for a moment and then disappeared behind the driving clouds, and everything grew dark. Then the moonlight came again brightly through the round opening and fell directly on Heidi's couch. Her cheeks were fiery red as she slept under the heavy coverlet, and she lay perfectly calm and peaceful on her little round arm. She must have been dreaming happy dreams, for a look of happiness was on her face. The grandfather gazed long at the sweetly sleeping child until the moon went behind a cloud again and it was dark. Then he went back to his own bed.

Chapter 3

In the Pasture

Heidi was awakened early in the morning by a loud whistle; and when she opened her eyes, a flood of sunshine was pouring through the round window on her bed and the hay close by, so that everything about shone like gold. Heidi looked round her in amazement and did not know where she was.

Then she heard her grandfather's deep voice outside, and everything came back to her mind—where she had come from, and that now she was up on the Alm with her grandfather and no longer with old Ursel. Ursel was always cold, so that she liked to sit by the kitchen fire or by the stove in her chamber. Heidi had been obliged to stay very near, so that the old woman could see where she was, because she was deaf and could not hear her. This had often been very tiresome to Heidi, who longed to run outside.

So she was very glad when she awoke in her new home and remembered how many strange things she had seen the day before and what she would see again that day, especially Schwänli and Bärli.

Heidi jumped quickly out of bed and in a few minutes had put on all that she wore the day before; it was very little. Then she climbed down the ladder and ran out in front of the hut. There already stood the goatherd Peter with his flock, and the grandfather was bringing Schwänli and Bärli out of the shed to join the other goats. Heidi ran up to him to say good morning to him and the goats.

"Would you like to go to the pasture, too?" asked the grandfather. Heidi was pleased with the idea and jumped for joy.

"But first wash and be clean, or else the sun will laugh at you when it is shining so brightly up there and sees that you are dirty; see, everything is ready for you."

The grandfather pointed to a large tub full of water standing before the door in the sunshine. Heidi ran to it and splashed and rubbed until she was all shining. Meanwhile the grandfather went into the hut and called to Peter, "Come here, general of the goats, and bring your haversack with you."

Peter, surprised, obeyed the call and brought along the little bag in which he carried his scanty dinner.

"Open it," said the old man; and he put in a large piece of bread and an equally large piece of cheese. Peter opened his round eyes as wide as possible in his amazement, for both pieces were half as large again as what he had brought for his own dinner.

"Now in goes the little bowl," continued the uncle, "for the child cannot drink the way you do, right from the goat; she doesn't know how. Milk two bowlfuls at noon for her, as she is to go with you and stay until you come down again; take care that she doesn't fall over the rocks; do you hear?"

Heidi came running up.

"Can the sun laugh at me now, grandfather?" she asked eagerly. In her fear of the sun she had rubbed her face, neck, and arms so vigorously with the coarse towel her grandfather had hung by the water tub that she looked as red as a lobster. Her grandfather smiled.

"No; now he has nothing to laugh at," he admitted. "But tonight, when you come home, you must go in all over, like a fish; for after running about like the goats you will have black feet. Now you can march along."

So she went merrily up the Alm. The wind in the night had blown away the last clouds; the sky was everywhere a deep blue, and in the midst stood the sun, shining on the green mountain; all the blue and yellow flowers opened their cups and looked up with gladness. Heidi jumped here and there and shouted for joy; for there were whole troops of delicate primroses together, and yonder it was blue with gentians, and everywhere in the sunshine smiled and nodded the tender-leaved golden rockroses. Heidi was so charmed by all these glistening, nodding flowers that she entirely forgot the goats and even Peter. She ran far ahead and then off on one side, for it shone red here and yellow there and enticed her in every direction. Wherever she went she picked quantities of the flowers and put them into her apron, for she wanted to carry them all home and put them into the hay in her sleeping room, that it might look there as it did here.

So Peter had to look everywhere; and his round eyes, which did not move quickly from one place to another, had more work than they could well manage, for the goats were as bad as Heidi. They ran hither and thither, and he was obliged to whistle and shout and swing his rod continually in order to drive all the stragglers together.

"Where have you gone now, Heidi?" he called almost angrily.

"Here," sounded from some unseen place. Peter could see no one, for Heidi was sitting on the ground behind a knoll, which was thickly covered with fragrant wild flowers. The whole air round was filled with the sweet odor, and Heidi had never breathed anything so delicious before. She sat down among the flowers and drew in long breaths of the perfume.

"Come along!" called Peter again. "You must not fall down over the cliffs; the uncle charged me not to let you."

"Where are the cliffs?" asked Heidi without stirring from the place, for every breath of wind brought the sweet fragrance to her with increasing charm.

"Up there, 'way up; we have still a long way to go; so come along now! And up at the very top sits the old robber-bird croaking."

That succeeded. Heidi immediately jumped up and ran to Peter with her apron full of flowers.

"You have enough now," he said, when they were once more climbing together. "Besides, you'll stay here forever, and if you pick them all you won't have any tomorrow."

The last reason convinced Heidi; besides, her apron was already so full that there was hardly room for more, and there must be some left for tomorrow. So she went along with Peter; and the goats behaved better and hurried along without delay, for they smelled the good herbage in the distance on the high pasture land.

The pasture where Peter usually went with his goats for the day lay at the foot of the high cliff. The lower part of this was covered with bushes and fir trees, but it rose toward heaven quite bald and steep. On one side of the mountain there were deep abysses. The grandfather was quite right in warning Peter about them.

When Peter reached this spot on the heights, he took off his bag and laid it carefully in a little hollow in the ground. He knew that the wind often rushed across in strong gusts, and he did not wish to see his precious possessions roll down the mountain. Then he stretched himself out on the ground in the sunny pasture to rest from the labor of climbing.

In the meantime Heidi had taken off her apron, rolled it up tightly with the flowers inside, and laid it close to the lunch bag. Then she sat down beside Peter and looked round her. The valley lay far below in the full morning sunshine. In front of her Heidi saw a great wide field of snow, stretching high up into the deep blue sky; on the left stood an enormous mass of rock, on each side of which a higher tower of bald, jagged cliffs rose into the sky and looked very sternly down on Heidi. The child sat as still as a mouse; everywhere there was a great, deep stillness; only the wind passed very softly and gently over the tender bluebells and the radiant golden rockroses, which were everywhere gaily nodding to and fro on their slender stems. Peter had gone to sleep after his labor, and the goats were climbing among the bushes.

She drank in the golden sunlight, the fresh air, the delicate fragrance of the flowers, and desired nothing more than to remain there forever. A good while passed in this way, and Heidi had gazed so often and so long at the lofty mountaintops that it seemed as if they all had faces and were gazing down quite familiarly at her, like good friends.

Then she heard above her a loud, shrill screaming and croaking, and as she looked up into the air the largest bird she had ever seen in her life was flying round on wide, outstretched wings and coming back in wider circles and screaming loud and piercingly over her head.

"Peter! Peter! Wake up!" cried Heidi at the top of her voice. "See, there is the robber-bird! See! See!"

Peter jumped up at the call and looked with Heidi at the bird, which was flying higher and higher in the blue sky. Finally it disappeared over the gray cliffs.

"Where has he gone now?" asked Heidi, who had watched the bird eagerly.

"Home to his nest," was Peter's answer.

"Is his home way up there? Oh, how lovely to be so high up! Why does he scream so?" asked Heidi again.

"Because he can't help it," explained Peter.

"Let us climb up there and see where his home is," proposed Heidi.

"Oh! Oh! Oh!" burst out Peter, uttering each exclamation with stronger disapproval. "No goat can get there, and the uncle said you must not fall over the cliff."

Then Peter suddenly began such a whistling and calling that Heidi did not know what was going to happen; but the goats must have understood the sound, for one after another they came jumping down until the whole flock was assembled on the green slope, some nibbling the spicy stalks, others running to and fro, and still others amusing themselves by butting one another with their horns.

Heidi jumped up and ran round among the goats. It was new and extremely amusing to her to see how the little creatures leaped about and played together, and Heidi made the personal acquaintance of each, for every one had a quite distinct individuality and its own peculiar ways.

Meanwhile Peter had brought out the bag and nicely arranged all four of the pieces of bread and cheese on the ground in a square, the larger pieces on Heidi's side, the smaller ones on his side; he knew just how many he had. Then he took the little bowl and milked sweet, fresh milk from Schwänli into it and placed it in the middle of the square. Then he called Heidi, but he had to call longer for her than for the goats, because she was so interested and pleased with the playing and frolicking of her new playmates that she saw and heard nothing else.

But Peter knew how to make himself understood. He called till he made the rocks above echo; and Heidi appeared, and the table he had laid looked so inviting that she danced round it for joy.

"Stop jumping; it is time to eat," said Peter. "Sit down and begin."

Heidi sat down.

"Is the milk mine?" she asked, looking with satisfaction at the neat square and the bowl in the middle.

"Yes," answered Peter, "and the two large pieces of bread and cheese are yours, too; and when you have drunk all the milk, you can have another bowlful from Schwänli, and then it is my turn.

"And where will you get your milk?" Heidi wanted to know.

"From my goat—from Schnecke.* Go to eating!" commanded Peter once more.

Heidi began with her milk, and as soon as she set down her empty bowl Peter rose and filled it again. Heidi broke some of her bread into it; the rest, a piece still larger than all Peter's bread, she handed over to him, with all her large portion of cheese, and said, "You may have that, I have enough."

Peter looked at Heidi in speechless amazement, for never in his life had he been able to say such a thing or give anything away. He hesitated a little, for he could not really believe that Heidi was in earnest. She went on offering the bread and cheese, and when he did not take it, she laid it down on his knee. Then he saw that she meant it for him, seized the prize, nodded his thanks, and then made the most satisfactory dinner of his goatherd life. Meantime Heidi watched the goats.

"What are their names, Peter?" she asked.

He knew them all well enough and could keep them in his head all the better because he had little else to store away there. So he began and without hesitation named one after the other, pointing to each one as he did so. Heidi listened with the closest attention to his explanation, and before long she could distinguish them from one another and call each by name; for they all had their peculiarities, which anyone might remember, but it was necessary to look at them closely, and this she did.

There was the big Türk with his powerful horns. He was always

* *Schnecke = snail*

trying to butt all the others, and if he came near, most of them ran away and would have nothing to do with their rough comrade. The brave Distelfinck,* a slender, nimble little goat, was the only one that did not avoid him, but often ran at him three or four times in succession so swiftly and skillfully that the big Türk would stand still in astonishment and make no further attack; for Distelfinck looked very warlike and had sharp horns.

Then there was the little white Schneehöpli,† always bleating so touchingly, so beseechingly, that Heidi ran to her again and again and put her arms round her head to comfort her. But now the child hurried to her once more, for her mournful young voice was again raised in appeal. Heidi threw her arm round the little creature's neck and asked quite sympathetically, "What is the matter, Schneehöpli? Why do you cry so?"

The goat trustingly pressed close to Heidi's side and became perfectly quiet.

Peter called out from where he was sitting, with frequent interruptions while he took a bite and a swallow, "She does so because the old one doesn't come with her anymore. They sold her and sent her to Maienfeld day before yesterday; so she doesn't come up on the Alm any longer."

"Who is the old one?" asked Heidi.

"Why, the mother, of course," was the reply.

"Where is the grandmother?" asked Heidi again.

"Hasn't any."

"And the grandfather?"

"Hasn't any."

"You poor Schneehöpli," said Heidi, drawing the little creature tenderly toward her. "Don't cry so anymore, for, you see, I will come with you every day, and then you won't be alone; and if you want anything, you can come to me.

* *Distelfinck = gold finch*

† *Schneehöpli = little snowhopper*

Schneehöpli rubbed her head contentedly against Heidi's shoulder and bleated no more.

By far the prettiest and cleanest of the goats were Schwänli and Bärli, who were decidedly superior in their behavior, and usually went their own way; they especially avoided the troublesome Türk and treated him with scorn.

The animals had begun to climb up to the bushes again, each one after his own fashion: some leaping carelessly over everything, others cautiously seeking out the good herbs as they went along, while Türk tried his horns here and there —first in one place and then in another.

Schwänli and Bärli climbed prettily and gracefully, and whenever they found fine bushes, there they stationed themselves and nibbled them. Heidi stood with her hands behind her back, watching them all with the closest attention.

"Peter," she said to the boy, who had thrown himself down again on the ground, "the prettiest of them all are Schwänli and Bärli."

"Of course they are," was the reply. "The Alm-Uncle brushes and washes them and gives them salt and has the best shed."

Suddenly Peter jumped up and fairly leaped after the goats. Heidi ran after him; she felt that something must have happened, and she could not remain behind. Peter ran through the midst of the goats to the side of the mountain, where the rocks descended steep and bare far below, and where a careless goat, going near, might easily fall over and break all its bones. He had seen the venturesome Distelfinck jumping along in that direction; he reached there just in time, for at that instant the little goat came to the very edge of the precipice. Just as it was falling, Peter flung himself down on the ground and managed to seize one of its legs and hold it fast. Distelfinck bleated with anger and surprise, to be held so by his leg and hindered from continuing his merry course, and struggled obstinately onward. Peter screamed, "Heidi, help me!" for he couldn't get up and was almost pulling off Distelfinck's leg.

Heidi was already there and instantly understood their sorry plight. She quickly pulled up from the ground some fragrant herbs and held them under Distelfinck's nose and said soothingly, "Come, come, Distelfinck, you must be sensible! See, you might fall off and break your bones, and that would give you frightful pain."

The goat quickly turned round and eagerly nibbled the herbs from Heidi's hand. Meanwhile Peter had succeeded in getting on his feet and had seized the cord which held the bell round Distelfinck's neck. Heidi seized it on the opposite side, and the two together led the runaway back to the peacefully feeding flock.

When Peter had the goat in safety once more, he raised his rod to beat him soundly as a punishment, and Distelfinck timidly drew back, for he saw what was going to happen. But Heidi cried, "No, Peter! No, you must not beat him! See how frightened he is!"

"He deserves it," snarled Peter and was going to strike the goat.

But Heidi seized his arm and cried indignantly, "You shall not do it; it will hurt him! Let him alone!"

Peter looked in astonishment at the commanding Heidi, whose black eyes snapped at him. He hesitatingly dropped his rod.

"He can go if you will give me some of your cheese again tomorrow," said Peter, yielding; for he wanted some reward for his fright.

"You may have it all—the whole piece—tomorrow and every day; I do not want it," said Heidi with ready assent. "And I will give you a good part of my bread, too, as I did today. But then you must never, never beat Distelfinck, nor Schneehöpli, nor any of the goats."

"It's all the same to me," remarked Peter; and this was as good as a promise with him. Then he let the culprit go, and the happy Distelfinck leaped high in the air and then bounded back into the flock.

Thus the day had passed away unnoticed, and the sun was just ready to go down behind the mountains. Heidi sat down on the ground again and silently gazed at the bluebells and the rockroses glowing in the evening light; and all the grass seemed tinted with gold, and the cliffs above began to gleam and sparkle. Suddenly Heidi jumped up and exclaimed, "Peter! Peter! It's on fire! It's on fire! All the mountains are burning, and the big snow field over there is on fire, and the sky! Oh, see! See! The high cliff is all burning! Oh, the beautiful fiery snow! Peter, get up! See! The fire reaches up to the robber-bird! Look at the rocks! See the fir trees! Everything, everything is on fire!"

"It's always so," said Peter good-naturedly, peeling the bark from his rod. "But it is no fire."

"What is it, then?" asked Heidi, running back and forth in order to look on every side; for she could not see enough, it was so beautiful everywhere.

"What is it, Peter? What is it?" cried Heidi again.

"It comes so of itself," explained Peter.

"Oh, see! See!" cried Heidi in great excitement. "Suddenly it grows rosy red! Look at the snow and the high, pointed rocks! What are their names, Peter?"

"Mountains don't have names," he replied.

"Oh, how lovely! See the snow all rosy red! And oh, on the rocks above there are ever and ever so many roses! Oh, now they are turning gray! Oh! Oh! Now it is all gone! It is all gone, Peter!" And Heidi sat down on the ground and looked as distressed as if everything were really coming to an end.

"It will be just the same again tomorrow," explained Peter. "Get up! We must go home now."

Peter whistled and called the goats together, and they started on the homeward journey.

"Will it be like that every day—every day when we go to the pasture?" asked Heidi, listening eagerly for some decided assurance as she walked down the mountain by Peter's side.

"Usually," was the reply.

"But really tomorrow again?" she wanted to know.

"Yes; yes, tomorrow, certainly!" assured Peter.

Then Heidi was happy once more, but she had received so many impressions, and so many things were going round in her mind, that she was perfectly silent until they reached the hut and saw her grandfather. He was sitting under the fir trees, where he had also made a seat and was in the habit of waiting there in the evening for his goats.

Heidi ran straight up to him, followed by Schwänli and Bärli; for the goats knew their master and their shed. Peter called out to Heidi, "Come again tomorrow! Good night!" He was pleased to have Heidi go with him.

Heidi darted back, gave Peter her hand, and assured him that she would accompany him again; then she sprang into the midst of the departing flock, threw her arms once more round Schneehöpli's neck, and said confidingly, "Sleep well, Schneehöpli, and remember that I will go with you again tomorrow and that you must never bleat so mournfully again."

Schneehöpli seemed pleased and looked thankfully into Heidi's face and then leaped gaily after the other goats.

Heidi came back under the fir trees.

"Oh, grandfather, it was so beautiful!" she exclaimed even before she had reached him—"the fire and the roses on the cliffs and the blue and yellow flowers; and see what I have brought you!"

Whereupon Heidi shook all her wealth of flowers out of her folded apron in front of her grandfather. But what a sight the poor little flowers made! Heidi no longer recognized them. They were all like hay, and not a single cup was open.

"Oh, grandfather, what is the matter with them?" cried Heidi, quite shocked. "They were not like that; why do they look so now?"

"They like to stand out in the sunshine and not to be shut up in your apron," said the grandfather.

"Then I will never bring any more home. But, grandfather, what made the robber-bird scream so?" asked Heidi urgently.

"You must jump into the water now, while I go to the shed and fetch the milk; afterward we will go into the house together and have supper. Then I will tell you about it."

So it was; and later, when Heidi sat on her high stool before her little bowl of milk, next her grandfather, she again asked the question, "Why did the robber-bird keep croaking and screaming so, grandfather?"

"He is mocking at the people down below, because so many sit together in the villages and make one another wicked. So he mocks at them: 'It would be much better for you to leave one another and let each go his own way and climb up to some mountaintop, as I do!'"

The grandfather spoke these words so wildly that the robber-bird's screaming came back to Heidi's mind still more forcefully.

"Why have the mountains no names, grandfather?" asked Heidi again.

"They have names," he replied, "and if you can describe one to me so that I can recognize it, I will tell you what it is called."

Then Heidi described the rocky mountain, with its two high towers, just as she had seen it, and the grandfather, well pleased, said, "Very good! I know it; it is called Falknis.* Did you see any more?"

Then Heidi described the mountain with the big snow field, which had been on fire, then turned rose color, and then suddenly grew pale and wan.

"I know that, too," said the grandfather. "That is the Scesaplana. So it pleased you up in the pasture, did it?"

Then Heidi told him about everything that had happened throughout the day—how lovely it had been; and she asked her grandfather to tell her where the fire at evening had come from, for Peter could not tell her.

"You see," the grandfather explained, "the sun does it. When he says good night to the mountains, he sends to them his most beautiful rays so that they may not forget him until he comes back again in the morning."

This pleased Heidi, and she could hardly wait for another day to come so that she could go up to the pasture and see once more how the sun said good night to the mountains. But first she had to go to sleep, and she slept soundly the whole night long on her bed of hay and dreamed of bright shining mountains and their red roses, in the midst of which Schneehöpli merrily ran and jumped.

* *Falcon's nest*

Chapter 4

At the Grandmother's

On the following morning the bright sun appeared again, and Peter came with his goats, and they all went together up to the pasture; and so it happened day after day. Heidi grew very brown and strong and healthy from this outdoor life, and she was as happy as a bird.

It was now autumn, and the wind was beginning to blow louder over the mountains; so the grandfather said one day, "You must stay here today, Heidi; the wind with one puff could blow a little thing like you over all the rocks down into the valley."

But when Peter heard this in the morning, he looked very unhappy, for he saw real misfortune before him. He did not know how to pass the time; it was so tiresome when Heidi was not with him. He missed his hearty dinner. Moreover, the goats were so contrary these days that he had twice as much trouble with them; they were so accustomed to Heidi's company that they would not go along, but ran off in every direction, because she was not with them.

Heidi was never unhappy, for she always found something about her to enjoy. She would have preferred to go with Peter and the goats to the pasture, to the flowers, and up to the robber-bird, where there were so many things to do, with all the different goats; but still her grandfather's hammering and sawing and carpentering were very interesting to Heidi. It pleased her that he was just preparing the pretty round goat cheeses. Since she had to stay at home, it was particularly delightful to watch the remarkable operations of her grandfather as he bared both arms and stirred the cheese in the big kettle.

But more attractive than all else to Heidi on such windy days was the roaring and rushing in the three old fir trees behind the hut. Wherever she happened to be, she had to run to them every little while, for nothing was so fascinating and wonderful as this deep, mysterious sound up in the treetops. Heidi would stand under them and listen; she was never tired of seeing and hearing how the wind roared and rocked the trees with such might.

The sun was no longer hot, as in summer, and Heidi brought out her shoes and stockings and also her little coat; for it grew cooler and cooler. When she stood under the fir trees the wind blew through her as if she were a thin leaf, but she kept running back again and could not stay in the house when she heard the wind.

Then it grew cold, and Peter breathed on his hands when he came early in the morning, but not for long, for suddenly one night a deep snow fell. When the sun rose, the whole Alm was white, and not a single green leaf was to be seen anywhere about.

After this, goatherd Peter came no more with his flock; and Heidi looked with amazement out of the little window, for it was beginning to snow again; and big flakes fell thick and fast, until the snow came up to the window, and then still higher, until they could not open the window, and they were completely buried in the little house. This made Heidi so merry that she kept running from one window to the other to see how the snow was increasing and whether it would cover the entire hut, so that they would need to have a light in the middle of the day. It was not so bad as that; and the following day the grandfather went out with his shovel, for the storm was ended. He piled up great heaps of snow, so that there seemed to be mountains of it all round the hut.

Now the windows and the door were free, and this was fortunate; for as Heidi and her grandfather were sitting in the afternoon on their three-legged stools, suddenly there was a great knocking and stamping against the threshold, and finally the door opened. It was Peter the goatherd; he had not kicked against the door through rudeness, but in order to beat off the snow from his shoes. Indeed, Peter was covered with snow, for he had been obliged to struggle through the high drifts; so that great lumps remained clinging to him, frozen fast by the sharp cold. But he had not given up, for he was anxious to reach Heidi, whom he had not seen for a whole long week.

"Good afternoon," said he as he entered, then placed himself as near as possible to the fire and made no further remark; but his whole face beamed with pleasure at being there. Heidi looked at him wonderingly; for now that he was so near the fire, he began to thaw all over, so that he looked like a little waterfall.

"Well, general, how are you?" asked the grandfather. "Now you are without an army and must bite your slate pencil."

"Why must he bite his slate pencil, grandfather?" asked Heidi at once with curiosity.

"In winter he has to go to school," explained the grandfather. "There you learn to read and write, and often it is hard work; so it helps a little if you bite your slate pencil. Isn't it so, general?"

"Yes, it is so," said Peter.

Heidi's interest in the matter was now aroused, and she had to ask Peter a great many questions about the school and everything that happened and was to be seen and heard there. As much time was always spent in any conversation in which Peter was obliged to take part, the result was that meanwhile he was able to get well dried from top to toe. It was always a great effort for him to put his thoughts into words—to express his meaning; but this time it was unusually difficult, for he had scarcely succeeded in giving one answer before Heidi put two or three more unexpected questions and mostly such as required a whole sentence in reply.

The grandfather had kept quite still during this conversation, but the corners of his mouth had twitched with amusement, and this was a sign that he was listening.

"Well, general, now you have been under fire and need strengthening. Come, stay to supper with us!"

Whereupon the grandfather rose and brought the evening meal from the cupboard, and Heidi pushed the stools to the table. Next the wall there was still another seat, which the grandfather had made and fastened there. Now that he was no longer alone, he had fashioned here and there all sorts of seats for two; for Heidi had a way of always keeping near him wherever he went. So they all three had good seats;

and Peter opened his round eyes very wide when he saw what a big piece of the fine dried meat the Alm-Uncle laid on his thick slice of bread. Peter had not had anything so good for a long time. When the pleasant meal was over, it began to grow dark, and Peter started for home. When he had said "good night" and "God bless you" and was already in the doorway, he turned round once more and said, "Next Sunday I will come again—a week from today; and you must come to my grandmother's sometime; she said so."

It was a new idea to Heidi that she should go to visit someone, but it took root on the spot, and on the following morning Heidi's first words were: "Grandfather, now I must really go down to the grandmother's; she expects me.

"There is too much snow," replied the grandfather, putting her off. But the purpose was deeply seated in Heidi's mind. After that not a day passed when Heidi did not say five or six times, "Grandfather, now I must really go; the grandmother is expecting me."

On the fourth day, when the cold was so bitter that it cracked and creaked with every footstep outdoors, and the whole covering of snow was frozen hard all about, and yet the beautiful sun looked in at the window, Heidi, as she sat on her high stool eating her dinner, began her little speech again: "Today I must really go to the grandmother's; she will be tired of waiting for me."

Then the grandfather rose from the dinner table, went up to the hayloft, brought down the thick bag that served as Heidi's bed covering, and said, "Well, come along!"

The child was greatly delighted and skipped after him out into the glistening world of snow. In the old fir trees it was now quite still; the white snow lay on every bough, and the trees sparkled and shone all over in the sunshine so gloriously that Heidi jumped up and down with delight and kept exclaiming, "Come out, grandfather! Come out! The fir trees are all covered with real silver and gold!"

The grandfather had gone into the shop and now came out with a wide sled. It had a handle fastened to the side, and from the low seat one could hold the feet out in front against the snowy ground and steer with one or the other in the required direction.

After the grandfather had first looked all round the fir trees with Heidi, he seated himself on the sled, took the child in his lap, wrapped her up in the bag, so that she might be warm and comfortable, and held her tight with his left arm, as this was very necessary for the coming journey. Then with his right hand he seized the handle and gave a push with both feet. The sled shot away down the mountain with such swiftness that Heidi thought she was flying through the air like a bird and shouted with joy.

Suddenly the sled stood still in front of Peter the goatherd's hut. The grandfather put the child on the ground, unwrapped her covering, and said, "Now go in, and when it begins to grow dark, come out again and start along on the way home."

Then he turned round with his sled and drew it up the mountain.

Heidi opened the door and went into a little room which looked black. There was a fireplace in it and some bowls on a stand. This was the kitchen. Then came another door, which Heidi also opened. This led into a small sitting room; for this was not a cheese maker's hut, like her grandfather's, with one single, large room and a loft above it, but a very old little house, where everything was small, narrow, and old-fashioned.

When Heidi stepped into the little sitting room, she stood right in front of a table by which sat a woman mending Peter's jacket. Heidi immediately recognized it. In the corner an old, bent grandmother sat spinning. Heidi knew at once who she was. She went straight to the spinning wheel and said, "How do you do, grandmother? I have come to see you. Did you think it was a long time before I came?"

The grandmother raised her head and sought for the hand held out to her. When she found it, she felt it for some time thoughtfully; then she said, "Are you the child staying up with the Alm-Uncle? Are you Heidi?"

"Yes, yes," replied the child. "I have just come down with my grandfather on the sled."

"Is that possible! Your hand is so warm! Say, Brigitte, did the Alm-

Uncle himself come down with the child?"

Peter's mother, Brigitte, who was mending by the table, had risen and was now examining the child with curiosity from head to foot; she said, "I don't know, mother, whether the uncle himself came with her or not; it is not likely; the child may be mistaken."

But Heidi looked straight at the woman and said sturdily, "I know very well who wrapped me up in the coverlet and brought me down on the sled. It was my grandfather."

"Then there must be something in what Peter said last summer about the Alm-Uncle, although we thought he was not right," said the grandmother. "Who could really have believed that such a thing was possible? I thought the child wouldn't live three weeks up there! How does she look, Brigitte?"

Brigitte had studied her so thoroughly in the meantime that she could well describe her appearance.

"She has a delicate form like Adelheid," she replied, "but she has black eyes and curly hair, like Tobias and also like the old man up there. I believe she looks like them both."

Meanwhile Heidi was not idle; she had looked round and noticed everything. Now she said, "See, grandmother! There is a shutter that keeps swinging back and forth. My grandfather would drive in a nail at once to hold it fast. It will break a pane of glass. See, see!"

"Oh, you good child!" said the grandmother. "I cannot see it, but I can hear it and much more besides the shutter. Everything creaks and rattles when the wind blows, and it comes in everywhere. Everything is loose; and often in the night when both the others are asleep, I am so anxious and afraid lest the whole house should tumble down over our heads and kill us all three; and there is no man to mend anything about the hut, for Peter doesn't know how."

"But why can't you see how the shutter swings, grandmother? See! There it goes again—there, there, there!" and Heidi pointed with her finger directly toward the place.

"Ah, child! l can see nothing at all, nothing at all; the shutter or nothing else," said the grandmother mournfully.

"But if I go out and open the shutter wide so that it will be quite light, can you see then, grandmother?"

"No, no, not even then! No one can make it light for me again!"

"But if you go out in the white snow, then it will surely be light for you. Come with me, grandmother; I will show you.

Heidi took the grandmother by the hand to lead her out, for she was beginning to be distressed because it did not seem light anywhere to the old woman.

"Let me sit still, you good child! It would be dark to me even in the snow and in the light. My eyes cannot see!"

"But then in the summertime, grandmother," said Heidi, still anxiously seeking some way out of the difficulty, "you know when the sun comes down quite hot and then says 'good night' to the mountains, and they shine fiery red, and all the yellow flowers glisten; then it will be light to you, won't it?"

"Ah, child! I can never see them anymore. The fiery mountains and the golden flowers above us will nevermore be bright to me on earth—nevermore."

Then Heidi burst into loud weeping. Full of distress, she kept sobbing, "Who can make it light again for you? Can no one? Can no one at all?"

The grandmother tried to comfort the child, but she did not soon succeed. Heidi hardly ever cried; but when she once began, it was almost impossible for her to recover from her grief.

The grandmother had tried every means to soothe the child, for it went to her heart to have her sob so pitifully. Finally she said, "Come, dear Heidi, come here! I want to tell you something. When a person cannot see, it is so pleasant to hear a friendly word, and I like to hear you talk. Come, sit down near me and tell me what you do up there and what your grandfather does. I used to know him well, but for many years I have heard nothing about him, except through Peter; but Peter doesn't say much."

Then a new idea came to Heidi's mind. She quickly wiped away her tears and said comfortingly, "Just wait, grandmother; I will tell my grandfather all about it. He will make it light for you again, and he will fix the hut so that it won't tumble down. He can make everything all right."

The grandmother remained silent. Then Heidi began with great liveliness to tell about her life with her grandfather and the days she spent in the pasture; about her present life in the winter, and what her grandfather made out of wood—benches and stools and lovely cribs to put hay in for Schwänli and Bärli, and a large new water tub for bathing in summer, and a new milk bowl and spoon. Heidi grew still more eager in describing the beautiful things which were made out of a piece of wood, and how she stayed near her grandfather and watched him, and how quickly he did everything. The grandmother listened with great interest and from time to time interrupted her with, "Do you hear that, Brigitte? Do you hear what she says of the uncle?"

Suddenly the story was interrupted by a great thumping at the door, and in stamped Peter. The boy immediately stood still and opened his round eyes wide in astonishment at the sight of Heidi, and then a good-natured grin spread over his face as she said, "Good afternoon, Peter!"

"Is it possible that he has already come home from school!" exclaimed the grandmother in surprise. "No afternoon for many a year has passed so quickly! Good afternoon, Peter! How did you get on with the reading?"

"Just the same," answered Peter.

"Dear, dear!" said the grandmother with a little sigh. "I thought there might be a change! Think! You will be twelve years old next February!"

"Why should there be a change, grandmother?" asked Heidi at once with interest.

"I only thought he might be able to learn something," said the grandmother, "learn to read, I mean. Up there on the shelf I have an old prayer book with beautiful hymns in it which I have not heard for so long that I cannot remember them; so I thought if Peterli could only learn, he would perhaps be able to read some of the verses to me. But he cannot learn; it is too hard for him."

"I think I must get a light, it is already quite dark," said Peter's mother, who had been busy mending the jacket all the while. "The afternoon has gone before I was aware of it, either."

Then Heidi jumped up from her chair, quickly reached out her hand and said, "Good night, grandmother! I must go home right away, if it is growing dark"; and Peter and his mother shook hands with her, one after the other, and accompanied her to the door. But the grandmother called out anxiously, "Wait, wait, Heidi! You must not go alone. Peter must go with you; do you hear? And take care of the child, Peter. Don't let her fall down, and don't let her stand still, for she might freeze. Do you hear? And has she a good thick scarf round her neck?"

"I haven't any scarf at all; but I shall not freeze," Heidi called back. Then she went out the door and slipped away so quickly that Peter could hardly follow her.

But the grandmother called anxiously, "Run after her, Brigitte, run! The child will be frozen—out so in the night. Take my shawl. Run quickly!"

Brigitte obeyed. But the children had gone only a few steps up the mountain when they saw the grandfather coming down, and in a moment he was with them.

"Very good, Heidi," said he, "you have kept your word!" He wrapped the coverlet round the child once more, took her in his arms and climbed up the mountain.

Brigitte saw this and went back into the hut with Peter and told the grandmother in great surprise all about it. The grandmother also was surprised and kept saying, "God be praised and thanked that he is so good to her! God be praised and thanked! If he will only let her come to see me again; for the child did me so much good! What a kind heart she has! How amusingly she talks!" And until she went to bed she kept repeating, "If she will only come again! Now there is something still left in the world to give me pleasure!"

Brigitte agreed with her every time, and Peter nodded his head approvingly and stretched his mouth wide with delight, saying, "It's no surprise to me!"

Meanwhile Heidi, wrapped in her bag, had much to say to her grandfather; but as her voice did not sound clearly through the eight-fold wrap, and he could not understand a word, he said, "Wait a little while, until we get home; then tell me about it."

As soon as he reached the hut and had taken off Heidi's wrap, she said, "Grandfather, tomorrow we must take the hammer and the big nails and fasten the shutter at the grandmother's house, and drive a good many more nails; for everything creaks and rattles there."

"We must? We must do so? Who told you that?" asked the grandfather.

"Nobody told me so; I knew it without," replied Heidi, "for everything is loose and it makes the grandmother anxious and afraid when the wind blows; and she can't sleep. She thinks: 'Now everything will fall down on our heads.' And nobody can make it light anymore for the grandmother! She doesn't know how anyone can. But you can surely, grandfather! Only think how sad it is for her to be always in the dark! And nobody can help her but you! Tomorrow we will go; won't we, grandfather?"

Heidi clung to her grandfather and looked up at him with undoubting confidence. The old man gazed at the child for a little while, then said, "Yes, Heidi; we will make everything fast at the grandmother's hut, so that there will be no more rattling. Tomorrow we will do so."

Then the child jumped for joy all round the room and cried, "Tomorrow we will do it! Tomorrow we will do it!"

The grandfather kept his word. The following afternoon they took the same ride on the sled. The old man set the child down before the door and said, "Now go in, and when it is night come back." Then he laid the bag on the sled and went round the house.

Scarcely had Heidi opened the door and run into the room, when the grandmother called out from her corner, "Here comes the child! It is the child!"

She dropped her thread and stopped the wheel for joy, and held out both hands.

Heidi immediately pushed the little low chair quite near, sat down in it, and had a great many more things to tell her and to ask her. But suddenly there was a heavy pounding on the house. It startled the grandmother so that she nearly upset the spinning wheel and, trembling, cried out, "Oh, dear me! it has come at last; the hut is all tumbling to pieces."

But Heidi held her fast by the arm and said comfortingly, "No, no, grandmother; don't be afraid, it is grandfather with his hammer; he is going to mend everything so that you won't be worried and afraid any longer."

"Oh! Is it possible? Is such a thing possible? So the dear Lord has not entirely forgotten us!" exclaimed the grandmother. "Did you hear that, Brigitte, did you hear what it is? It is really a hammer! Go out, Brigitte, and if it is the Alm-Uncle tell him he must come in a moment and let me thank him."

Brigitte went out. The Alm-Uncle was just driving new fastenings into the wall; Brigitte went toward him and said, "I wish you good afternoon, uncle, and so does my mother; and I want to thank you for doing us such a service, and so does my mother indoors. Surely no one else would do such a thing for us, and we want to thank you, for surely—"

"That will do," interrupted the old man. "What you think of the Alm-Uncle I already know. Just go back into the house; I can find out for myself what needs to be done here."

Brigitte at once obeyed, for the uncle had a way which people did not usually oppose. He pounded and hammered all round the hut; then he climbed the narrow little staircase up under the roof and kept on hammering until he had driven the last nail he had brought with him. Meanwhile it had begun to grow dark; he had hardly come down and drawn his sled from behind the goat shed when Heidi stepped out from the door. The grandfather wrapped her up in his arms and carried her as on the previous day, drawing the sled after him.

Thus the winter passed. After many long years a joy had come into the blind grandmother's dreary life, and her days were no more long and dark; for now she always had something pleasant to look forward to. From early morning she listened for the tripping footstep, and when the door opened and the child actually came dancing in, then she always exclaimed joyfully, "God be praised! She has come again!"

Heidi would sit down by her side and prattle and talk merrily about everything she knew; it made the time pass so quickly that the grandmother did not notice it, and not once did she ask as formerly, "Brigitte, is the day nearly over?"

Every time that Heidi closed the door behind her the grandmother would say, "How short the afternoon has been, hasn't it, Brigitte?" and Brigitte would reply, "To be sure, it seems to me we have hardly put away the dinner plates."

And the grandmother would say again, "If only the good Lord will preserve the child for me and keep the Alm-Uncle kind. Does she look well, Brigitte?" and every time Brigitte would answer, "She looks like a rosy apple."

Heidi had also a great fondness for the old grandmother, and whenever it came to her mind that no one, not even her grandfather, could make it light for her again, a great feeling of sorrow came over her; but the grandmother assured her that she suffered least when she was with her, so Heidi came down on the sled every fine winter's day. The grandfather, without making any objection, brought her, always carrying his hammer and other things; and he spent many an afternoon working about Peter's hut. It had a good result; there was no more creaking and rattling, and the grandmother said she should never forget the uncle, for she had not been able to sleep well for many a long winter.

Chapter 5

Two Visits and Their Results

Quickly passed the winter, and still more quickly the merry summer following; and a new winter was already drawing to an end. Heidi was as happy and contented as the birds of the air, and rejoiced more and more every day in the approaching spring, when the warm south wind would blow through the fir trees and drive away the snow; then the bright sunshine would call forth the blue and yellow flowers, and the days in the pasture would come again—days which to Heidi brought the greatest pleasure that earth could give.

Heidi was now in her eighth year; she had learned all sorts of handiwork from her grandfather. She could go round with the goats as if she were one of them, and Schwänli and Bärli followed her like trusty dogs, bleating loudly for joy if they merely heard her voice.

This winter Peter had already brought word twice from the schoolteacher in Dörfli that the Alm-Uncle ought to send the child living with him to school, for she was more than old enough and should have gone the winter before. The uncle had sent word back both times that if the schoolteacher wanted anything of him he would find him at home, but that he would not send the child to school. This message Peter had faithfully delivered.

When the March sun had melted the snow on the slopes, and the snowdrops were in bloom everywhere in the valley, when the fir trees on the Alm had shaken off their burden of snow, and their branches again waved merrily—then Heidi in her delight kept running back and forth from the house to the goat shed, and from the goat shed to the fir trees, and then into the hut to her grandfather to tell him how much larger the piece of green ground had grown under the trees. Then she would immediately run back to look again, for she could not wait until everything should be green once more, and the lovely summer with its leaves and bloom return to the mountain.

One sunny March morning, when Heidi was running back and forth in this way, and was jumping over the doorsill for about the tenth time, she nearly fell backward into the house from fright; for suddenly there appeared before her an old man all in black, who looked at her very earnestly. But when he saw how startled she was, he said kindly, "You must not be afraid of me; I love children. Give me your hand! You must be Heidi; where is your grandfather?"

"He is sitting at the table, carving round spoons out of wood," replied Heidi, opening the door.

It was the old pastor from Dörfli, who had known the uncle well years before, when he still lived in the valley and was one of his neighbors. He stepped into the hut, went up to the old man, who was bending over his wood carving, and said, "Good morning, neighbor!"

The grandfather looked up in surprise; the next instant he rose and replied, "Good morning, pastor." Then he offered him his stool, saying, "If the pastor does not object to a wooden seat, here is one.

The pastor sat down. After a moment he said, "I have not seen you for a long time, neighbor."

"Nor have I seen you, pastor," was the answer.

"I come today to talk with you about something," continued the pastor. "I think you already know what the matter is which I am going to speak about, and I want to hear what you plan to do."

The pastor remained silent and looked at the child, who was standing in the doorway and closely watching the stranger.

"Heidi, go out to the goats," said the grandfather. "You may take a little salt along and stay with them until I come."

Heidi immediately disappeared.

"The child should have been sent to school a year ago, and she certainly ought to have gone this winter," said the pastor. "The teacher has sent you word about it, but you have made no fitting reply. What do you intend to do with her, neighbor?"

"I do not intend to send her to school," was the answer.

The pastor looked in surprise at the old man as he sat with folded arms on his bench and looked very decided.

"What are you going to make of the child?" then asked the pastor.

"Nothing; she grows and thrives with the goats and the birds; she is well enough with them, and she learns no harm from them."

"But the child is neither a goat nor a bird; she is a human being. If she learns no harm from such companions, neither does she learn anything else; she ought to learn something, and the time for it has arrived. I have come to tell you now, neighbor, so that you may be able to think it over and make your plans during the summer. This is the last winter that the child can spend without any teaching; next winter she must go to school, and every day."

"I shall not do it, pastor," said the old man decidedly.

"Do you really suppose, then, that there is no means of bringing you to terms if you will go on so obstinately in your unreasonable behavior?" said the pastor somewhat warmly. "You have been about the world a great deal and have had an opportunity to see and learn much, and I should give you credit for better sense, neighbor."

"Indeed!" said the old man; and his voice showed that he was no longer so perfectly calm in his mind. "And does the pastor suppose that I would really send a delicate child next winter on icy mornings through storm and snow down the mountain, a two hours' journey, and let her come back again at night, when it often blusters and rages so that any one of us would be lost in the wind and snow, and she only a little child? Possibly the pastor can recall her mother, Adelheid; she used to walk in her sleep and have ill turns. Shall the child, too, be made to suffer from such a struggle? Just let anyone come and try to force me! I will go into every court with her, and then we shall see who is going to force me!"

"You are quite right, neighbor," said the pastor with friendliness. "It would not be possible to send the child from here to school. But I can see that she is dear to you; for her sake do what you ought to have done long ago: come down into Dörfli and live once more with human beings. What kind of life is this up here, alone and bitter toward God and man? If anything should happen to you up here, who would help you? I cannot understand in the least why you are not half frozen all winter long in your hut, and how can the delicate child endure it?"

"The child has young blood and good shelter; that I can assure you, pastor. Moreover, I know where there is wood, and also when it is a good time to get it; the pastor ought to look into my shed; there is enough there so that the fire in my hut never goes out all winter long. It is not for me to go down into the valley as the pastor suggests; the people down there despise me and I despise them, so it is better for both that we remain apart."

"No, no; it is not good for you; I know what the trouble is," said the pastor earnestly. "As to the people despising you down in the valley, it is not so bad. Believe me, neighbor, seek to make peace with your God; ask for His pardon if you have done any wrong, and then come and see how differently the people regard you, and how well it can still be with you."

The pastor rose, held out his hand to the old man, and said again with heartiness, "I count upon it, neighbor, that next winter you are to come down with us, for we are good old friends. I should feel very sorry if you had to be forced; give me your hand on it that you will come down and live among us again, at peace with God and man.

The Alm-Uncle gave his hand to the pastor, but said firmly and decidedly, "The pastor means well toward me, but I cannot do what he expects; that I tell him surely and finally. I shall not send the child, neither shall I come down myself."

"Then God help you!" said the pastor, and went sadly out of the hut and down the mountain.

The Alm-Uncle was out of sorts. In the afternoon when Heidi said, "Now let us go to the grandmother's," he replied shortly, "Not today."

He did not speak again all day, and on the following morning when Heidi asked, "Are we going to the grandmother's today?" he still answered shortly and merely said, "We shall see.

Before the bowls had been put away after dinner another visitor came to the door. It was Aunt Dete. She had on her head a fine hat with a feather in it, and a dress which swept up everything on the floor, and in the hut lay all sorts of things which would not improve a dress.

The uncle looked at her from top to toe and said not a word. But Aunt Dete had a very friendly speech in her mind, for she immediately began to praise him by saying that Heidi was looking so well that she hardly recognized her, and that it was plain to be seen that she had not fared ill with her grandfather. She had really always intended to take her away again, for she understood very well that the little one must be a trouble to him, but never at any time before had she been able to find a place for her. But day and night she had wondered how she could provide for the child, and today she had come because she had suddenly heard of something which would be such good luck to Heidi that she could hardly believe it. She had gone at once to see about the matter, and now she could say it was as good as settled, and not one in a hundred thousand was so fortunate as Heidi.

"Some very wealthy relatives of my mistress, who live in almost the finest house in all Frankfurt, have an only daughter who is obliged to sit all the time in a wheelchair, because she is lame and not well in other ways. So she is almost always alone and obliged to study alone with a teacher, which is very dull for her; and, besides, she would like to have a playmate in the house."

This had been spoken about at her employer's house, and her mistress, who felt great sympathy for the little invalid, was anxious to find such a companion as the housekeeper described.

The housekeeper had said she wanted an unspoiled child, not like those seen every day. Then Aunt Dete had at once thought of Heidi and hastened immediately to tell her all about the child and her character; and the lady engaged to have her come. It was impossible to tell what good fortune was before Heidi, for when she was once there, if she pleased the people, and something might possibly happen to the only daughter—there was no knowing, she was so sickly—and if the people should not care to be left without any child, then the most unheard-of good luck might—

"Will you ever finish?" interrupted the uncle, who had not said a word all this time.

"Bah," retorted Dete, tossing her head. "You act exactly as if I had told you the most ordinary thing in the world, and there isn't a single person throughout all Prättigau who wouldn't thank God in heaven if I brought such news to them as I have brought to you.

"Take it to anyone you like; I will have none of it," said the uncle bluntly.

Dete went off like a rocket and said, "Well, if that is what you think about it, uncle, I will tell you what I think; the child is now eight years old and can do nothing and knows nothing, and you will not let her learn anything. You will not send her to school nor to church; that they told me down in Dörfli; and she is my own sister's child. I have to answer for what happens to her; and when a child can have such good fortune as Heidi, there can be only one person to prevent it, that one who cares for nobody and wishes nobody any good. But I won't give in; that I can tell you; and the people are all in my favor; there isn't a single person down in Dörfli who will not help me, and is not against you; so take heed if you don't care to be brought before the court, uncle; there are things that might be brought up which you would not like to hear, for when a man once gets into court many things are hunted up that he has forgotten all about."

"Silence!" roared the uncle; and his eyes blazed like fire. "Take her and be gone! Never bring her into my sight again. I never want to see her with feathers in her hat and words in her mouth such as you have spoken today!"

The uncle strode out of the house.

"You have made my grandfather angry," said Heidi; and her black eyes snapped at her aunt in no friendly way.

"He will soon be all right again. Now come," urged the aunt, "where are your clothes?"

"I will not come," said Heidi.

"What do you say?" continued the aunt; then she somewhat changed her tone of voice and went on in a half-friendly, half-annoyed way, "Come, come along, you don't know any better; you can't imagine what a good time you will have." She went to the cupboard, took out Heidi's things and put them together.

"Now come, take your little hat, it doesn't look very well, but it will do for once; put it on and make haste to come along."

"I shall not come," answered Heidi.

"Don't be so foolish and stubborn, like the goats; you must have learned it from them. Listen to me; your grandfather is angry; you have just heard him say that we must never come into his sight again; he wants you to go with me now, and you must not make him more angry. You haven't the least idea how lovely it is in Frankfurt, and how many things you will see there; and if you don't like it you can come back here; then the grandfather will be good-natured again."

"Can I turn right round and come back again tonight?"

"Oh, come along! I tell you, you can come home if you want to. Today we will go as far as Maienfeld, and tomorrow morning early we will get into the train, and in that you can get home again in no time; it's like flying."

Aunt Dete took the bundle of clothes on her arm, and Heidi by the hand, and they started down the mountain.

As it was not yet time to go to the pasture, Peter still went to school down in Dörfli, or was supposed to go there; but he took a holiday now and then, for he thought it was of no use to go to school; reading was not necessary, but a little wandering about and looking for large rods was profitable because he could make use of them. So he was just coming toward his hut from the farther side with a visible result of that day's efforts in a huge long bundle of thick hazel rods which he carried on his shoulder. He stood still and stared at the two approaching figures until they reached him.

"Where are you going?" he asked.

"I am hurrying to Frankfurt with my aunt," replied Heidi, "but I will first go in to see the grandmother, for she is expecting me."

"No, no; no talking, it is already too late," said the aunt hastily, and holding the struggling Heidi fast by the hand. "You can see her when you come back; so come along!"

Whereupon the aunt dragged Heidi off with her and did not let go, for she was afraid, if she went in, the child might refuse to go away, and that the grandmother might take her part. Peter ran into the hut and beat on the table with his whole bundle of rods, making such a frightful noise that the whole house trembled; the grandmother sprang up from her spinning wheel in alarm and cried out aloud. Peter had to give vent to his feelings.

"What is the matter? What is the matter?" cried the grandmother with great distress; and the mother, who had been sitting by the table and was almost startled out of her wits by the noise, said in her naturally patient way, "What is the matter, Peterli? What makes you so wild?"

"Because she has taken Heidi away with her," explained Peter.

"Who? Who? Where, Peterli, where?" asked the grandmother with new distress; she quickly guessed what had happened, for her daughter had told her a short time before that she had seen Dete go up to the Alm-Uncle's. All trembling in her haste, the grandmother opened the window and called out beseechingly, "Dete, Dete, don't take the child away from us! Don't take Heidi away from us!"

The two travelers heard the voice, and Dete must have understood what the grandmother said, for she took hold of the child more firmly than ever and ran as fast as she could. Heidi held back and said, "The grandmother is calling; I want to go to her."

But the aunt would not allow it and soothed the child by telling her that they must hurry in order not to be too late, and that the next morning they could travel farther and she could then see whether it pleased her well enough in Frankfurt to be willing to stay there. If she wanted to come back home again, she could do so at once; and then she could bring something to the grandmother which would delight her. This prospect pleased Heidi. She began to hurry without further objection.

"What can I bring home to the grandmother?" she asked after a while.

"Something good," said the aunt, "some lovely, soft white rolls that will please her; for she can hardly eat the hard black bread any longer."

"Yes; she always gives it back to Peter and says, 'It is too hard for me.' I have seen that myself," stated Heidi. "So let us go fast, Aunt Dete; then, perhaps, we shall reach Frankfurt today, so that I can soon be back again with the rolls."

Heidi then began to run so fast that Dete, with her bundle in her arms, could hardly keep up with her. But she was very glad that she went so swiftly; for they were coming to the first houses in Dörfli, and there everybody would make remarks and ask questions, which might set Heidi to thinking again. So she hurried straight through, and the child pulled so hard at her hand that all the people could see that she was obliged to hasten to please the child. So she merely replied to those who questioned and called to her from every door and window, "You see I can't stop now, for the child is in a hurry, and we have still far to go."

"Are you taking her away? Is she running away from the Alm-Uncle? It's only a wonder that she is still alive! And yet what rosy cheeks she has!"

Such remarks as these came from every side; and Dete was glad that she came through the place without delay and without being obliged to make any explanation, and also that Heidi said never a word, but only pushed on in the greatest haste.

From that day on, the Alm-Uncle looked more ill-natured than ever when he came down and passed through Dörfli. He spoke to no one; and with his cheese basket on his back, his enormous staff in his hand, and his thick, wrinkled brows, he looked so threatening that the women said to the little children, "Take care! Get out of the Alm-Uncle's way or he may hurt you!"

The old man had nothing to do with anyone in Dörfli, but went through there far down into the valley, where he sold his cheeses and bought his supply of bread and meat. When he passed along through Dörfli the people all stood in groups behind him, and everyone knew some strange thing about the Alm-Uncle; how he grew more wild-looking, and no longer even so much as greeted anyone. All were agreed that it was fortunate that the child was able to escape; for they had seen how she hurried away as if she were afraid the old man was coming after her to bring her back.

The blind grandmother was the only one who stood by the Alm-Uncle; and she always told everyone who came up to her house, to bring spinning or to get yarn, how good and painstaking he had been to the child, and what he had done for her and her daughter; how many afternoons he had worked about their little house, which would surely have tumbled to pieces without his help. So this information also reached Dörfli; but most people who heard it said that perhaps the grandmother was too old to understand rightly about it; for she could no longer hear well, and she could not see at all.

The Alm-Uncle showed himself no more at Peter's hut; it was a good thing that it had been so well repaired, because it remained for a long time untouched.

The blind grandmother now began the day with sighs, and not a day passed that she did not say sorrowfully, "Ah! With the child all joy and good have been taken away from us, and the days are so empty! If I could only hear Heidi's voice once more before I die!"

Chapter 6

A New Chapter and Entirely New Scenes

In the house of Herr Sesemann, in Frankfurt, the little sick daughter, Klara, reclined in her comfortable wheelchair. She spent the whole day in it and was pushed from one room to another. She was now in the so-called library, next the large dining room, and here all sorts of articles were scattered about for comfort, showing that it was used as the living room. From the beautiful, large bookcase one could see how it had been named, and that it was the place where the little lame girl received her daily instruction.

Klara had a pale, thin face, out of which looked two gentle blue eyes, at this moment directed toward the large wall clock, which seemed to go unusually slow; for Klara, who was hardly ever impatient, now said with some uneasiness, "Isn't it time yet, Fräulein Rottenmeier?"

Fräulein Rottenmeier sat very upright in a little sewing chair and was embroidering. She wore a mysterious wrap, a large cape, or sort of cloak, which gave her a solemn appearance, and was emphasized by a kind of high dome, which she had on her head. Fräulein Rottenmeier, since the death of Klara's mother many years before, had been in charge of everything in the Sesemann household. Herr Sesemann was away most of the time and left the whole house in Fräulein Rottenmeier's care, but with the condition that his little daughter should have a voice in everything, and that nothing should be done against her wishes.

While Klara, with signs of impatience, was for the second time asking Fräulein Rottenmeier whether it was not time for the expected guest to arrive, Dete, holding Heidi by the hand, was standing at the entrance door below, asking the coachman, Johann, who had just jumped down from the carriage, whether she might venture to disturb

Fräulein Rottenmeier at so late an hour.

"That is not my business," growled the coachman. "Ring for Sebastian, inside there in the corridor."

Dete did as he told her; and the butler, with big buttons on his coat and round eyes almost as big in his head, came down the stairs.

"I would like to ask whether I may venture to disturb Fräulein Rottenmeier at this hour."

"That is not my business," answered the butler. "Ring the other bell for the maid, Tinette"; and without further information Sebastian disappeared.

Dete rang again. This time the maid Tinette appeared on the stairs, with a little cap, dazzlingly white, on the middle of her head and a scornful expression on her face.

"What is it?" she asked from the stairs, without coming down. Dete repeated her request.

Tinette disappeared, but soon came back again and called down the stairs, "You are expected."

Dete, with Heidi, then went up the stairs and, following Tinette, entered the library. Here Dete remained politely standing by the door; she still held Heidi fast by the hand, for she was not quite sure what the child might take it into her head to do in this strange place.

Fräulein Rottenmeier slowly rose from her seat and came nearer, in order to examine the newly arrived companion for the daughter of the house. Heidi's appearance did not seem to please her. She had on her plain cotton dress and her old crushed straw hat. Her eyes peered forth very innocently from under it and looked with unconcealed amazement at the construction on the lady's head.

"What is your name?" asked Fräulein Rottenmeier, after having looked searchingly for some minutes at the child, who never took her eyes away from her.

"Heidi," she replied distinctly, in a ringing voice.

"What? What? That can surely be no Christian name. Then you can't have been baptized. What name was given you in baptism?" asked Fräulein Rottenmeier further.

"That I do not know," replied Heidi.

"What an answer!" exclaimed the lady, shaking her head. "Dete, is the child foolish or pert?"

"If the lady will allow me, I will speak for the child, for she is very inexperienced," said Dete, after she had given Heidi a little nudge on the sly for her unbecoming answer. "She is neither foolish nor pert, for she knows nothing about it; she means just what she says. But this is the first time she has ever been in a gentleman's house, and she knows nothing about good manners; she is willing and quick to learn if the lady will have patience. She was baptized Adelheid, like her mother, my late sister."

"Well! That is a name that can be pronounced," observed Fräulein Rottenmeier. "But, Dete, I must tell you that she is a remarkable-looking child for her age. I informed you that Fräulein Klara's companion must be of her own age, in order to follow the same studies with her and, especially, to share her occupations. Fräulein Klara is more than twelve years old; how old is this child?"

"With the lady's permission," Dete began again, "I can't quite recollect just how old she is; to be sure, she must be somewhat younger, but not very much. I can't say exactly; but she may be about the tenth year, or nearly that, I should think."

"I am eight now; grandfather said so," explained Heidi. The aunt nudged her again; but Heidi had not the least idea why and was not at all disturbed.

"What? Only eight years old!" exclaimed Fräulein Rottenmeier with some vexation. "Four years too little! What does it mean? What have you learned? And what books have you studied?"

"None," said Heidi.

"What? what? How did you learn to read then?" asked the lady again.

"I have never learned to read; neither has Peter," stated Heidi.

"Good gracious! You cannot read! You really cannot read!" exclaimed Fräulein Rottenmeier with the greatest horror. "Is it possible that you are unable to read? What have you learned, then?"

"Nothing," said Heidi with exact truthfulness.

"Dete," said Fräulein Rottenmeier, after some minutes, in which she tried to calm herself, "this is not according to the agreement. How could you bring me this creature?"

But Dete was not so easily disturbed; she answered eagerly, "If the lady will allow me, the child is exactly what I thought the lady wanted; the lady explained to me that she must be quite different and not at all like other children, and so I brought this little one; for the larger ones among us are not so different, and I thought this one answered the description perfectly. But I must be going. My mistress is expecting me; if she will allow me, I will come again soon and see how the child gets along."

With a curtsy Dete went out the door and down the stairs as fast as she could go. Fräulein Rottenmeier stood still for a moment, then ran after Dete. It suddenly occurred to her that she wished to talk with the aunt about a number of things if the child was really going to remain; and here the child was, and, as Fräulein Rottenmeier saw, the aunt was determined to leave her.

Heidi remained on the spot by the door where she had stood from the first. Until then Klara had watched everything in silence from her chair. Now she beckoned to Heidi: "Come here!"

Heidi went to the wheelchair.

"Would you rather be called Heidi or Adelheid?" asked Klara.

"My name is Heidi and nothing else," was Heidi's reply.

"Then I will always call you so," said Klara. "I like the name for you; I have never heard it before, but I have never seen a child before that looks like you. Have you always had such short, curly hair?"

"Yes, I think so," answered Heidi.

"Did you want to come to Frankfurt?" asked Klara again.

"No; but tomorrow I am going back home again to carry the grandmother some white rolls," explained Heidi.

"You are a strange child!" said Klara. "They have brought you to Frankfurt on purpose to stay with me and study with me, and you see now it will be very funny, because you don't know how to read at all, and there will be something entirely new in the study hours. It has often been so frightfully tiresome and has seemed as if the morning would never end. You see, the Herr Kandidat comes every morning at ten o'clock, and then the lessons begin and last until two, and it is so long! The Herr Kandidat often puts his book close to his face, as if he had suddenly grown nearsighted, but he is only yawning frightfully behind it, and Fräulein Rottenmeier, too, takes out her big handkerchief every now and then and buries her whole face in it as if she were very much touched by what we are reading; but I know perfectly well that she is only yawning terribly. Then I want to yawn so badly, but I have to swallow it down, for if I yawn only one single time Fräulein Rottenmeier brings the cod-liver oil and says I am getting faint. Cod-liver oil is the very worst thing to take, so I prefer to smother the yawns. But now it will be less tiresome, for I can listen while you learn to read."

Heidi shook her head quite thoughtfully when she heard about learning to read.

"But, Heidi, you must learn to read, of course; everyone has to, and the Herr Kandidat is very good—he is never cross, and he will explain everything to you. But you see, when he explains anything, if you don't understand at all about it you must just wait and say nothing, or else he will explain a great deal more and you will understand still less. But afterward, when you have learned something and know it, then you will understand what he meant."

Just then Fräulein Rottenmeier came into the room; she had not succeeded in calling Dete back and was evidently disturbed by it, for she had not been able to tell her exactly in what respect the child was not according to the agreement, and since she did not know what to do to retrace her steps she was all the more disturbed, as she herself had proposed the whole thing.

She went from the library to the dining room, and from there back again, and then immediately turned round and went to Sebastian, who passed his round eyes thoughtfully over the table, which was already laid, to see if there was any fault to be found with his work.

"Think your great thoughts tomorrow, and today get ready for us to come to the table."

With these words Fräulein Rottenmeier passed by Sebastian and called Tinette in such an ungracious tone that she came with even shorter steps than usual, and stood before her with such a mocking face that Fräulein Rottenmeier herself did not dare to speak angrily to her; so her vexation increased.

"The little visitor's room is to be put in order, Tinette," said the lady with forced calmness. "Everything is ready, but the furniture needs to be dusted."

"It is well worthwhile," said Tinette sneeringly, and went out.

Meanwhile Sebastian had opened the double doors of the library with considerable noise, for he was very angry, but did not dare to give vent to his feelings in words before Fräulein Rottenmeier; he then went quite calmly into the library to push out the wheelchair. While he was arranging the handle at the back of the chair Heidi placed herself in front of him and fixed her eyes upon him. He noticed this and suddenly burst forth, "Now what is there so remarkable to look at?" he growled at Heidi, in a way he would not have spoken if he had seen Fräulein Rottenmeier.

She was just coming into the room when Heidi replied, "Thou lookst just like Peter, the goatherd."

The lady clasped her hands in horror. "Is it possible!" she groaned half aloud. "She is saying thou to the servants! The creature has the most primitive ideas!"

The chair came rolling along, and Sebastian placed Klara at the table.

Fräulein Rottenmeier sat next her and beckoned to Heidi to take the place opposite. No one else came to the table, and as the three sat far apart there was plenty of room for Sebastian to serve his dishes. Next Heidi's plate lay a lovely white roll; the child cast longing looks at it. The likeness which Heidi had discovered must have aroused her entire trust in Sebastian, for she sat as still as a mouse and did not move until he held out the large tray and offered her the fried fish;

then she pointed to the roll and said, "Can I have that?"

Sebastian nodded, and glanced at Fräulein Rottenmeier, for he wondered what impression the question would make on her. In a twinkling Heidi seized her roll and put it into her pocket. Sebastian made a face to keep from laughing, for he knew very well that this was not allowable. He remained standing silently by Heidi, for he did not dare to speak, and neither did he dare to move away until he was bidden. Heidi looked at him for some time in amazement, and then asked, "Shall I eat some of that?"

Sebastian nodded again.

"Then give me some," she said, looking calmly at her plate.

Sebastian's face grew very thoughtful, and the tray in his hand began to tremble dangerously.

"You may put the tray on the table and come back again later," said Fräulein Rottenmeier, looking severely at him.

Sebastian at once disappeared.

"As for you, Adelheid, I must positively give you some ideas; I see that," continued Fräulein Rottenmeier with a deep sigh. "In the first place, I will tell you how to behave at the table"; and the lady explained clearly and exactly everything that Heidi had to do. "Then," she went on, "I must impress it upon you particularly that you are not to speak to Sebastian at the table, unless you have some order to give, or some necessary question to ask."

She then told her how she was to address the different members of the household, ending with: "Klara will tell you how she wishes you to call her."

"Klara, of course," said the little invalid.

Then followed a multitude of instructions about rising in the morning and going to bed, about coming in and going out, about shutting doors, and about orderliness in general. Meantime Heidi's eyes closed, for she had been up since five o'clock and had taken a long journey. She leaned back in her chair and fell asleep. When Fräulein Rottenmeier finally came to the end of her instructions, she said, "Now think this all over! Have you understood everything?"

"Heidi has been asleep for a long time," said Klara, looking much amused; the supper hour had not passed so quickly in a long time.

"I never in all my life saw the like of this child!" exclaimed Fräulein Rottenmeier in great vexation; and she rang the bell so violently that Tinette and Sebastian both came rushing in together. In spite of all the confusion, Heidi did not wake, and they had the greatest difficulty in arousing her sufficiently to get her to her sleeping room, first through the library, then through Klara's bedroom and Fräulein Rottenmeier's to the corner chamber, which was now ready for the little girl.

Chapter 7

Fraulein Rottenmeier Has an Uncomfortable Day

When Heidi awoke, on her first morning in Frankfurt, she could not understand what she saw. She rubbed her eyes hard, then looked up again; everything was the same. She was sitting in a high white bed in a large room; where the light came in hung long, long white curtains; close by stood two chairs with large flowers on them; then there was a sofa with the same flowers, and a round table in front of it, and in the corner was a washstand on which were things that Heidi had never seen before.

Suddenly she remembered that she was in Frankfurt, and everything that had happened the day before came back to her mind; and finally she recalled quite clearly the lady's instructions, as far as she had heard them.

Heidi jumped from the bed and dressed herself. She went first to one window and then to the other, for she wanted to see the sky and earth outside; she felt as if she were in a cage behind the long curtains. She could not push them aside, so she crawled in behind them in order to reach the window. But this was so high that her head hardly came up far enough to let her see out. Heidi did not find what she was looking for. She ran from one window to the other and then back again; but there was always the same thing before her eyes—walls and windows, and then walls and then windows again.

This puzzled her. It was still early in the morning, for she was accustomed to rise early on the Alm, and then to run outdoors immediately to see if the sky was blue and the sun already up; if the fir trees were murmuring, and the blue flowers had opened their eyes. As a little bird, placed for the first time in a handsome, glittering cage, flies back and forth and tries every bar to see if it cannot slip between and fly out and regain its freedom, so Heidi kept running from one window to the other, trying to open them, for she felt that there must be something to be seen besides walls and windows; she felt sure that the ground underneath, with the green grass and the last melting snow on the cliffs, must come into sight, and she longed to see it.

But the windows remained firmly closed, no matter how hard the child tugged and pulled and tried to get her little fingers under the sash. After some time, when she found that her efforts were of no use, she gave up the plan and wondered how it would be if she were to go outdoors and round behind the house until she should come to some grass, for she remembered that the evening before she had walked over nothing but stones in front of the house. There was a knock at the door, and Tinette immediately thrust her head in and said shortly, "Breakfast's ready!"

Heidi did not in the least understand that these words meant an invitation; Tinette's scornful face seemed to warn her not to come too near her rather than to give a friendly summons, and Heidi so understood and acted accordingly. She took the little footstool out from under the table, placed it in a corner, sat down on it, and waited to see what would happen. After some time she heard a bustling, and Fräulein Rottenmeier, again in a state of irritation, came and called into Heidi's room, "What is the matter with you, Adelheid? Don't you understand what breakfast means? Come down!"

Heidi understood this, and at once followed her.

Klara had been sitting some time in her place in the dining room and gave Heidi a friendly greeting. She looked much more contented than usual, for she expected all sorts of strange things to happen that day. The breakfast passed without any disturbance; Heidi ate her bread and butter properly enough, and after the meal was over Klara was rolled back into the library. Heidi was bidden by Fräulein Rottenmeier to follow and remain with Klara until the Herr Kandidat came to begin the lessons. When the two children were alone Heidi said at once, "How do you see outdoors and way down to the ground here?"

"We open the window and look out," replied Klara, amused at the question.

"But the windows don't open," said Heidi sadly.

"Well! Well!" exclaimed Klara, "you can't open them, and I can't help you; but when you see Sebastian, he will open one for you."

It was a great relief to Heidi to know that the windows could open and that she could look out, for her room had seemed to her like a prison.

Klara then began to ask Heidi about her home; and Heidi was delighted to tell her about the Alm, the goats, and the pasture, and everything she was so fond of.

In the meantime the Herr Kandidat arrived; but Fräulein Rottenmeier did not take him as usual into the library, for she wished to talk with him first, and so asked him into the dining room, where she sat down in front of him, and in great excitement described her embarrassing situation, and how it had come about.

She had written some time before to Herr Sesemann in Paris, where he was staying, that his daughter had for a long time desired to have a companion in the house, and that she herself believed that it would encourage Klara in the study hours, and give her interesting society the rest of the time. In reality the plan was a very desirable one for Fräulein Rottenmeier herself, as she was anxious to have someone there to relieve her from entertaining the sick girl—a task which was often too much for her. Herr Sesemann had replied that he would willingly grant his daughter's wish, but with the condition that her playmate should be treated in every way as Klara's equal; for he would have no children tormented in his house—"a really very unnecessary remark from Herr Sesemann," added Fräulein Rottenmeier, "for who wants to torment children?"

She then went on to tell the Herr Kandidat how terribly disappointed she had been in the child, and related all the strange things Heidi had done since she had been in the house, showing not only that he would have really to begin his instruction with the alphabet, but that she, too, had to commence at the very beginning in every kind of training. She saw only one way out of this unfortunate situation, and that was for the Herr Kandidat to declare that two children so different could not be taught together without great harm to the advanced pupil; this would be a sufficient reason to Herr Sesemann for putting an end to the matter and allowing the child to be immediately sent back where she came from; she would not dare to undertake this without his consent, because the master of the house knew that the child had come.

But the Herr Kandidat was very careful and never one-sided in his judgment.

He spoke many consoling words to Fräulein Rottenmeier and gave the opinion that if the young girl was backward in one way she might be so advanced in other ways that with well-planned instruction they would be brought into harmony. When Fräulein Rottenmeier saw that the Herr Kandidat did not favor her, but would undertake to teach A-B-Cs, she opened the door into the library for him, and after he had gone in closed it quickly behind him and remained on the other side, for she had a horror of A-B-Cs.

She strode up and down the room, considering how the servants should address Adelheid. Herr Sesemann had written that she must be treated as his daughter; and this command had to be carried out, especially in regard to the servants, thought Fräulein Rottenmeier. But she was not able to think about it long without interruption, for suddenly from the library came a frightful crash as of something falling, and then a call to Sebastian for help. She rushed into the room. There on the floor everything lay in a heap—books, copybooks, inkstand, and on top of all the rest the table cover, from underneath which a stream of ink flowed across the whole length of the room.

Heidi had disappeared.

"Just look at that!" exclaimed Fräulein Rottenmeier, wringing her hands. "Table cover, books, and work basket, all in the ink! Such a thing never happened before! There's no doubt about it, it is that wretched creature!"

The Herr Kandidat stood in perfect dismay gazing at the destruction which could be regarded only in one light—as very disturbing. Klara, on the other hand, watched the unusual occurrence and its result with a look of perfect delight and simply said by way of explanation, "Yes, Heidi did it, but not on purpose; she really must not be blamed; she was only in such a fearful hurry to get away, and pulled the cover with her, and so everything fell with it to the floor. Several carriages went by, one after the other, so she rushed out; perhaps she had never seen a carriage before."

"There, isn't it just as I told you, Herr Kandidat? The creature hasn't an idea about anything! Not a suspicion what a lesson hour is, that she ought to sit still and listen. But where is the unlucky child? If she has run away, what would Herr Sesemann say to me?"

Fräulein Rottenmeier darted out and down the stairs. There in the open doorway stood Heidi, looking, quite perplexed, up and down the street.

"What is it? What is the matter with you? Why have you run away?" demanded Fräulein Rottenmeier of the little girl.

"I heard the fir trees roar, but I don't know where they are, and I don't hear them any longer," answered Heidi, looking blankly in the direction where the rolling of the carriages had died away, a noise which in Heidi's ears had seemed like the raging of the wind in the firs, so that she had followed the sound in the highest glee.

"Firs! Are we in the woods? What a notion! Come up and see what you have done!"

Whereupon Fräulein Rottenmeier went upstairs again; Heidi followed her and was very much astonished to see the great damage done, for in her delight and haste to hear the fir trees she had not noticed what she was dragging after her.

"You have done that once; you must not do it again," said Fräulein Rottenmeier, pointing to the floor. "When you are having lessons you must sit still in your chair and pay attention. If you cannot do it by yourself, I shall have to fasten you to your seat. Do you understand?"

"Yes," replied Heidi, "and I will sit still now"; for she began to understand what she was expected to do.

Tinette and Sebastian by this time had to come to put the room in order, and the Herr Kandidat went away, for all further teaching had to be given up. There had been no excuse for yawning that morning.

In the afternoon Klara always had to rest a long time, and Heidi could then busy herself as she pleased; so Fräulein Rottenmeier had explained to her in the morning. When Klara had lain down to rest in her chair after dinner, Fräulein Rottenmeier went to her room. Heidi was glad to have the time to herself, for she had in her mind a plan which she was anxious to undertake, but she would have to have someone's help. Therefore she placed herself in the middle of the hall, in front of the dining room, in order that the person she wished to see might not escape her. Sure enough, in a little while Sebastian came up the stairs with the large tea tray, bringing the silver up from the kitchen to put away in the china closet. When he reached the last stair Heidi stepped up to him, saying, "I would like to ask you something," and added, as if to make peace with him, "but it is really not wrong, as it was this morning"; for she noticed that he looked a little cross, and she thought it was on account of the ink on the carpet.

Sebastian then laughed so loud that Heidi looked at him in amazement, for she hadn't noticed anything amusing.

"All right, go ahead, Mamselle."

"My name isn't Mamselle," said Heidi, a little vexed in her turn, "my name is Heidi."

"That's all right; Fräulein Rottenmeier told me to call you so," explained Sebastian.

"Did she? Well, then, I must be called so," said Heidi meekly; for she had noticed that everything had to be as Fräulein Rottenmeier said.

"Now I have three names," she added with a sigh.

"What did the little Mamselle want to ask?" said Sebastian as he went into the dining room and was putting away the silver in the closet.

"How do you open the windows, Sebastian?"

"This way," he replied, swinging one of the large windows wide open.

Heidi went to it, but she was too small to be able to see anything; she reached only to the window sill.

"There, now the little girl can look out and see what there is below," said Sebastian, bringing a high wooden stool and setting it down. Heidi climbed up with great delight, and was able at last to take the longed-for look out the window. But she immediately drew her head in, evidently much disappointed.

"There is nothing to see at all but the stony street," said the child mournfully. "If you go clear round the house, what do you see on the other side, Sebastian?"

"Just the same," was the answer.

"But where do you go to see way down across the whole valley?"

"You have to climb up into some high church tower, like the one over there with the golden dome above it. From up there you can see away off ever so far."

Then Heidi quickly climbed down from the stool, ran out the door, down the stairs, and went out into the street. But she did not find it as she had imagined it would be. When she had seen the tower through the window, she had fancied she would only have to go across the street and it would be just in front of her. She went down the entire length of the street, but without coming to the tower, and she could no longer see it anywhere; and she came to another street and then another, and so on, but still she did not see the tower. A great many persons passed her, but they were all in such a hurry that Heidi thought they had no time to tell her anything about it. Finally she saw a boy standing on the corner of the next street; he was carrying a small hand organ on his back and a very strange animal in his arms. Heidi ran up to him and asked, "Where is the tower with the golden dome at the very top?"

"Don't know," was the answer.

"Who can tell me, then, where it is?" asked Heidi again.

"Don't know."

"Don't you know any other church with a high tower?"

"Certainly I know one."

"Come and show me where it is."

"Show me first what you will give me if I do."

The boy held out his hand. Heidi searched in her pocket.

She drew out a little picture, on which was painted a garland of red roses; she looked at it for a little while, for she disliked to part with it. That very morning Klara had given it to her; but to look down into the valley, across the green slopes!

"There," said Heidi, holding out the picture to him, "will you take that?"

The boy drew his hand back and shook his head.

"What do you want, then?" asked Heidi, delighted to put her picture back into her pocket.

"Money."

"I haven't any, but Klara has, and she will give me some; how much do you want?"

"Four pennies.

"Well, then, come along."

The two accordingly went through a long street, and on the way Heidi asked her companion what he was carrying on his back, and he explained that under the cloth he had an organ which made wonderful music when he turned the handle. Suddenly they came to an old church with a high tower; the boy stood still and said, "There!"

"But how can I get in?" asked Heidi when she found that the doors were closed.

"Don't know," was the answer.

"Do you think I could ring here as I do for Sebastian?"

"Don't know."

Heidi had noticed a bell in the wall and now pulled it with all her might.

"If I go up there you must wait down here, for I don't know the way back, and you must show me."

"What will you give me if I do?"

"What shall I have to give you, then?"

"Four pennies more."

A key was turned in the old lock on the inside, and the creaking door opened; an old man stepped out and looked at first surprised and then rather angrily at the children and said, "How did you dare to ring for me to come down? Can't you read what it says under the bell? 'For those who wish to ascend the tower.' "

The boy pointed to Heidi and said not a word.

Heidi replied, "I want to go up into the tower."

"What do you want to do up there?" asked the tower-keeper. "Did someone send you here?"

"No," answered Heidi. "I only want to go up so that I can look down."

"Go home, and don't play any more tricks on me, or you won't get off so easily another time!"

Whereupon the tower-keeper turned round and was about to shut the door, but Heidi held him by the coattail and said pleadingly, "Only just this once!"

He looked round, and Heidi's eyes gazed up at him so beseechingly that he quite changed his mind; he took hold of the child's hand and said in a kindly tone, "If you are so anxious to go, come with me."

The boy sat down on the stone step in front of the door and signified that he did not care to go with them.

Heidi, holding the tower-keeper's hand, climbed many, many steps, which became smaller and smaller; finally she went up an extremely narrow staircase, and then she was at the top. The keeper lifted Heidi up and held her to the open window.

"There, now look down," he said.

Heidi saw below her a sea of roofs, towers, and chimneys. She drew her head back quickly and said in a tone of disappointment, "It is not at all what I thought it would be."

"Is that so? What does a little girl like you know about a view? Well, now come down, and don't ring at a church door again!"

The keeper put Heidi on the floor and started down the narrow stairs in front of her. On the left, where they began to be wider, there was a door which opened into the keeper's room; close by, where the floor extended out under the sloping roof, stood a large basket, and in front of it sat a big gray cat, growling, for in the basket lived her family, and she wished to warn every passer-by not to disturb them. Heidi stood still and looked amazed, for she had never seen such a huge cat before; in the old tower there lived whole flocks of mice, so the cat had no difficulty in catching half a dozen little ones every day.

The tower-keeper noticed Heidi's surprise and said, "Come, you may look at the kittens; she won't hurt you while I am here."

Heidi went toward the basket and screamed with delight. "Oh, the cunning little creatures! The lovely kittens!" she exclaimed again and again, running back and forth round the basket, in order to watch the amusing frolic and play of seven or eight little kittens as they crawled and jumped and tumbled over one another.

"Would you like one?" asked the tower-keeper, pleased to see Heidi dance with delight.

"For my own? To keep always?" asked Heidi, excited and hardly able to believe in such good luck.

"Yes, to be sure; you can have more than one—you can have them all, if you have room for them," said the man, glad of a chance to dispose of the kittens without having to harm them.

Heidi was highly delighted. The kittens would have so much room in the big house, and how surprised and pleased Klara would be when the pretty creatures arrived!

"But how can I carry them?" asked Heidi, and was going to take some of them up in her hands at once, but the big cat jumped up on her arm and growled so fiercely that she drew back greatly frightened.

"I will bring them to you, only tell me where," said the keeper, stroking the old cat to make her good-natured again, for she was his friend and had lived in the tower with him for a good many years.

"To Herr Sesemann's big house. There is a golden head of a dog with a big ring in his mouth on the front door," explained Heidi.

This detail was not necessary, for the tower-keeper had sat in the tower for many long years and knew every house far and wide;

besides, Sebastian was an old acquaintance of his.

"I know where it is," he remarked, "but whom shall I bring the things to, and whom shall I ask for? You don't belong to Herr Sesemann, do you?"

"No; but Klara will be so delighted to have the kittens!"

The tower-keeper was ready to go on down the stairs, but Heidi could hardly tear herself away from the entertaining sight.

"If I could only carry one or two with me—one for myself and one for Klara! Why can't I?"

"Well, wait a little," said the keeper; and he carried the old cat carefully into his little room, put her into the cupboard, shut the door, and came back. "Now take two!"

Heidi's eyes shone with delight. She chose a white kitten and a striped yellow-and-white one, and put one in her right pocket and the other in the left. Then she went down the stairs.

The boy was still sitting on the steps outside, and when the keeper had closed the door after Heidi she said, "Which is the way to Herr Sesemann's house?"

"Don't know," was the answer.

Heidi then began to describe, as well as she knew how, the front door, the windows, and the steps; but the boy shook his head; he knew nothing about it.

"You see," Heidi went on, "out of one window you look at a big, big gray house, and the roof goes so"; and with her forefinger she described a sharp point in the air.

Then the boy jumped up; all he needed was some such sign in order to find the way. He started off on the run and Heidi after him, and in a short time they stood directly in front of the door with the big brass knocker. Heidi rang the bell. Sebastian soon appeared, and when he saw Heidi he exclaimed urgently, "Quick! Quick!"

Heidi ran in great haste, and Sebastian closed the door; he had not noticed the boy standing disappointed outside.

"Quick, Mamselle!" urged Sebastian again. "Go right into the dining room; they are already at the table. Fräulein Rottenmeier looks like a loaded cannon; but what made the little Mamselle run away so?"

Heidi went into the dining room. Friiulein Rottenmeier did not look up, and Klara said nothing; there was an uncomfortable silence. Sebastian pushed up Heidi's chair. When she was once seated in her place Fräulein Rottenmeier began, with a stern face and a very solemn voice, "Adelheid, I will talk with you later; now I have only this to say: you have behaved very badly, and really deserve to be punished for leaving the house without asking permission, without anyone knowing a thing about it, and wandering about until so late in the day; I never heard of such conduct."

"Meow," sounded as the apparent answer.

Then the lady grew angry. "What, Adelheid," she exclaimed, raising her voice, "after such behavior, do you dare to play a naughty trick? You had better be very careful, I assure you!"

"I didn't—" began Heidi.

"Meow! Meow!"

Sebastian put his tray down on the table and rushed out.

"That is enough," Fräulein Rottenmeier tried to say; but she was so excited that her voice no longer sounded.

"Get up and leave the room!"

Heidi, much frightened, rose from her chair and tried once more to explain.

"I really didn't—"

"Meow! Meow! Meow!"

"But, Heidi," said Klara, "when you see how angry you are making Fräulein Rottenmeier, why do you keep saying 'meow'?"

"I am not doing it; it is the kittens," Heidi at last was able to say without interruption.

"What? What? Cats? Kittens?" screamed Fräulein Rottenmeier. "Sebastian! Tinette! Find the horrible creatures and take them away!"

Whereupon the lady rushed into the library and fastened the door in order to be safe, for to Fräulein Rottenmeier kittens were the most dreadful things in the world. Sebastian was standing outside the door and had to stop laughing before he could enter the room again. While he was serving Heidi, he had noticed a little cat's head peeping out of her pocket, and when it began to meow he could hardly contain himself long enough to set his tray on the table. At last he was able to go back calmly into the room, some time after the distressed lady had called for help. Everything was then perfectly quiet and peaceful; Klara was holding the kittens in her lap, Heidi was kneeling by her side, and both were playing to their great delight with the two tiny, graceful creatures.

"Sebastian," said Klara as he entered, "you must help us; you must find a bed for the kittens where Fräulein Rottenmeier will not see them, for she is afraid of them, and will have them taken away; we want to keep the cunning things and bring them out whenever we are alone. Where can you put them?"

"I will take care of them, Fräulein Klara," replied Sebastian willingly. "I will make a fine bed for them in a basket, and put it where the timid lady will never come."

Sebastian went on with his work, chuckling to himself all the while, for he thought: "This isn't the last of it!" and he did not at all dislike to see Fräulein Rottenmeier a little distressed.

Some time after, when it was almost time to go to bed, Fräulein Rottenmeier opened the door a very little way and called through the crack, "Have the horrible creatures been taken away?"

"Yes, indeed! Yes, indeed!" answered Sebastian, who had kept busy in the room, expecting this question. Quickly and quietly he took the two kittens out of Klara's lap and disappeared with them.

Fräulein Rottenmeier put off until the following day the special scolding that she had intended to give Heidi; for she felt too exhausted that night, after all the vexation, anger, and fright, which in turn Heidi had unconsciously stirred in her. She drew back in silence, and Klara and Heidi followed quite content, for they knew their kittens were in a good bed.

Chapter 8

Disturbances in the Sesemann House

On the following morning Sebastian had no sooner opened the front door for the Herr Kandidat and showed him into the library than someone else rang the bell, but with such force that Sebastian rushed down the stairs with all his might, for he thought, "No one rings like that except Herr Sesemann himself; he must have come home unexpectedly."

He pulled open the door; a ragged boy with a hand organ on his back stood before him.

"What do you mean?" said Sebastian to him. "I will teach you how to pull doorbells! What do you want here?"

"I want to see Klara," was the reply.

"You dirty street urchin, you! Can't you say 'Fräulein Klara,' as the rest of us do? What have you to do with Fräulein Klara?" asked Sebastian savagely.

"She owes me eight cents," explained the boy.

"You are certainly not right in your mind! How do you know, anyway, that there is such a person as Fräulein Klara here?"

"I showed her the way yesterday; that makes four cents; and then I showed her the way back again; that makes four more!"

"You see what a fib you are telling; Fräulein Klara never goes out; she is not able to go out. Get you gone where you belong before I start you!"

But the boy was not at all frightened; he remained calmly standing still and said coolly, "But I saw her on the street. I can describe her; she had short, curly black hair, and her eyes are black, and her dress brown, and she doesn't talk as we do."

"Oho!" thought Sebastian, chuckling to himself. "That is the little Mamselle, who has been in more mischief." Then he said, pulling boy in, "You're quite right; follow me and wait at the door until I come out again. If I let you come in, you must play something; it will please Fräulein Klara."

He went upstairs, knocked at the library door, and was called in.

"There is a boy here who wishes to see Fräulein Klara herself," announced Sebastian.

Klara was very much delighted at this unusual occurrence.

"He may come right in," she said. "May he not, Herr Kandidat, if he wants to speak to me?"

The boy soon entered the room, and, according to his instructions, he immediately began to play his organ. In order to avoid the A-B-Cs, Fräulein Rottenmeier was busying herself with all sorts of things in the dining room. Suddenly she stopped to listen. Did the sound come from the street? and so near? How could the sound of a hand organ come from the library? And yet—really! She rushed through the long dining room and threw open the door. There—she could hardly believe it—there in the middle of the library stood a ragged organ-grinder, playing his instrument most busily. The Herr Kandidat seemed trying to say something, but the words failed to come. Klara and Heidi were listening with beaming faces to the music.

"Stop! Stop immediately!" exclaimed Fräulein Rottenmeier, coming into the room. Her voice was drowned by the music. Then she ran toward the boy, but suddenly she felt something between her feet; she looked on the floor; a horrible black creature was crawling under her skirts—a turtle. Fräulein Rottenmeier jumped in the air as she had not done before for many years, then screamed at the top of her voice, "Sebastian! Sebastian!"

Suddenly the organ-grinder stopped, for this time her voice was heard above the music. Sebastian, doubled up with laughter, stood outside the half-open door, for he had seen the jump Fräulein Rottenmeier had made. Finally he entered. Fräulein Rottenmeier had thr[illegible]rself into a chair.

[illegible]ith them both, the boy and that creature! Send them away [illegible] Sebastian!" she cried to him. Sebastian readily obeyed.

He led out the boy, who had quickly seized his turtle; then, pressing something into his hand, he said, "Eight for Fräulein Klara, and eight for playing. You did well"; whereupon he closed the door.

Quiet was once more restored in the library; the studies were resumed, and Fräulein Rottenmeier had settled herself in the room, in order that her presence might prevent a similar dreadful occurrence. After the study hours she intended to investigate the case and punish the guilty one, so that it would not be forgotten.

Soon there came another knock at the door, and Sebastian again came in with the information that a large basket had been brought, which was to be given immediately to Fräulein Klara herself.

"To me?" asked Klara in surprise and curious to know what it might be. "Let me see at once what it looks like."

Sebastian brought in a covered basket and then hastened away.

"I think you had better finish your studies first and then open the basket," remarked Fräulein Rottenmeier.

Klara could not imagine what had been sent to her; she gazed with longing eyes at the basket.

"Herr Kandidat," she said, stopping short while she was declining a word, "may I not take just one little peep to see what is in the basket and then go right on with my lessons?"

"From one point of view I might be in favor of it, from another against it," replied the Herr Kandidat, "the reason for it would be that if your whole attention is directed toward this object—"

His remark could not be finished. The cover of the basket was not fastened, and suddenly, one, two, three, and then two, and then even more little kittens jumped out into the room and began to scamper round so unaccountably fast that it seemed as if the whole room were full of the tiny creatures. They jumped over the Herr Kandidat's boots, bit his trousers, climbed up Fräulein Rottenmeier's dress, crawled round her feet, leaped up into Klara's chair, scratched, groped about, and mewed; there was utter confusion.

Klara was charmed and kept exclaiming, "Oh, what cunning little creatures! How gaily they jump about! See! Look, Heidi, here, there!

Look at that one!"

Heidi with delight ran after them into every corner. The Herr Kandidat, hindered from going on with his teaching, stood by the table, lifting first one foot and then the other to avoid the annoyance. Fräulein Rottenmeier at first sat speechless with horror; then she began to scream at the top of her voice, "Tinette! Tinette! Sebastian! Sebastian!" She did not even dare to rise from her chair, lest all the dreadful little creatures might jump at her at once.

Finally Sebastian and Tinette answered her repeated calls for help and put the kittens, one after another, back into the basket and carried them to the bed made for the two kittens that had arrived the night before.

On this day again there had been no opportunity for yawning during the study hours. Late in the evening, when Fräulein Rottenmeier had recovered enough from the excitement of the morning, she called Sebastian and Tinette up into the library to make a thorough inquiry about the disgraceful proceedings. Then it came out that Heidi, in her expedition of the previous day, had been the cause of all that had happened. Fräulein Rottenmeier sat there pale with anger, and at first could find no words to express her feelings. She made a sign for Sebastian and Tinette to leave the room. She then turned to Heidi, who was standing by Klara's chair and had no idea what wrong she had done.

"Adelheid," she began in a severe voice, "I know only one punishment which could have any effect on you, for you are a barbarian; but we shall see whether you will not become civilized down in the dark cellar with lizards and rats, so that you will never let such things happen again."

Heidi listened calmly and wonderingly to her sentence, for she had never been in a frightful cellar; the room adjoining the Alm hut, which her grandfather called the cellar, and where the cheese and fresh milk were kept, was a pleasant, inviting place, and she had never seen any rats and lizards.

But Klara raised great objections to this: "No, no, Fräulein

Rottenmeier, you must wait until papa is here; he has already written that he is coming soon, and I will tell him everything; then he will say what is to be done with Heidi."

Fräulein Rottenmeier dared make no objection to this. She rose, saying somewhat bitterly, "Very well, Klara, very well; but I too shall have a word to say to Herr Sesemann."

Whereupon she left the room.

Then followed two or three peaceful days, but Fräulein Rottenmeier did not get over her distress; her disappointment in Heidi kept coming before her eyes, and it seemed to her that since the little girl had made her appearance in the Sesemann house everything had gone wrong and could never again be set right.

Klara was well contented; the days no longer seemed dull. It was Heidi who made the study hours pass quickly. The alphabet always confused her and she could never learn it. When the Herr Kandidat was in the midst of explaining and writing the forms of the letters, and, to make them clearer, compared one to a little horn and another to a beak, she would exclaim with delight: "It is a goat!" or "It is the robber-bird!" The description awakened all sorts of thoughts in her brain, but no idea of the alphabet.

In the late afternoon hours Heidi would again sit beside Klara and tell her all about the Alm and her life there, until her longing for it became so intense that she would cry out, "I really must go home now! Tomorrow I really must go!"

But Klara always quieted these attacks and showed Heidi that she must surely remain until her papa came home; then they would see what would happen.

One happy thought which Heidi secretly enjoyed helped her to give in and become contented once more. This was, that every day she remained she would be able to add two more rolls for the grandmother. Every noon and night beside her plate lay a lovely white roll, which she immediately put into her pocket, for she could not eat the bread when she thought how the grandmother had none at all and was hardly able any longer to eat the hard black bread.

Every day after dinner Heidi sat for two long hours quiet and alone in her room, for she was not allowed to run outdoors in Frankfurt as she did on the Alm; she understood this now and never did it anymore. Neither did she dare to talk to Sebastian in the dining room, for Fräulein Rottenmeier had forbidden that also; and she never dreamed of speaking to Tinette, whom she always avoided, for Tinette spoke to her in a scornful tone and was continually laughing at her, and Heidi understood her perfectly. So Heidi sat thinking to herself how the Alm was growing green again, how the yellow flowers were glistening in the sunshine, and how bright everything was—the snow and the mountains and the whole wide valley. She often felt as if she could not bear it any longer, so great was her yearning to be there. Her aunt had told her, moreover, that she might go home whenever she liked.

So it happened that one day she packed up her rolls in great haste in the big red shawl, put on her straw hat, and started. But at the very door she encountered Fräulein Rottenmeier just returning from a walk. She stood still and in blank amazement gazed at Heidi from top to toe, and her eyes rested especially on the full red shawl. Then she broke forth: "What kind of expedition is this? What does it mean? Have I not strictly forbidden you to go wandering about again? Now you are trying to start out another time, and looking for all the world like a tramp.

"I am not going to wander about; I only want to go home," replied Heidi, frightened.

"What? What? Go home? You want to go home?" Fräulein Rottenmeier wrung her hands in distress. "Run away! If Herr Sesemann knew that! Run away from this house! Don't let him ever hear of it! And what is it that doesn't suit you in his house? Are you not better treated than you deserve? Is there anything you need? Have you ever in your whole life had a home, or a table, or the service that you have here? Tell me!"

"No," replied Heidi.

"I know that perfectly well," continued the lady in great excitement. "You lack nothing, nothing at all; you are the most ungrateful child I ever heard of, and you don't know how well off you are."

Then all Heidi's hidden feelings broke forth: "Indeed I am going home, for I have been away so long that Schneehöpli must be crying for me all the time, and the grandmother is expecting me, and Distelfinck will be beaten if Peter has no cheese, and here you never see how the sun says good night to the mountains; and if the robber-bird should fly over Frankfurt he would scream still louder, because so many people live together and make each other wicked, and do not go up on the cliffs where it would be good for them."

"Mercy, the child is crazy!" exclaimed Fräulein Rottenmeier; and as she darted in alarm up the stairs she ran hard against Sebastian, who was coming down.

"Bring up that miserable creature at once!" she called to him as she rubbed her head, for she had received no gentle bump.

"Yes, yes, I'm all right, thank you," answered Sebastian, for he had been hit still harder.

Heidi still stood, with flaming eyes, on the same spot, and her whole body trembled with excitement.

"Well, what have you been doing now?" asked Sebastian gaily; but when he saw that Heidi did not move he patted her kindly on the shoulder and said comfortingly, "Pshaw! Pshaw! The little Mamselle must not take it so to heart; just be merry, that is the best way! She almost broke my head just now, but don't be frightened! Well? Still on the same spot? We must go upstairs; she said so."

Heidi then went up the stairs, but very slowly and quietly, and not at all as she was accustomed to go. That made Sebastian feel sorry. He went behind her and spoke encouraging words to her: "You mustn't give way! You mustn't be so sad! Only be brave about it! We have had a very sensible little Mamselle, who has never cried since she has been with us; other little girls cry a dozen times a day; that is well known. The kittens are gay, too, upstairs; they jump all round the floor and act like mad. By and by shall we go up there together and look at them, when the lady in there is away?"

Heidi nodded her head slightly, but so sadly that it went to

Sebastian's heart, and he looked at Heidi quite feelingly as she stole away to her room.

At suppertime that day Fräulein Rottenmeier said not a word, but kept throwing strangely sharp glances at Heidi, as if she expected her suddenly to do some unheard-of thing; but Heidi sat as still as a mouse at the table and did not stir; she neither ate nor drank; but she had put her bread quickly into her pocket.

On the following morning, when the Herr Kandidat came upstairs, Fräulein Rottenmeier motioned to him secretly to come into the dining room, and here she confided to him her worry lest the change of air, the unusual manner of life, and the new impressions had driven the child out of her senses; and she told him how Heidi had tried to run away, and repeated to him as much as she could remember of her strange words.

But the Herr Kandidat calmed Fräulein Rottenmeier and told her he knew that, on the one hand, Adelheid was certainly somewhat unusual, but, on the other hand, she was in her right mind, so that, little by little, with the right kind of treatment, he would be able to work out what he had in view. He found the case more serious because he had not yet succeeded in teaching her the alphabet, for she couldn't seem to grasp the letters.

Fräulein Rottenmeier felt calmer and let the Herr Kandidat go to his work. Late in the afternoon she remembered Heidi's appearance on her intended journey, and she determined to furnish the child's wardrobe with some of Klara's clothing before Herr Sesemann should appear. She consulted with Klara about it, and as she agreed with her, and wished to give Heidi a quantity of dresses and linen and hats, the lady went to Heidi's room to look into her closet and to examine the things she already had, and decide what should be kept and what disposed of. But in a few moments she came back again, looking very much disgusted.

"What a discovery I have made, Adelheid!" she exclaimed. "I never heard of such a thing! In your closet, a clothes closet, Adelheid, in the bottom of this closet, what do I find? A pile of little rolls! Bread, I say,

Klara, in a clothes closet! And such a pile stowed away!"

"Tinette!" she then called into the dining room. "Take away the old bread in Adelheid's closet and the crushed straw hat on the table."

"No! No!" screamed Heidi. "I must have the hat, and the rolls are for the grandmother"; and Heidi was about to rush after Tinette, but was held fast by Fräulein Rottenmeier.

"Stay here, and the rubbish will be taken away and put where it belongs," she said decidedly, holding Heidi back.

But Heidi threw herself down by Klara's chair and began 'to cry in such despair, louder and louder, and more bitterly, and sobbed again and again in her distress, "Now the grandmother won't have any rolls. They were for the grandmother; now they are all gone and she won't have any!"

It seemed as if her heart would break. Fräulein Rottenmeier ran out. Klara was alarmed and puzzled by her distress.

"Heidi, Heidi, don't cry so!" she begged. "Only listen to me! Don't be so troubled; see, I promise you I will give you just as many rolls for the grandmother, or even more, when you go home, and then they will be fresh and soft, and those would become very hard, and were so already. Come, Heidi, don't cry so anymore!"

It was long before Heidi could control her sobs; but she understood Klara's comforting words and took them to heart, else she would never have been able to stop crying. But she had to be reassured of her hope again and again, and so she kept asking Klara, while her sobs still interrupted her speech, "Will you really give me, for the grandmother, just as many as I had?"

And Klara kept saying, "Yes, indeed I will, and more, too; so be happy again."

Heidi came to supper with her eyes all red from weeping, and when she saw her little roll she had a fresh outbreak of sobbing; but this time she quickly controlled herself, for she realized that she had to behave at mealtime.

Sebastian this time kept making the most meaning gestures whenever he came near Heidi; he would point to his own head, then to

Heidi's, then he would nod and wink as if to make her understand, "Be comforted! I have looked out for everything and made it all right."

When Heidi a little later went to her room, and was about to get into bed, she found her little crumpled straw hat hidden under the bedspread. With perfect delight she snatched the old hat out; in her joy she crumpled it still more, and then, tying it up in a handkerchief, she thrust it down into the deepest corner of her closet. Sebastian had hidden it under the bedspread; he had been in the dining room at the same time with Tinette when she was called, and he had heard Heidi's cry of distress. Then he had followed Tinette, and when she came out of Heidi's room with an armful of bread, and the hat on top of it all, he had snatched the hat, exclaiming, "I will take care of that!"

So in great delight he had rescued it for Heidi, and that was what he meant at table by his comforting gestures.

Chapter 9

The Master of the House Hears of Strange Doings

A few days after this there was a great bustle in the Sesemann house, and hurried running up and down stairs, for the master of the house had just returned from his journey. Sebastian and Tinette were bringing in one package after another from the well-laden carriage, for Herr Sesemann always brought home many beautiful things.

He went first of all to his daughter's room to greet her. Heidi was sitting beside her, for it was late in the afternoon, when the two were always together. Klara greeted her father with great tenderness, for she loved him dearly, and the good papa showed no less affection toward his little Klara. Then he reached out his hand to Heidi, who had quietly withdrawn into a corner, and said kindly, "And this is our little Swiss girl, I suppose; come here and give me your hand! That's right! Now tell me, are you and Klara good friends? You do not quarrel and get cross, and then cry and make up, and then begin all over again?"

"No, Klara is always good to me," replied Heidi.

"And Heidi has never tried to quarrel, papa," quickly added Klara.

"That's good; I am glad to hear that," said her papa as he rose. "But now you must allow me, Klärchen, to get some luncheon, for I have had nothing to eat today. Later I will come back to you, and you shall see what I have brought home."

Herr Sesemann went into the dining room, where Fräulein Rottenmeier was overseeing the laying of the table for his midday meal. After Herr Sesemann had sat down, and the lady, looking like a living picture of gloom, had taken a seat opposite him, the master of the house said to her, "Fräulein Rottenmeier, what am I to think? You have put on a truly alarming face at my return. What is the matter?

Klara is very lively."

"Herr Sesemann," began the lady with great earnestness, "Klara is also disturbed; we have been frightfully deceived."

"How so?" asked Herr Sesemann, calmly sipping his coffee.

"We had decided, as you know, Herr Sesemann, to have a companion for Klara in the house, and as I knew very well how particular you were to have only good and noble friends for your daughter, I fixed my mind on a young Swiss girl, expecting to see such a person appear as I had often read about—one who, sprung up in the pure mountain air, so to speak, goes through life without touching the earth."

"I think," remarked Herr Sesemann, "that Swiss children touch the earth, if they move along, otherwise they would have wings instead of feet."

"Ah, Herr Sesemann, you know what I mean," continued the Fräulein. "I mean one of those well-known forms living in the pure mountain regions, who pass by us like an ideal breath."

"But what would my Klara do with an ideal breath, Fräulein Rottenmeier?"

"No, Herr Sesemann, I am not joking; the matter is more serious to me than you think; I have been frightfully, really quite frightfully deceived."

"But how so frightfully? The child doesn't seem to me so very frightful," remarked Herr Sesemann calmly.

"You should know just one thing, Herr Sesemann, only one—what sort of people and animals this creature has filled your house with in your absence; the Herr Kandidat can tell you about that."

"With animals? What am I to understand by that, Fräulein Rottenmeier?"

"It is not to be understood; this creature's whole conduct is past understanding, except from one point of view, that she has attacks of being out of her mind."

Up to this time Herr Sesemann had not taken the matter seriously; but "out of her mind"? This might result seriously for his daughter. Herr Sesemann looked at Fräulein Rottenmeier very closely, as if he wished first to assure himself that she herself was not troubled in that way. Just at this moment the door opened and the Herr Kandidat was ushered in.

"Ah, here comes our Herr Kandidat, who will give us an explanation!" exclaimed Herr Sesemann to him. "Come, come and sit down by me!" and he held out his hand to him.

"The Herr Kandidat will drink a cup of black coffee with me, Fräulein Rottenmeier. Sit down, sit down; don't be formal! And now tell me, my dear sir, what is the matter with the child who has come into my house to be a companion for my daughter, and whom you are teaching? What is the story about her bringing animals into the house, and what is the matter with her mind?"

The Herr Kandidat had first to express his pleasure at Herr Sesemann's safe return and bid him welcome home; but Herr Sesemann urged him to give his opinion about the matter in question. So the Herr Kandidat began, "If I were to speak my mind about the character of this little girl, I should first of all speak especially of the fact that if, on the one hand, she shows a lack of development, which through a more or less neglected education, or, to express it better, caused by a somewhat tardy instruction, on the contrary, her good qualities unquestionably show the effect of living a long while in the Alps, which, if it doesn't exceed a certain length of time, without doubt has its good side—"

"My dear Herr Kandidat," interrupted Herr Sesemann, "you are really giving yourself too much trouble; tell me, has the child alarmed you by bringing in animals, and what do you think of her society for my little daughter?"

"I don't wish in any way to offend the young girl," the Herr Kandidat began again, "for if she, on the one hand, shows a certain kind of social inexperience, due to the more or less wild life in which she moved up to the time of her coming to Frankfurt, which coming—"

"Pray excuse me, Herr Kandidat, don't trouble yourself; I will—I must hasten to look after my daughter."

Whereupon Herr Sesemann hurried out of the room and did not

return. He went into the library and sat down beside his little daughter; Heidi rose from her seat. Herr Sesemann turned toward the child, saying, "Look here, little girl, bring me—wait a moment—bring me—" Herr Sesemann did not exactly know what he wanted, but he wished to send Heidi away for a little while; "bring me a glass of water."

"Fresh water?" asked Heidi.

"Yes, indeed! yes, indeed! quite fresh!" answered Herr Sesemann.

Heidi disappeared.

"Now, my dear little Klara," said her papa, while he drew near to his daughter and took her hand in his, "tell me clearly and distinctly what sort of animals your companion brought into the house, and why Fräulein Rottenmeier should think that she is sometimes not quite right in her head; can you tell me that?"

Klara was able to do so, for the worthy lady in her horror had spoken to her also about Heidi's puzzling words, the meaning of which was clear to Klara. She first told her father about the turtle and the kittens, and then explained to him Heidi's remark which had so shocked Fräulein Rottenmeier. Herr Sesemann burst into a hearty laugh.

"So you don't care to have me send the child home, Klärchen; you are not tired of her?" asked her father.

"No, no, papa; don't do that!" begged Klara. "Since Heidi has been here something always happens every day, and the time goes so quickly; not at all as it did before she came, when nothing ever happened! Heidi tells me so many things."

"Very good, very good, Klärchen; and here comes your little friend back again. Have you brought cool, fresh water?" asked Herr Sesemann as Heidi offered him a glass of water.

"Yes, fresh from the well," replied Heidi.

"Did you run to the well yourself, Heidi?" asked Klara.

"Yes, indeed; it is perfectly fresh, but I had to go a long way, for there were so many people at the first well. So I went through the whole street, but there were just as many people at the second well; then I went to another street, and there I got the water; and the gentleman with the white hair sent his regards to Herr Sesemann."

"So your expedition was very successful?" said Herr Sesemann, laughing. "And who is this gentleman?"

"He was passing by the well, and then stood still and said, 'As you have a glass, you might give me a drink; to whom are you going to take the water?' And I said, 'To Herr Sesemann.' Then he laughed very loud and told me to give you his regards, and also said, 'Herr Sesemann ought to enjoy it.' "

"Who could it have been? How did the gentleman look?" asked Herr Sesemann.

"He laughed pleasantly and had a big gold chain and a gold thing with a large red stone hanging from it, and there was a horse's head on his cane."

"That is the doctor"—"That is my old doctor," said Klara and her father at the same time; and Herr Sesemann laughed again to himself at the thought of his friend and how he would regard this new way of having his supply of water brought to him.

That same evening, while Herr Sesemann and Fräulein Rottenmeier were sitting alone in the dining room and talking over all sorts of household matters, he told her that his daughter's companion was to remain in the house; he thought that the child was in a normal condition, and his daughter found her society very pleasant and more enjoyable than any other.

"I wish, therefore," he added very positively, "to have this child always treated kindly, and that her peculiarities shall not be considered as sins. If you should not be able to deal with the child alone, you have the prospect of valuable assistance, for my mother is coming very soon to my house to make a long visit, and she manages everyone, no matter how peculiar he may be. You are well aware of that, Fräulein Rottenmeier?"

"Yes, indeed, I know that, Herr Sesemann," replied the lady, but not with an expression of relief at the assured prospect of help.

Herr Sesemann had only a short time to remain at home now, for after two weeks, business called him back to Paris, and as his little daughter would not consent to his going away so soon, he consoled her with the promise of a visit from her grandmamma, who might be expected in a few days.

Herr Sesemann had hardly left home when a letter came announcing that Frau Sesemann had started from Holstein, where she lived on an old estate. She would arrive at a certain hour on the following day, and the carriage was to be sent to the railway station for her.

Klara was greatly delighted by the news, and told Heidi that evening so much about her grandmamma that Heidi, too, began to talk about the "grandmamma"; and Fräulein Rottenmeier looked at her disapprovingly, but the child did not think this anything strange, as she felt continually under her disapproval. When she started later to go to her room, Fräulein Rottenmeier called her first into hers, and explained then and there that she must never use the name "grandmamma," but must address her as "gracious lady."

"Do you understand this?" asked the lady as Heidi looked at her somewhat doubtfully; but she gave her such a forbidding look in return that Heidi asked for no more explanation, although she did not understand the title.

Chapter 10

A Grandmamma

On the following evening there were great expectations and lively preparations in the Sesemann house, and it was plain to be seen that the expected lady was of great importance there, and that everyone felt deep respect for her. Tinette had put a brand-new white cap on her head, and Sebastian had collected a great number of footstools, so that the lady might find one under her feet wherever she might sit down. Fräulein Rottenmeier, very erect, went through the rooms inspecting everything, as if to show that even though a second ruling power was near at hand, her own, for all that, had not come to an end.

The carriage rolled up to the door, and Sebastian and Tinette rushed down the stairs; Fräulein Rottenmeier in a dignified way followed slowly after, for she knew that she had to appear to welcome Frau Sesemann. Heidi had been told to go to her room and to wait there until she was called, for the grandmamma would first go to see Klara and would wish to see her alone. Heidi sat down in a corner and repeated what she was to say to Frau Sesemann. She did not have long to wait before Tinette thrust her head a very little way in at the door and said sharply, as usual, "Go into the library."

Heidi had not dared to ask Fräulein Rottenmeier for an explanation about the manner of addressing the grandmamma, but she thought the lady must have made a mistake, for until now she had always heard a person called Frau or Herr, with the name following; so she settled the matter thus in her own mind. As she opened the door into the library, the grandmamma called out to her in a friendly voice, "Ah, here is the child! Come here to me and let me look at you."

Heidi went to her and in her clear voice said distinctly, "How do you do, Lady Gracious?"

"And why not!" said the grandmamma, laughing. "Is that what you say at home? Did you hear that in the Alps?"

"No; no one among us has that name," answered Heidi earnestly.

"Neither has anyone here," said the grandmamma, again laughing, and patted Heidi affectionately on the cheek. "It's no matter! In the nursery I am grandmamma, and you shall call me so. You can remember that, can't you?"

"Yes, I can," said Heidi confidently. "I always called you so before."

"Well, you understand now!" said the grandmamma, nodding her head quite merrily. Then she took a good look at Heidi, nodding her head again from time to time, and Heidi looked very earnestly into her eyes, for they had such an expression of kindness that they made her feel quite at her ease, so that she could not look away. She had such beautiful white hair, and round her head a lovely lace frill, and two broad strings fluttered from her cap, and moved continually as if a light breeze hovered round the grandmamma; and this seemed to Heidi very peculiar.

"And what is your name, child?" then asked the grandmamma.

"My name is just Heidi; but if I must be called Adelheid, I'll answer to that." Heidi hesitated, for she felt a little guilty since she still made no reply if Fräulein Rottenmeier called unexpectedly, "Adelheid!" for it did not really seem to her that this was her name, and Fräulein Rottenmeier was just coming into the room.

"Frau Sesemann will doubtless admit," broke in Fräulein Rottenmeier, "that I had to choose a name which could be pronounced without so much difficulty, for the sake of the servants."

"My dear Rottenmeier," replied Frau Sesemann, "if a person is named Heidi, and she is accustomed to the name, I call her so and let it remain so!"

Fräulein Rottenmeier was very much troubled because the old lady continually addressed her by her last name alone; but there was nothing to be done about it; the grandmamma always had her own way, and there was no help for it. Besides, her five senses were keen and sound, and she always knew what was going on in the house.

On the day after her arrival, when Klara lay down at the usual time after dinner, the grandmamma took a seat in an easy chair by her side, and closed her eyes for a few moments; then she jumped up, for she was immediately awake again, and went out into the dining room; there was no one there. "She is asleep," she said to herself; then went to Fräulein Rottenmeier's room and knocked loudly on the door. After some time the Fräulein appeared, and started back somewhat alarmed by the unexpected visit.

"Where does the child stay at this time, and what does she do? I should like to know about it," said Frau Sesemann.

"She sits in her room, where she might busy herself with something useful, if she had the slightest desire to do anything; but Frau Sesemann ought to know what strange things this creature often plans, and really carries into effect —things which I could hardly speak about in polite society."

"I should do the same if I had to sit there alone as this child does, I assure you, and you would see how you would speak of my nonsense in polite society. Now bring the child out and fetch her to my room; I want to give her some pretty books I have brought with me."

"That is just the trouble; it is indeed!" exclaimed Fräulein Rottenmeier, wringing her hands. "What can the child do with books? In all this time she has not even learned her A-B-Cs; it is really impossible to get a single idea into this creature's head; the Herr Kandidat can tell you about that! If this excellent man didn't possess the patience of an angel from heaven, he would long ago have given up trying to teach her."

"This is very strange; she doesn't look like a child who cannot learn the alphabet," said Frau Sesemann. "Now bring her to me; she can first look at the pictures in the books."

Fräulein Rottenmeier was anxious to make further remarks, but Frau Sesemann had already turned round and was hurrying back to her own room. She was very much surprised to hear of Heidi's stupidity, and thought she would make an investigation, but not with the Herr Kandidat, though she really valued him on account of his good character; she always spoke to him in a particularly friendly way, whenever she met him, but then hurried away, in order not to be drawn into conversation with him, for his manner of expressing himself was rather annoying to her.

Heidi came into the grandmamma's room and opened her eyes wide when she saw the gay pictures in the large books which the lady had brought with her. Suddenly Heidi screamed aloud when the grandmamma turned a new leaf; she looked at the figures with gleaming eyes, then all at once bright tears rushed to them, and she began to sob as if her heart would break. The grandmamma examined the picture. It was a lovely green pasture, where all sorts of animals were feeding and nibbling the green shrubs. In the middle stood the shepherd, leaning on a long staff and gazing at the happy creatures. It seemed as if there were a golden light over it all, for the sun was just going down beyond the horizon.

The grandmamma took Heidi by the hand.

"Come, come, child," she said in a friendly way, "don't cry, don't cry. The picture made you remember something; but see, there is a lovely story about it, which I will tell you this evening, and there are a great many more beautiful stories in the book, which can be read and repeated. Come, we must have a little talk together. Dry your tears, and now stand right here in front of me, so that I can look straight at you; there, that's right; now we are happy again."

But it was still some time before Heidi could stop sobbing. The grandmamma gave her a good while to recover, merely saying encouragingly now and then, "There, that's good; now we are happy again together."

When she finally saw that the child was quieted she said, "Now you must tell me something, my child. How do you get along in the study hours with the Herr Kandidat? Are you studying well, and have you learned something?"

"Oh, no!" answered Heidi, sighing. "But I knew that it couldn't be learned."

"What could not be learned, Heidi? What do you mean?"

"People can't learn to read; it is too hard."

"What an idea! And where did you hear this news?"

"Peter told me so, and he knows about it. He has to keep trying, but he can never learn; it is too hard."

"Well, Peter is a strange fellow! But, see here, Heidi, you must not always take for granted what Peter tells you; you must try for yourself. Surely you have not listened with all your mind to the Herr Kandidat, and looked at the letters."

"It's of no use," asserted Heidi with a tone of entirely giving in to what could not be helped.

"Heidi," said the grandmamma, "now I am going to tell you something: you have not learned to read yet because you believed Peter; but now you must believe me, and I tell you, really and truly, that you can learn to read in a short time, like a great many children, who are like you and not like Peter. And now you must know what will happen when you can read. You have seen the shepherd in the beautiful green pasture. As soon as you can read you shall have the book for your own, so that you can learn his whole story, just as if someone told it to you; all that he is doing with his sheep and goats, and all the remarkable things that happened to him. You would like to know this, wouldn't you, Heidi?"

Heidi had listened with the most eager attention, and now she said, with beaming eyes, and drawing a deep breath, "Oh, if I could only read now!"

"It will come, and it won't take long; that I can see already, Heidi. And now we must look after Klara; come, we will take the lovely books with us." And the grandmamma took Heidi by the hand and went with her into the library.

Since the day when Heidi had wanted to go home, and Fräulein Rottenmeier had scolded her on the steps and told her how naughty and ungrateful she had shown herself by wishing to run away, and that it would be a good thing if Herr Sesemann never knew about it, a change had taken place in the child. She had the idea that she could not go home if she wished, as her aunt had told her, but that she must stay in Frankfurt for a long, long time, perhaps forever. She had also understood that Herr Sesemann, when he came home, would think her very ungrateful, and she imagined that Klara and her grandmamma would think so too. So Heidi dared tell no one that she wanted to go home, for she did not wish to cause the grandmamma to be cross, like Fräulein Rottenmeier. But in her heart the burden grew heavier and heavier; she could no longer eat; every day she grew a little paler. At night she often lay awake for a long, long time; for as soon as she was alone, and all was still round her, everything came so lifelike before her eyes—the Alm and the sunshine on it and the flowers! And when finally she fell asleep, she would see in her dreams the red pointed cliffs of Falknis, and the fiery snow field of the Scesaplana, and in the morning she would awake and, full of joy, be ready to run out of the hut; suddenly she was in her big bed in Frankfurt, so far, far away, and could not go home! Then Heidi would bury her head in her pillow and weep very softly so that no one might hear her. Heidi's unhappiness did not escape the grandmamma's notice. She let some days pass by to see if there would be any change in her—if her downheartedness would pass away. But as Heidi remained the same, and the grandmamma could often see early in the morning that she had been crying, she called the child one day into her room and said with the greatest kindness, "Now tell me, Heidi, what is the matter? Is something grieving you?"

But Heidi would not seem ungrateful to the kind grandmamma, for fear she might no longer be so friendly toward her; so she said sadly, "I cannot tell you."

"No? Can you not tell Klara?" asked the grandmamma.

"Oh, no, I can't tell anybody!" said Heidi decidedly, and looked so unhappy that the grandmamma pitied her.

"Come, my child," she said, "I want to tell you something. When we have a sorrow we cannot speak to anybody about, then we tell the dear God in heaven, and ask Him to help us, for He can take away every sorrow that troubles us. You understand that, don't you? You pray every night to the dear God in heaven, and thank Him for everything good, and ask Him to keep you from all harm, don't you?"

"Oh, no, I never do that!" answered the child.

"Have you never prayed, then, Heidi? Do you not know what it is?"

"I used to pray with the first grandmother, but it is so long ago that I have forgotten about it."

"You see, Heidi, the reason you are so sad is because you know no one that can help you. Just think what a good thing it is, when something troubles and distresses you in your heart, that you can go any moment to the dear Lord and tell Him everything, and ask Him to help you, when no one else can help you! And He can always help you and make you happy again."

A glad light came into Heidi's eyes. "Can I tell Him everything, everything?"

"Everything, Heidi, everything."

The child drew her hand out of the grandmamma's and said quickly, "May I go?"

"Certainly! Certainly!" was the reply; and Heidi ran away to her own room where she sat down on a footstool and, folding her hands, told the dear Lord everything that was in her heart, everything that made her sad, and asked Him, urgently and sincerely, to help her and let her go home to her grandfather.

A little more than a week had passed since this day, when the Herr Kandidat asked to see Frau Sesemann, as he wished to talk with her about an important matter. He was called into her room. Frau Sesemann politely offered him her hand.

"My dear Herr Kandidat, I am glad to see you! Sit down here by me"; and she pushed a chair toward him. "There, now tell me what brings you here; nothing unpleasant, no complaint?"

"On the contrary, gracious madam," began the Herr Kandidat, "something has happened which I no longer expected, and anyone who could have glanced at what went before, after thinking it all over, would have decided that what has actually happened and taken place in the most wonderful way was quite impossible, as if in opposition to all consistent to the—"

"Has the child Heidi possibly learned to read, Herr Kandidat?"

broke in Frau Sesemann.

The Herr Kandidat, taken aback, looked at the lady in speechless amazement.

"It is really quite wonderful," he said at last, "not only that the little girl, after all my thorough explanation and unusual pains, did not learn her A-B-Cs, but also, and especially, that in the shortest time after I had decided to give up the attempt, and without further explanation, to bring the bare letters, so to speak, before the little girl's eyes, she took hold of the reading overnight as it were, and then at once read the words with such correctness as I have seldom found with beginners. Almost equally wonderful to me is the gracious lady's keenness in immediately suspecting that this unlikely fact was possible."

"A great many wonderful things happen in the course of one's life," said Frau Sesemann, laughing with satisfaction. "Two things might happen fortunately; for instance, new interest in learning and a new method in teaching; and neither can do any harm, Herr Kandidat. Let us rejoice that the child has done so well, and let us hope for good progress."

Whereupon she accompanied the teacher out of the room and went quickly to the library, to assure herself that the delightful news was true. It was! There sat Heidi, reading a story to Klara, and with growing eagerness pushing into the new world opened to her; men and things suddenly became alive and stepped out of the black letters and took part in affecting stories.

That same evening, as they were sitting down to the table, Heidi found the large book with the beautiful pictures lying on her plate, and when she looked inquiringly at the grandmamma, Frau Sesemann said, nodding in a friendly way, "Yes, yes, now it belongs to you."

"For always? Even when I go home?" asked Heidi, blushing with delight.

"Certainly, for always!" said the grandmamma assuringly. "Tomorrow we will begin to read it."

"But you are not going home, not for a good many years, Heidi," broke in Klara. "If grandmamma goes away, you must surely stay with me."

Before she went to sleep Heidi had to look at her beautiful book in her own room, and from that day forth she liked nothing better than to sit with it, reading over and over again the stories belonging to the lovely pictures. In the evening the grandmamma would say, "Now Heidi will read to us"; and this delighted the child, for now she could read easily; and as she read the stories aloud they became much more beautiful, and she understood them better, and the grandmamma explained so much to her, and always told her still more about them. Heidi liked to look again and again at the green pasture and the shepherd in the midst of his flock, standing so contentedly, leaning on his long staff, for there he was still with his father's flock, following the merry lambs and goats, for this was his delight.

Then came the picture where he had run away from his father's house, and was in a strange land, obliged to tend the swine, and had grown very thin because he had nothing but husks to eat. The sun no longer shone so golden in this picture, and the land looked gray and gloomy. But there was still another picture to the story, in which the old father, with outstretched arms, was coming out of the house and running to welcome the penitent son, who, in a ragged jacket, was returning home discouraged and weak and ill. This was Heidi's favorite story, and she read it over and over again, both aloud and to herself; and she was never tired of hearing the explanation which the grandmamma gave. There were a great many other beautiful stories in the book, and with reading these and looking at the pictures the days passed away quickly, and the time soon drew near when the grandmamma had decided to go home.

Chapter 11

Heidi Improves in Some Respects, and in Others Grows Worse

The very afternoon when Klara was lying down, and Fräulein Rottenmeier, apparently in need of rest, mysteriously disappeared, the grandmamma sat down by Klara for a while, but after five minutes she was on her feet again, and always called Heidi to her room to talk with her, keep her busy, and amuse her in various ways. The grandmamma had pretty little dolls and pieces of the most marvelous bright-colored materials, which she showed Heidi how to make into dresses and aprons and cloaks for them; so the little girl unconsciously learned to sew. Now that Heidi could read, she always read some of her stories aloud to the grandmamma; and this gave her the greatest pleasure, for the more she read them the dearer they became to her. Heidi entered so eagerly into the characters and their experiences that she felt closely related to them and took more and more pleasure in their company. But she never looked quite happy, and there was no longer any merriment in her eyes.

It was the last week that the grandmamma was to spend in Frankfurt. She had called for Heidi to come into her room; Klara was taking her nap. When Heidi entered with her big book under her arm, the grandmamma motioned to her to come close to her, laid the book aside, and said, "Now come, my child, and tell me why you are not happy. Have you still the same trouble in your heart?"

"Yes," said Heidi, nodding.

"Have you told the dear Lord about it?"

"Yes."

"And do you pray every day that all may be well, and that He will make you happy?"

"Oh, no, I don't pray anymore now."

"What do you tell me, Heidi? What do I hear? Why don't you pray any longer?"

"It's of no use; the dear Lord did not listen; and I really believe," continued Heidi, somewhat excited, "when so many, many people in Frankfurt are praying together at night, the dear Lord cannot pay attention to them all, and so He has certainly not heard me."

"Why, how do you know that this is so, Heidi?"

"I prayed the same prayer every day for many long weeks, and the dear Lord never answered me."

"That is not so, Heidi! You mustn't have such an idea! You see, the dear Lord is a good Father to us all! He always knows what is good for us, if we do not know it. But if we want something from Him that is not good for us, He does not give it to us, but something much better, if we continue to pray to Him sincerely, and do not run away and lose all confidence in Him. You see, what you wished to ask of Him was not good for you just now; the dear Lord heard you; He can hear and see everyone at the same time, because He is God, and not a human being like you and me, and because He knew what was good for you, He thought to Himself, 'Yes, Heidi shall have what she asks for, but not until it is good for her, and when she will be quite happy about it. For if I should do now what she wants, and she finds afterwards that it would have been better if I had not done what she wished, then she would cry and say: "If only the dear Lord had not given me what I asked for! It is not so good as I thought it would be!"' And while the dear Lord was looking down to see whether you really trusted Him and came to Him every day and prayed when you needed anything, you have run away, no longer prayed, and quite forgotten Him.

"But, you see, when one does so, and the dear Lord no longer hears his voice in prayer, He forgets him, too, and lets him go whither he will. But when one is in trouble and complains, 'There is no one to help me!' we feel no pity for him, but say, 'You yourself ran away from the dear Lord, who could have helped you!' Do you want it to be so, Heidi, or will you go right away to the dear Lord and ask His forgiveness for having turned away from Him, and then pray every day, and trust

Him so that everything will be made right for you, and you may have a happy heart again?"

Heidi had listened very attentively; every word of the grandmamma's had gone to her heart, for the child had perfect confidence in her.

"I will go now, right away, and ask God to forgive me, and I will never forget Him again," said Heidi penitently.

"That is right, my child; He will help you at the right time, only be trustful!" said the grandmamma encouragingly; and Heidi ran away to her room at once and prayed earnestly and penitently to the dear Lord, and asked Him not to forget her, but to look down upon her again.

The day for the grandmamma's departure had come, and it was a sad day for Klara and Heidi; but the grandmamma managed it so that they were not aware that it was a sad day, but thought it rather a festival, until she went away in the carriage. Then the house seemed as empty and still as if everything had come to an end, and throughout the rest of the day Klara and Heidi sat as if lost, and did not know what would happen next.

The next day when the lessons were over, and it was time for the children to sit together as usual, Heidi came in with her book under her arm and said, "I am always, always going to read aloud to you; would you like to have me, Klara?"

Klara agreed to this proposal, and Heidi made haste to begin her task. But it was not long before it all came to an end, for Heidi had scarcely begun to read a story, which told about a dying grandmother, when she suddenly screamed aloud, "Oh, now the grandmother is dead!" She burst into pitiful weeping, for everything that Heidi read was to her actually taking place, and she believed nothing else than that the grandmother on the Alm was dead; so she cried louder and louder, "Now the grandmother is dead and I can never go to her, and she has never had a single roll!"

Klara tried to explain to Heidi that it was not the grandmother on the Alm, but an entirely different one, whom the story was telling about; but even when this mistake was finally made clear to the excited Heidi, she could not calm herself, and went on crying as if her heart would break, for the thought had been awakened in her mind that the grandmother really might die, and her grandfather too, while she was so far away, and then if she should go home after a long time, it would be so still and lifeless on the Alm, and she would be all alone, and could never again see those who were dear to her.

In the meantime Fräulein Rottenmeier had come into the room and had heard Klara's attempt to explain Heidi's mistake. But when the child still could not stop sobbing, she went with evident signs of impatience toward the children and said in a decided voice, "Adelheid, we have had enough of your useless screaming! I want to tell you something; if you ever again, while you are reading your stories, give vent to such an outbreak, I will take the book away from you and not return it."

This made an impression. Heidi turned pale with fright. The book was her dearest treasure. She hastily dried her tears and swallowed and choked down her sobs with all her might, so that no further sound was heard from her. This means took effect. Heidi did not cry again, no matter what she read; but many a time she had to make such an effort to control herself and not scream out that Klara often said, quite surprised, "Heidi, you are making the most frightful faces I ever saw!"

But the faces made no sound and did not offend Fräulein Rottenmeier, and when Heidi had overcome her attack of desperate sadness everything went on in the old way and passed along quietly. But Heidi lost her appetite and was so thin and pale that Sebastian could hardly bear to look on and see how the child let the nicest dishes pass by untouched. He often whispered to her encouragingly when he passed her something, "Take some of it, Mamselle, it is fine. Not such a little! A good spoonful, and another!" But his fatherly advice did no good. Heidi ate almost nothing at all, and at night when she lay down on her pillow everything at home instantly came before her eyes, and then, out of homesickness, she wept in her pillow very softly, so that no one might hear her.

A long time passed in this way. Heidi scarcely knew whether it was summer or winter, for the walls and windows, which were the only things to be seen from the Sesemann house, always looked the same, and she went out only when Klara was particularly well and could be taken for a drive in the carriage; and this was always very short, for Klara could not bear to go far. So they seldom went beyond walls and pavements, but usually turned round before they reached the suburbs; so that all they saw were beautiful wide streets, where plenty of houses and people were to be seen, but no grass and flowers, no fir trees, and no mountains; and Heidi's longing for a glimpse of the beautiful things she had been accustomed to increased every day. Now the mere name of one of these suggestive words was enough to cause an outbreak of pain, and Heidi had to struggle against it with all her might.

Thus passed the autumn and winter; and the sun had already become so dazzling on the white walls of the houses opposite that Heidi felt sure the time was drawing near for Peter to drive the goats up on the Alm again, and the golden rockroses would be glistening in the sunshine, and every evening all the mountains round would be on fire. Heidi would sit down in a corner of her lonely room and put both hands over her eyes, so that she might not see the sunlight on the walls opposite; and thus she would sit without stirring, silently fighting against her burning homesickness, until Klara called for her again.

Chapter 12

The Sesemann House Is Haunted

For several days Fräulein Rottenmeier had been going about the house, for the most part, in silence and wrapped in thought. If at dusk she went from one room to another, or through the long hall, she often looked round her and into the corners, giving a quick glance behind now and then, as if she thought someone might be coming softly after her and, unnoticed, pull her dress. She went alone into the living rooms only. If she had something to do on the upper floor where the handsomely furnished guest rooms were situated, or downstairs in the great mysterious hall in which every step gave a resounding echo, and the old senators, with their big white collars, looked down from the walls so sternly and steadily with their big eyes, she would pretend there was something to carry up or down, and she would summon Tinette and tell her she must come with her. Tinette did exactly the same; if she had any work to do upstairs or downstairs, she would call Sebastian and tell him he was to go with her, for she might have something to carry which she could not manage alone. Strange to say, Sebastian did exactly the same; if he was sent to the remote part of the house, he called Johann and directed him to accompany him, for fear he could not bring what was needed. Each one followed the other quite willingly, although there was really nothing to be carried, and each might have gone alone; but it seemed as if the companion always thought he might soon need the other for the same service. While this was going on upstairs, the cook, who had been in the house for many years, stood below, deep in thought among her pots, and shook her head and sighed, "That I should live to see this!"

For some time there had been something strange and weird going on in the Sesemann house. Every morning when the servants came down, the house door stood wide open, but no one was to be seen anywhere about who could give any account of the matter. The first few times when this happened all the chambers and rooms of the house were anxiously searched to see what had been stolen, for they thought a thief had broken into the house in the night and had escaped with what he had stolen; but such was not the case; not a single thing in the whole house was missing.

At night the door was not only double-locked, but also a wooden bar was put across; it made no difference, in the morning the door stood wide open; and no matter how early the servants in their excitement came down, there stood the door open; yet everything round about was wrapped in deep sleep, and the doors and windows in all the other houses were still firmly fastened.

At last Johann and Sebastian took courage, and, at Fräulein Rottenmeier's pressing request, prepared to spend the night below, in the room adjoining the great hall, to see what would happen.

Fräulein Rottenmeier got out some of Herr Sesemann's weapons and gave them to Sebastian.

The two men sat down on the appointed evening, and after being at first very talkative they became rather sleepy; whereupon they both leaned back in their chairs and were silent. When the old tower clock struck twelve, Sebastian grew bold and called to his companion; but he was not easy to waken; as often as Sebastian called to him he would turn his head from one side of the chair back to the other and go to sleep again. Sebastian now listened eagerly, for by this time he was wide awake. It was as still as a mouse everywhere; even in the street there was no sound to be heard. Sebastian did not go to sleep again, for it seemed to him weird in the deep stillness, and he called Johann in a subdued voice and shook him a little from time to time. Finally, when it had struck one o'clock, Johann woke up and realized why he was sitting in a chair and not lying in his bed. Suddenly he began to be very brave and called out, "Now, Sebastian, we must go out and see how things are; you needn't be afraid. Come after me."

Johann opened wide the room door, which had been left open a little, and stepped outside. At the same moment a sharp gust of air blew in from the open house door and put out the light which Johann held in his hand. He rushed back, almost threw Sebastian, who was standing behind him, backward into the room, then dragged him along, closed the door, and in feverish haste turned the key as far as it would go. Then he pulled out his matchbox and made a light again. Sebastian did not know just what had happened, for, standing behind the broad-shouldered Johann, he had not so plainly felt the draft of air. But when they could see each other by the light, Sebastian cried out from fright, for Johann was deadly pale and trembled like an aspen leaf.

"What is the matter? What was outside there?" asked Sebastian anxiously.

"The door was as wide open as it could be," gasped Johann, "and there was a white form on the steps; you see, Sebastian, it came up the steps, disappeared, and was gone."

Cold shivers ran down Sebastian's back. Then they sat down very close together and did not stir again until it was morning and people began to be moving in the street. Then they went out together, closed the open door, and went upstairs to tell Fräulein Rottenmeier about their experience. The lady was quite ready to talk, for the expectation of what might happen had kept her from sleeping. As soon as she learned what had occurred she sat down and wrote such a letter to Herr Sesemann as he had never received before. In it she said that her fingers were numb with fright. Herr Sesemann must immediately come home, for the most unheard-of things had happened there. Then she told him what had taken place; how the door was found wide open every morning, and in consequence no one in the house was any longer sure of his life, and that no one could tell what horrible results might follow this mysterious happening. Herr Sesemann replied by return mail that it was impossible for him to leave his business so suddenly to come home. The ghost story was very strange, and he hoped it was all past. Meanwhile, if there should be any further trouble, Fräulein Rottenmeier might write to Frau Sesemann and ask her to come to Frankfurt to their assistance; his mother would surely scatter the ghosts in a very short space of time, and after that they would never again venture to disturb his house.

Fräulein Rottenmeier was not pleased with the tone of this letter; the matter had made too little impression on him. She wrote immediately to Frau Sesemann, but she did not get any more satisfaction from this direction, and the reply contained some very sharp remarks. Frau Sesemann wrote that she did not think it worthwhile for her to travel from Holstein to Frankfurt because Rottenmeier saw ghosts. Moreover, a ghost had never been seen in the Sesemann house, and if there was one wandering round there now, it could be nothing but a living being, and Rottenmeier ought to be able to come to an understanding with it; if not, she should call the night watchman to her aid.

But Fräulein Rottenmeier was determined not to spend her days any longer in terror, and she knew how to help herself. Until then she had told the children nothing about the appearance of a ghost, lest they should be afraid to stay alone a single moment day or night, and that might have very uncomfortable consequences for her. Now she went straight to the library, where the two were sitting together, and in a low voice told them how a strange being appeared every night. Immediately Klara screamed out that she would not stay alone another moment, that her papa must come home, and Fräulein Rottenmeier must sleep in her room, and Heidi ought not to be alone either, or the ghost might come to her and do her some harm. She wanted them all to stay in the same room and to have a light burning all night, and Tinette must sleep near, and Sebastian and Johann must come down and spend the night in the hall, in order to scream and frighten away the ghost if it should come up the stairs.

Klara was very much excited, and Fräulein Rottenmeier had the greatest difficulty quieting her. She promised to write to her papa immediately, and to put her bed in Klara's room, and never to leave her alone again. They could not all sleep in the same room, but if Adelheid was afraid, Tinette must put up a couch in her room. But Heidi was more afraid of Tinette than of ghosts, for she had never even heard of such things, and she insisted that she was not afraid and preferred to remain alone in her room.

Hereupon Fräulein Rottenmeier flew to her writing table and wrote to Herr Sesemann how the mysterious proceedings which were repeated every night in his house had so affected his daughter's delicate health that the most serious results were to be expected. Examples were known of sudden epileptic seizures, or attacks of St. Vitus's dance, in similar cases, and his daughter was liable to any such misfortune if the house were not relieved from this state of terror.

This had some effect. Two days later Herr Sesemann was standing at his door and rang so violently that everyone in the house came hurrying forth, and each gazed at the other, for they believed nothing less than that the ghost was most impudently playing his evil tricks even in the daytime. Sebastian, on the floor above, cautiously peered out through a half-opened shutter; and just at that instant there was another ring at the bell, and this time so decided that no doubt was left in anyone's mind that it was a human hand behind the summons.

Sebastian had recognized the hand, dashed through the room, flew headfirst downstairs, but landed on his feet at the bottom and flung the front door open. Herr Sesemann did not stop to talk with him, but went immediately up to his daughter's room. Klara received her papa with a cry of joy, and when he saw her looking so cheerful and unchanged, his face, which had looked very stern, softened, and his expression grew more and more pleasant, as he heard from his daughter's own lips that she was as well as usual, and that she was perfectly delighted to have him at home again, and that she was most grateful to the ghost that was haunting the house, because it had caused her papa to come home.

"And what further pranks has the ghost been up to, Fräulein Rottenmeier?" asked Herr Sesemann with a comical expression around the corners of his mouth.

"Indeed, Herr Sesemann," replied that lady solemnly, "it is no laughing matter. I have no doubt at all that by tomorrow Herr Sesemann will find it serious enough; for what is going on in this house signifies that something terrible must have happened here in days gone by and has been kept secret."

"Well, I know nothing about it," observed Herr Sesemann, "but I must beg of you not to harbor any doubts about my most honorable ancestors. And now call Sebastian into the dining room; I wish to talk with him alone."

Herr Sesemann went into the dining room, and Sebastian made his appearance. Herr Sesemann had not failed to observe that Sebastian and Fräulein Rottenmeier were not the best of friends; so he had his suspicions.

"Come here, Sebastian," said he, beckoning the servant to enter. "Now tell me honestly, have you not yourself been playing the part of a ghost in order to tease Fräulein Rottenmeier a little? Tell me!"

"No, on my word; you must not think any such thing; I myself have not felt at all comfortable about the matter," replied Sebastian with unmistakable frankness.

"Well, if that is the case, I will show you and the brave Johann tomorrow how ghosts look by daylight. Shame upon you, Sebastian! A strong young fellow like you running away from ghosts! Now go at once to my old friend, Dr. Reboux, give him my compliments, and tell him he must come here without fail tonight at nine o'clock. I have come home from Paris on purpose to consult him. It is such a serious matter that he must spend the night with me; he must make his arrangements to do so. Do you understand, Sebastian?"

"Yes, indeed; yes, indeed! Herr Sesemann may be sure that I shall do as he says."

Sebastian left the room, and Herr Sesemann returned to his little daughter to quiet her fears about the ghost, which he was going that very day to put in its true light.

Punctually at nine o'clock, when the children had gone to sleep and Fräulein Rottenmeier had retired, the doctor appeared, showing still under his gray hair a very fresh face and two bright, kind, twinkling eyes. He looked somewhat anxious, but, as his friend greeted him, broke out into a hearty laugh and said, clapping him on the shoulder, "Well, well, for one who needs to be watched with, you look fairly hearty, old friend."

"Have patience, my dear doctor," replied Herr Sesemann, "the one you have to watch with will look worse when we have caught him."

"What! A sick person in the house and one that must be caught?"

"Far worse, doctor, far worse. A ghost in the house; the house is haunted!"

The doctor laughed aloud.

"A fine state of affairs, doctor!" continued Herr Sesemann. "It's a shame that my friend Rottenmeier cannot enjoy it. She is convinced that a former Sesemann is wandering about here and atoning for some dreadful deed."

"How did she find out about it?" asked the doctor, still very much amused.

Herr Sesemann now told his friend about the whole matter, and added that, in order to be prepared for whatever might happen, he had left two well-loaded revolvers where they were to watch; for either the affair was a very undesirable joke, which possibly some of the servants' acquaintances were playing, in order to frighten the people in the house during the master's absence—in that case a little scare, such as a good shot into the air, could not be unwholesome—else it was a case of thieves, who had taken this means to make the inmates of the house think they were ghosts, in order to be safer later, as no one would dare to venture forth; if this were so, a good weapon might come in handy.

During this explanation the gentlemen had gone downstairs and entered the same room where Johann and Sebastian had watched. On the table lay the two revolvers, and two candlesticks, each holding three lighted candles, stood in the center, for Herr Sesemann did not care to await the ghost in a dim light.

The door was now partly shut, so that too much light need not shine out into the hall to frighten away the ghost. Then the gentlemen seated themselves comfortably in their easy chairs and began to talk about all sorts of things, now and then taking a little refreshment, and so the clock struck twelve before they were aware of it.

"The ghost has spied us out and is not coming tonight at all," said the doctor.

"Have patience; it may come at one o'clock," replied his friend.

They went on with their talking. It struck one. It was perfectly still all about; even on the street there was no sound to be heard. Suddenly the doctor lifted his finger.

"Sh, Sesemann! Don't you hear something?"

They both listened. They heard the bar softly but quite distinctly pushed back, the key turned twice in the lock, and the door opened. Herr Sesemann reached for the revolver.

"You are not afraid?" said the doctor, rising.

"It is better to be cautious," whispered Herr Sesemann. Seizing a candlestick in his left hand, and the revolver in his right, he followed the doctor, who had preceded him, likewise provided with lights and a revolver. Quickly and silently they stepped out into the hall.

Through the wide-open door the pale moonlight came in and lighted up a white form, which stood motionless on the doorsill.

"Who is there?" the doctor thundered forth, so that it echoed through the entire length of the hall, and both gentlemen, with lights and weapons, went toward the figure. It turned round and gave a little scream. There stood Heidi, with bare feet, in her white night clothes, looking confused at the bright lights and the firearms, and shivering and trembling from head to foot like a little leaf in the wind. The gentlemen looked at each other in the greatest astonishment.

"I really believe, Sesemann, that it is your little water carrier," said the doctor.

"Child, what does this mean?" asked Herr Sesemann. "What are you going to do? Why have you come down here?"

White as snow from fright, Heidi stood there and said, scarcely able to make a sound, "I don't know."

Then the doctor stepped forward.

"Sesemann, the case belongs to my domain; go and sit down in your easy chair in there for a while. I will first of all take the child back where she belongs."

Whereupon he laid his revolver on the floor, took the trembling child by the hand, as a father would, and went upstairs with her.

"Don't be afraid, don't be afraid," he said kindly, as they went up. "Only be very quiet; there is no harm done, so never mind."

When they were in Heidi's room the doctor placed his light on the table, took Heidi in his arms, laid her in her bed and covered her up carefully. He sat down in a chair by the bed and waited until she was somewhat calmer and did not tremble in every limb. Then he took Heidi's hand and said soothingly, "There, now everything is all right; now tell me where you wanted to go."

"I didn't want to go anywhere," asserted Heidi. "I did not go down there myself; I was only there all at once."

"Indeed! And did you dream anything in the night, do you know, so that you saw and heard something very clearly?"

"Yes, every night I dream, and always the same thing. I think I am with my grandfather, and I hear the fir trees roaring outdoors, and I think, 'Now the stars are sparkling so brightly in the sky,' and I run swiftly and open the door of the hut, and it is so beautiful there! But when I wake up I am always in Frankfurt still." Heidi began to struggle and to swallow down the lump that rose in her throat.

"Hm! And do you ever have any pain anywhere? In your head or in your back?"

"Oh, no; only something presses here all the time, like a great stone."

"Hm! Somewhat as if you had eaten something and then afterward wished you could give it back again?"

"No, not like that; but so heavy, as if I must cry hard."

"Indeed! And then do you cry right out loud?"

"Oh, no, I don't dare to do that; Fräulein Rottenmeier has forbidden that."

"Then you swallow it down till another time, don't you? Really! Well, you like to stay in Frankfurt, do you not?"

"Oh, yes," she replied faintly; but it sounded as if she meant the opposite.

"Hm! And where did you live with your grandfather?"

"Always on the Alm."

"It is not particularly pleasant there, but rather dreary, is it not?"

"Oh, no; it is so lovely there, so lovely!"

Heidi could say no more; the recollection of it all, the excitement she had just passed through, and the long restrained weeping overpowered the child; the tears rushed from her eyes in streams, and she broke into loud, violent sobbing.

The doctor rose; he laid Heidi's head gently on the pillow and said, "There, now cry a little—it can do no harm—and then go to sleep, and be happy in your sleep; tomorrow everything will be all right."

Then he went downstairs.

When he was once more in the room where they had been watching, he drew an easy chair opposite his waiting friend and explained to him, while Herr Sesemann listened with eager expectation, "Sesemann, in the first place, your little protégé walks in her sleep; all unconsciously she has opened the door every night like a ghost and put all your servants into a fever of fright. In the second place, the child is wasting away from homesickness, so that she is almost reduced to a little skeleton and will soon be entirely so; something must be done for her at once! For the first evil and for the nervous excitement existing in a high degree there is but one remedy, namely, to send the child immediately back to her native mountain air; for the second, there is but one medicine, and that the very same thing. So send the child home tomorrow; that is my advice."

Herr Sesemann rose from his chair. He walked up and down the room in the greatest excitement; then he exclaimed, "A sleepwalker! Sick! Homesick! Wasted away in my house! All this in my house! And no one noticed it or knew anything about it! And do you think, doctor, that I will send the child, who came fresh and healthy into my house, back to her grandfather miserable and wasted away? No, doctor, you cannot expect that; I can't do that; that I will never do. Take the child in hand, put her under treatment, do what you like, but make her sound and healthy, and then I will send her home if she wants to go; but first give her your aid!"

"Sesemann," replied the doctor earnestly, "think what you are doing! Her condition is no illness that can be cured with powders and pills. The child has no delicate nature; if you send her back now to the bracing mountain air, to which she is accustomed, she will be perfectly well again; if not—you would not like to send her back beyond all help to her grandfather, or never send her back at all, would you?"

Herr Sesemann stood still in astonishment.

"Well, if this is your advice, doctor, there is only one way; it must be followed immediately."

With these words Herr Sesemann took his friend's arm and walked about with him to talk the matter over still further. Then the doctor started to go home, for much time had passed during their conversation, and the bright morning light was coming through the house door, which was opened this time by the master of the house.

Chapter 13

Up the Alm on a Summer Evening

Herr Sesemann climbed the stairs in the greatest excitement and went with a firm step to Fräulein Rottenmeier's sleeping room. Here he rapped so unusually loud on the door that the good lady woke from sleep with a cry of terror. She heard Herr Sesemann's voice outside:

"Pray hasten to come into the dining room; preparations must be immediately made for a journey."

Fräulein Rottenmeier looked at her clock; it was half past four in the morning; she had never risen at such an hour in her life before. What could have happened? Curiosity and anxious foreboding made everything she touched go wrong, and she made slow progress in dressing, for she kept hunting about uneasily in her room for the things she had already put on.

Meanwhile Herr Sesemann went the entire length of the hall and furiously rang every one of the bells used to summon the different servants, so that in each separate room a terrified form jumped out of bed and hurried to dress, for one and all thought the same thing, that the ghost had seized the master of the house, and this was his call for help.

So they came down one after another, each looking more terrified than the last, and stood in surprise before the master of the house, for he was walking up and down the room, looking fresh and cheerful, and not at all as if a ghost had frightened him.

Johann was immediately sent to put the horses and carriage in order, to be brought round later on. Tinette was ordered to waken Heidi at once, and to make her ready to take a journey. Sebastian was ordered to hasten to the house where Heidi's aunt was at service and to bring her back. Fräulein Rottenmeier had meanwhile succeeded in getting dressed, and everything was all right except her headdress, which was on crooked, so that from a distance she looked as if her face were on backward. Herr Sesemann ascribed her perplexing appearance to the fact that she had been awakened so early, and proceeded at once to business. He explained to the lady that she was to get a trunk without delay, and to pack up all the things belonging to the Swiss child—Herr Sesemann usually spoke of Heidi in this way, as her name was somewhat unfamiliar to him—and also a good part of Klara's clothes, that the child might have everything that was necessary to take with her; but all must be done quickly and without stopping to question.

Fräulein Rottenmeier stood as if rooted to the floor and stared at Herr Sesemann in amazement. She had expected that he was going to tell her in confidence some horrible story of his ghostly experience the night before, and she would not have been displeased to hear it now in the clear morning light; instead of that came these very commonplace and particularly inconvenient commands. She could not at once overcome her surprise. She still stood speechless, expecting something further.

But Herr Sesemann had no intention of making further explanations; he let the lady stand where she was and went to his daughter's room. As he supposed, the unusual stir in the house had awakened her, and she was listening to everything and wondering what was going on.

Her father sat down by her bed and told her what the ghost really was, and that in the doctor's opinion Heidi was in a very bad condition, and that her nightly wanderings would become more extensive, and perhaps she might climb up to the roof, and that would be very dangerous. So he had decided to send the child home at once, for he could not be responsible for her; and Klara must be content, for she could see that this was necessary.

Klara was very painfully surprised by this news, and at first wanted to find some way out of the difficulty, but it was of no use; her father remained firm in his decision; but he promised to take Klara the following year to Switzerland, if she would be reasonable now and not grieve. So Klara yielded to what could not be helped; she asked that

Heidi's trunk should be brought into her room and packed there, so that she might put in some things Heidi would enjoy; and this her papa willingly granted; indeed, he even encouraged Klara to give the child a fine outfit.

Meanwhile Aunt Dete had arrived and stood with great expectation in the entrance; for to be summoned at this unusual time must mean something extraordinary. Herr Sesemann went out to her and told her how it was with Heidi, and that he wished she would take the child home at once, that very day. The aunt looked very much disappointed. She had not expected such news. She still remembered very distinctly the parting words the uncle had spoken to her: never to come before his eyes again; and having taken the child to him, and then brought her away, it did not seem advisable to take her back again. So she did not consider the matter long, but said, with great earnestness, that unfortunately it would be quite impossible for her to take the journey that day, and the next day she could think of it still less, and the day after that it would be utterly impossible on account of the work to be done then, and after that she would be no better able to go.

Herr Sesemann understood the aunt's excuses and dismissed her without saying anything further. He then summoned Sebastian and told him that he was to prepare immediately to take a journey; he was to go that very day with the child as far as Basle, and the next day to take her home. Then he could return at once; he would have no statement to make, for Herr Sesemann was sending a letter to the grandfather which would explain everything.

"There is one thing more of great importance, Sebastian," said Herr Sesemann in conclusion, "and I want you to look out for it carefully. I am acquainted at the hotel in Basle, the name of which I have written down here on my card for you. Show my card there, and a good room will be given you for the child; you must provide for yourself. Go first into the child's room and fasten all the windows so securely that they can be opened only with great force. When the child is in bed go and fasten the door outside, for the child wanders round in the night and might run into danger in a strange house if she went out and tried to open the house door; do you understand?"

"Aha! That was it, was it? That was it!" exclaimed Sebastian in the greatest surprise, for a great light had just been thrown on the ghosts.

"Yes, that was it! That was it! And you are a coward, and you can tell Johann that he is another, and all of you together a ridiculous set of men."

Having said this, Herr Sesemann went to his room and sat down to write a letter to the Alm-Uncle.

Sebastian stood amazed in the middle of the room and repeated over and over again to himself, "If only I hadn't let that coward of a Johann pull me back into the room, but had gone after the little white figure, as I undoubtedly should have done!" for now the bright sunshine distinctly lighted up every corner of the dark room.

Meanwhile Heidi, entirely unsuspicious of what was going to happen, stood waiting in her Sunday frock, for Tinette had merely roused her from sleep, taken her clothes out of the closet and put them on hurriedly without saying a word. She never talked with the ignorant Heidi, for she considered her beneath her notice.

Herr Sesemann walked with his letter into the dining room, where the breakfast was already served, and asked, "Where is the child?"

Heidi was called. When she approached Herr Sesemann to say "good morning" to him, he looked into her face inquiringly.

"Well, what do you say to it, little one?"

Heidi looked up at him in amazement.

"You don't know anything about it even now," said Herr Sesemann, laughing. "Well, you are going home today, right away."

"Home?" repeated Heidi, unable to speak aloud, and turned white as snow. For a little while she could hardly get her breath, she was so surprised by the unexpected news.

"Don't you want to know something about it?" asked Herr Sesemann, laughing.

"Oh, yes, I do," she now was able to gasp; and she turned deep red.

"Good, good!" said Herr Sesemann encouragingly, while he seated himself and motioned to Heidi to do the same. "And now eat a hearty breakfast and then into the carriage and away."

But Heidi could not swallow a mouthful, although through obedience she tried to force herself to eat; she was in such a state of excitement that she did not know whether she was awake or dreaming, or whether she would not suddenly awaken and be standing at the door in her nightgown.

'Sebastian must take plenty of luncheon," said Herr Sesemann to Fräulein Rottenmeier, who was just entering the room. "The child cannot eat, of course not. Go in to Klara until the carriage comes," he added kindly, turning to Heidi.

This was what Heidi wished, and she ran out of the room. In the middle of Klara's room stood a huge trunk, with the cover still wide open.

"Come, Heidi, come!" Klara called to her. "See what I have had packed for you! Come, do you like it?"

And she showed her a quantity of things—dresses and aprons, underwear and sewing materials—"And see here, Heidi," and Klara held up a basket triumphantly. Heidi peeped in and jumped high in her delight, for inside lay twelve lovely, round white rolls, all for the grandmother. The children in their glee entirely forgot that the moment had come for them to part, and when suddenly the call was heard—"The carriage is ready!"—there was no time left to be sad.

Heidi ran to her room; her beautiful book from the grandmamma must still be there; no one could have packed it; it lay under her pillow, for Heidi could not be parted from it day or night. That was laid in the basket on the bread. Then she opened her closet to see if there was anything left that had not been packed. To be sure—the old red shawl still lay there, for Fräulein Rottenmeier had not thought it worth packing. Heidi wrapped it round something else and laid it on top of the basket, so that the red parcel was very plainly to be seen. Then she put on her fine hat and left her room.

The two children had to say a speedy farewell, for Herr Sesemann was already there to take Heidi down to the carriage. Fräulein Rottenmeier stood at the head of the stairs to bid Heidi good-bye.

When she noticed the strange red bundle, she took it quickly out of the basket and threw it on the floor.

"No, Adelheid," she said, still finding fault, "you cannot leave this house so; you do not need to carry off such a thing as that. Now good-bye."

After this Heidi did not dare to pick up her bundle again, but she looked beseechingly at the master of the house, as if she were having her greatest treasure taken from her.

"No, no," said Herr Sesemann in a very decided voice, "the child shall carry home whatever gives her pleasure, and if she takes away kittens or turtles we will not get excited about it, Fräulein Rottenmeier."

Heidi quickly picked up her bundle from the floor and her eyes beamed with gratitude and pleasure.

When Heidi reached the carriage Herr Sesemann held out his hand to the child and said to her with friendly words that she must think of him and his daughter Klara. He wished her a happy journey, and Heidi thanked him very prettily for all the kindness he had shown her and finally said, "And I leave a thousand good-byes for the doctor, and thank him many times," for she had noticed how he had said to her the night before, "And tomorrow everything will be all right." Now it had all come true, and Heidi thought he was the cause of it.

Then the child was lifted into the carriage, and the basket and the lunch box and Sebastian followed. Herr Sesemann called out once more in a friendly voice, "A pleasant journey!" and the carriage rolled away.

Soon after, Heidi was sitting in the train and holding her basket firmly in her lap, for she would not let it out of her hands for a moment; the precious rolls for the grandmother were inside, and she had to watch them carefully and delight her eyes with a look at them every now and then. Heidi sat as still as a mouse for several hours, for now she began to realize that she was on the way home to her grandfather on the Alm, to the grandmother, and Peter, the goatherd; one thing after another came before her eyes—all that she was going to see again—and she imagined how everything would look at home, and new thoughts kept arising in her mind; suddenly she said anxiously, "Sebastian, are you sure that the grandmother on the Alm is not dead?"

"No, no," said he soothingly. "We hope she's not dead. She must be still alive."

Then Heidi became absorbed again in her own thoughts; only now and then she peeped into her basket, for her greatest desire was to lay all the rolls on the grandmother's table. After some time she said again, "Sebastian, if we could only be perfectly sure that the grandmother is still alive."

"Yes, indeed! Yes, indeed!" replied her companion, half asleep. "She's still alive; I don't see any reason why not."

After a while Heidi's eyes also closed; after the disturbance of the previous night and the early start, she was so heavy with sleep that she did not awaken until Sebastian shook her by the arm and called out to her, "Wake up! Wake up! We must get out now, we are in Basle!"

On the following morning they journeyed for several hours more. Heidi again sat with the basket in her lap, for on no account would she give it up to Sebastian; but today she did not speak, for with each hour her eagerness became more intense. Then suddenly, when Heidi was not thinking about it, came the loud call—"Maienfeld!" She jumped up from her seat, and Sebastian did the same, for he too had been surprised. Now they stood outside with the trunk, and the train was whistling farther on up the valley. Sebastian looked longingly after it, for he much preferred traveling on in that safe and easy way to undertaking a journey on foot, which had to end in climbing a mountain, and might be hard and dangerous besides, in this country where everything was still half wild, as he supposed. He therefore looked carefully about him for some advice concerning the safest way to Dörfli. Not far from the railway station stood a little wagon, drawn by a lean horse; into this a broad-shouldered man was loading several large bags, which had been brought by the train. Sebastian stepped up to him and questioned him about the way.

"All ways are safe here," was the short reply.

Then Sebastian asked him about the best way one could go without falling into the abysses, and also how a trunk could be taken to Dörfli. The man looked at the trunk and measured it with his eyes; then he said that, if it was not too heavy, he would take it in his wagon, since he himself was going to Dörfli. So some words were exchanged, and finally the two arranged that the man would take both the child and the trunk with him, and that the child could be sent from Dörfli up the Alm with someone that evening.

"I can go alone; I know the way from Dörfli up the Alm," said Heidi, for she had been listening attentively while they were making the bargain. A heavy load was taken from Sebastian's mind when he found himself so suddenly released from the prospect of climbing the mountain. He now secretly beckoned Heidi to one side and handed her a heavy package and a letter to her grandfather, and explained to her that the package was a present from Herr Sesemann, which must be put in the bottom of her basket, under the bread, and that she must take care of it, so that it should not be lost, or Herr Sesemann would be frightfully cross about it, and would never get over it all his life long; the little Mamselle must surely remember this.

"I will not lose it," said Heidi reassuringly, and placed the package and the letter in the bottom of the basket. The trunk was put into the wagon, and then Sebastian lifted Heidi with her basket up to the high seat, held out his hand to bid her good-bye, and once more urged her, with all sorts of signs, to keep her eyes on the contents of her basket; for the driver was near, and Sebastian was all the more cautious because he knew that he ought to go with the child himself to the end of her journey. The driver swung himself up on the seat beside Heidi, and the wagon rolled off toward the mountain, while Sebastian, glad to escape the dreaded mountain journey, sat down in the station to wait for the' returning train.

The man on the wagon was the baker of Dörfli, and he was carrying home his bags of meal. He had never seen Heidi, but like everyone else in Dörfli he knew about the child that had been brought to the

Alm-Uncle. Besides, he had known Heidi's parents and at once guessed that she was the much-talked-of little girl. He wondered somewhat why the child was so soon coming home again, and during the journey began to talk with Heidi.

"You are the child who was up with the Alm-Uncle, your grandfather, aren't you?"

"Yes."

"Did you fare badly that you have already come home from so far?"

"No, I did not; no one can fare better than I did in Frankfurt."

"Why are you running home then?"

"Only because Herr Sesemann allowed me, or I should not be coming home."

"Bah! Why didn't you prefer to stay there, if you were only allowed to come home?"

"Because I would a thousand times rather be at home with my grandfather on the Alm than do anything else in the world."

"Perhaps you'll think differently when you get up there," growled the baker. "But I wonder," he said to himself, "if she can know how it is."

Then he began to whistle and said nothing more, and Heidi looked round her and began to tremble inwardly from excitement, for she recognized the trees by the way, and over yonder stood the lofty peaks of the Falknis Mountain looking down at her, as if they were greeting her like good old friends. And Heidi greeted them in return, and with every step forward Heidi's expectation grew more eager, and she felt as if she would have to jump down from the wagon and run with all her might until she was up there. However, she remained still and did not move, but trembled all over. As they came into Dörfli the clock was just striking five. In a moment a crowd of women and children gathered round the wagon, and the neighbors came out to it, for the child and trunk on the baker's cart had attracted the attention of all the inhabitants, and each one wanted to know where they had come from and where they were going.

When the baker had lifted Heidi down, she said quickly, "Thank you, my grandfather will come for my trunk"; and she would have run away, but she was held fast on every side, and there was a tumult of voices, each asking something different. Heidi pressed through the crowd with such anxiety on her face that they unwillingly made room for her and let her pass, and one said to another, "You see how frightened she is; she has every reason to be."

Then they began to tell one another how the Alm-Uncle for a year past had been worse than ever, and would not speak a word to anyone, and when anyone came in his way he made a face, as if he would like to kill him; and if the child knew anything in the world about it, she would not run to the old dragon's nest. But here the baker interrupted their remarks by saying he knew more about it than all the rest, and then told them, with an air of mystery, how a gentleman had brought the child as far as Maienfeld, parted from her in a very friendly way, and had at once, without any bargaining, paid the fare he asked, besides adding a fee; and, more than all, he could say surely that the child had been well off where she was, and that she was anxious to come back to her grandfather. This news caused great surprise and was immediately spread through all Dörfli, so that there was not a house that evening where it was not repeated that Heidi had been anxious to come back from a life of luxury to her grandfather.

Heidi ran up the mountain from Dörfli as fast as she could; but now and then she would suddenly stand still, for she quite lost her breath; the basket on her arm was heavy for her, and besides the way grew steeper and steeper the higher she went. Heidi had only one thought: "Will the grandmother still be sitting in the corner at her spinning wheel; has she not died in all this time?"

Now Heidi saw the hut up in the hollow on the Alm, and her heart began to throb; she ran still faster; her heart kept beating louder and louder. Now she was up there—she could hardly open the door, she trembled so—but now!—She ran into the middle of the little room and stood there, completely out of breath and unable to speak.

"O heavens!" sounded from the corner. "Our Heidi used to run in like that! Ah, if only I could have her with me once more while I live!

Who has come in?"

"Here I am, grandmother; here I am, really!" exclaimed Heidi.

Rushing into the corner and into the grandmother's lap, she seized her arm and her hands and snuggled up to her, and was unable to say anything more from delight. At first the grandmother was so overcome that she could not speak a word; then she began to stroke Heidi's curly hair with her hand and kept saying again and again, "Yes, yes, it is her hair; and it is her voice; ah, dear Lord, that Thou shouldst have permitted me this!"

And two great tears of joy dropped from her blind eyes on Heidi's hand.

"Are you here, Heidi? Are you really here?"

"Yes, yes, really, grandmother," said Heidi with all assurance. "But do not cry; I am very surely here again and will come to you every day and never go away again; and you won't have to eat hard bread for many days, for see, grandmother, do you see?"

And Heidi now took one roll after another out of her basket, until she had piled up all twelve in the grandmother's lap.

"O child! O child! What a blessing you have brought me!" exclaimed the grandmother, when the rolls did not come to an end, but one kept following another. "But the greatest blessing is you yourself, child!" Then she seized hold of Heidi's curly hair and stroked her hot cheeks and said again, "Say just a word more, child; say something more, so that I can hear you.

Heidi then told the grandmother how she had suffered, fearing that the grandmother might die while she was away and not have the white rolls, and that Heidi would never, never be able to go to her.

Then Peter's mother came in, and for a moment stood still in astonishment. Then she exclaimed, "Surely, it is Heidi! How can it be possible!"

Heidi rose and shook hands with her, and Brigitte could not wonder enough at Heidi's appearance, and she walked round the child, saying, "Grandmother, if you only could see what a beautiful dress the child has on and how she looks; I hardly know her. And does the little hat trimmed with feathers, on the table, belong to you also? Just put it on, so I can see how you look in it."

"No, I will not," said Heidi decidedly. "You can have it; I don't need it any longer, I still have my own."

Whereupon Heidi opened her little red bundle and took out her old hat, which had become still more bent during the journey than it was before. But that troubled Heidi little; she had never forgotten how, when she was leaving her grandfather, he had called after her that he never wanted to see her in a hat trimmed with feathers, and that was why Heidi had kept her old hat so carefully, for she always thought of the time when she should go home to him.

But Brigitte said she must not be so foolish; the new hat was splendid, and she might sell it to the teacher's little daughter in Dörfli, and get a good deal of money for it, if she did not care to wear it. But Heidi was firm in her decision and laid the hat gently in the corner behind the grandmother, where it was entirely hidden. Then Heidi took off her lovely dress, and she folded the red scarf over her underwaist, in which she now stood with bare arms, and then seized the grandmother's hand, saying, "Now I must go home to my grandfather, but tomorrow I will come to you again; good night, grandmother."

"Yes, come again, Heidi; come again tomorrow morning," said the grandmother; and she pressed Heidi's hand between her own and could hardly let her go.

"Why have you taken off your beautiful dress?" asked Brigitte.

"Because I would rather go to my grandfather without it, or he might not know me; you hardly knew me in it."

Brigitte went out the door with Heidi, and said a few words secretly to her, "You can keep on the dress, he will know you; but you must take care of yourself, for Peterii says the Alm-Uncle is always very cross now and never says a word."

Heidi said "good night" and went on up the mountain with her basket on her arm. The evening sun shone all round on the green Alm, and now the snow field on Scesaplana came into sight and gleamed in the distance.

Every few steps Heidi had to stand still and look round, for the high mountains were behind her as she climbed. Now a red glow fell over the grass at her feet; she turned round; there—she had forgotten the splendor, and never had seen it in her dreams like this—the rocky peaks on Falknis flamed up to the sky, the broad snow field was all aglow, and rosy clouds were drifting high above. The grass all round on the Alm was golden; from all the heights it glimmered and gleamed down, and below, the far-reaching valley swam in a golden vapor.

While Heidi stood in the midst of all this glory, bright tears of joy and rapture ran down her cheeks, and she had to fold her hands, and, looking up to heaven, thank the dear Lord aloud that He had brought her back home again, and that everything, everything was still so beautiful, and even more beautiful than she had thought, and that it all was hers once more. And Heidi felt so happy and so rich in the great glory that she could not find words to express her thankfulness to the dear Lord.

Not until the light all about began to fade could Heidi move away from the place. But then she ran so fast up the mountain that it was not long before she saw the boughs of the fir trees above the roof, and then the roof itself, and then the whole hut, and on the seat beside it sat her grandfather, smoking his pipe; and over the hut the old fir trees were rocking their branches and roaring in the evening wind. Then Heidi ran all the faster, and before the Alm-Uncle could really see what was coming the child rushed up to him, threw her basket on the ground, and hugged the old man. In her excitement at seeing him again she was unable to say anything, except to keep exclaiming, "Grandfather! Grandfather! Grandfather!"

Neither did the grandfather say anything. For the first time in many years his eyes grew moist, and he had to pass his hand over them. Then he loosened Heidi's arms from his neck, took her on his knee, and looked at her for a moment.

"So you have come home again, Heidi," he said then. "How is it? You don't look particularly fine. Did they send you away?"

"Oh, no, grandfather," Heidi answered quickly and decidedly, "you must not think that; they were all so good—Klara and the grandmamma and Herr Sesemann. But you see, grandfather, I could hardly bear to wait any longer to come home again to you, and I often thought I should smother, it choked me so; but I really never said anything about it, because it would be ungrateful. And then suddenly one morning Herr Sesemann called me very early; but I believe the doctor was the cause of it; but perhaps it tells all about it in the letter"—whereupon Heidi jumped down on the ground, took her letter and her round package out of the basket and laid them both in her grandfather's hand.

"That belongs to you," he said, laying the package beside him on the seat. Then he took the letter and read it through; without saying a word he put it into his pocket.

"Do you think you can drink milk with me still, Heidi?" he then asked, while he took the child by the hand to lead her into the hut. "But take your money with you; you can buy a bed with it, and clothes enough to last you for two or three years."

"I really don't need it, grandfather," said Heidi. "I have a bed already; and Klara packed up so many clothes for me that I shall really never need any more."

"Take it, take it, and put it in the cupboard; you will be able to use it sometime."

Heidi obeyed and skipped after her grandfather into the hut, where, delighted to see everything again, she ran into every corner and up the ladder; but there she suddenly stood still and called down, somewhat concerned, "Oh, grandfather, I no longer have any bed!"

"You will soon have another," sounded from below. "I didn't know that you would return; now come and get your milk!"

Heidi came down and took her seat on her high stool in the old place, and then grasped her little bowl and drank as eagerly as if she had never had anything so precious within her reach before, and when she put down her bowl, with a deep breath, she said, "There is nothing in all the world so good as our milk, grandfather."

A shrill whistle sounded outside. Heidi shot out the door like lightning. There was the whole flock of goats, skipping, jumping, and leaping down from the heights above, and Peter in their midst. When he saw Heidi he stood perfectly still, as if rooted to the spot, and stared at her speechless. Heidi called out, "Good evening, Peter!" and rushed in among the goats. "Schwänli! Bärli! Do you know me still?"

The goats must have recognized her voice, for they rubbed their heads against her and began to bleat madly for joy, and Heidi called them all by name, one after the other, and they all ran like wild creatures in confusion and crowded round her. The impatient Distelfinck jumped high into the air and over two other goats, in order to get near her at once, and the timid Schneehöpli gave the big Türk a very determined thrust and pushed him aside, so that he stood looking much amazed at the daring, and raised his beard in the air to show that it was he.

Heidi was beside herself with joy to see all her old companions once more; she threw her arms round the little affectionate Schneehöpli again and again, stroked the violent Distelfinck, and was pushed and jolted hither and thither by the fond, trusting goats until she came quite near to Peter, who remained standing in the same place.

"Come down, Peter, and say good evening to me!" Heidi called to him.

"Are you really back again?" he finally managed to say in his astonishment; and then he came forward and took Heidi's hand, which she had been offering him for some time, and asked, as he always did when he was returning home at evening, "Will you come with me again tomorrow?"

"No, not tomorrow, but the day after, perhaps; for to-morrow I must go to the grandmother's."

"It is good to have you back again," said Peter, making all sorts of queer faces from huge delight; then he started homeward; but he had never before had such difficulty with his goats, for when he had at last, with coaxing and threatening, succeeded in collecting them about him, and Heidi had walked away with one arm round Schwänli's and the other about Bär!i's neck, they all with one accord turned round again and ran after the three. Heidi had to go into the shed with her two goats and shut the door, or Peter would never have succeeded in getting away with his flock.

When the child came back into the hut she found her bed already made up again, wonderfully high and fragrant, for the hay had not been in long, and the grandfather had very carefully spread the clean linen sheet over it. Heidi lay down on it with great delight and had a refreshing sleep, such as she had not enjoyed for a whole long year. During the night her grandfather left his couch at least ten times, climbed the ladder and listened carefully to see if Heidi was still asleep and was not restless, and looked at the window where the moon used to shine in on Heidi's bed, to see if the hay he had stuffed into it was still there, for the moon should be kept out henceforth. But Heidi slept right on and wandered about no longer, for her great, hungry longing was satisfied; she had seen all the mountains and cliffs in the evening glow again, she had heard the fir trees roaring, she was at home again on the Alm.

Chapter 14

Sunday When the Church Bells Ring

Heidi stood under the swaying branches of the fir trees, waiting for her grandfather, who was going to fetch the trunk from Dörfli while she stayed with the grandmother. The child could hardly wait to see the grandmother again and to hear how the rolls had tasted; yet the time did not seem long to her, for she could not listen enough to the tones of her native sighing fir trees above her, and drink in all the fragrance and brightness of the green pastures and their golden blossoms.

The grandfather came out of the hut, took a look round him, and then said in a satisfied tone, "Well, now we can go."

It was Saturday, and on that day it was the Alm-Uncle's custom to clean and put everything in order in the hut, in the shed, and all about; today he had taken the morning for this, in order to go with Heidi in the afternoon, and so everything all round looked neat and to his satisfaction. At Peter's hut they parted and Heidi ran in. The grandmother had already heard her step, and called out to her affectionately, "Have you come, child? Have you come again?"

Then she grasped Heidi's hand and held it very tightly, for she still feared that the child might be taken away from her again. And now the grandmother had to tell how the rolls had tasted, and she said she had been so refreshed by them that she thought she was much stronger that day than she had been for a long time. Peter's mother added that the grandmother was much worried lest the rolls should soon be gone and she had eaten only one roll the day before and that day together, and she really could not gain much strength; they would last only a week if she should eat one a day. Heidi listened attentively to Brigitte and remained for some time thinking. Then she found a way out of the difficulty.

"I know now what I will do, grandmother," she said with eager delight. "I will write a letter to Klara, and she will surely send me as many more rolls and twice as many as there are, for I had a great pile just like them in my closet, and when they were taken away from me Klara said she would give me just as many more, and she will do so."

"Dear me!" said Brigitte, "that is a good idea; but think, they would grow hard, too. If we only had a spare penny now and then; the baker down in Dörfli makes them, but I am hardly able to pay for the black bread."

Then a bright, joyful light spread over Heidi's face.

"Oh, I have a tremendous lot of money, grandmother!" she exclaimed triumphantly, and danced up and down with delight. "Now I know what I can do with it. Every single day you must have a new roll, and two on Sunday, and Peter can bring them up from Dörfli."

"No, no, child!" said the grandmother in disapproval. "That cannot be. The money was not given you for that; you must give it to your grandfather, and he will tell you what you are to do with it."

But Heidi would not be disturbed in her delight; she shouted and danced round the room and exclaimed again and again, "Now the grandmother can eat a roll every day and will grow quite strong again, and—O grandmother!" she cried with new delight. "If you should grow so well, it would really become light to you again; it is perhaps only because you are so weak."

The grandmother was silent; she did not wish to disturb the child's pleasure. In her dancing round, Heidi suddenly spied the grandmother's old hymn book, and a new and delightful thought came to her.

"Grandmother, I can read quite well now; shall I read a song out of your old book?"

"Oh, yes!" said the grandmother, overcome with delight. "Can you really do that, can you do that?"

Heidi climbed up in a chair and took down the book, covered thick with dust, for it had long lain there undisturbed. She then wiped it clean, sat down with it on her stool beside the grandmother, and asked what she should read.

"Whatever you like, child, whatever you like"; and the grandmother sat with eager expectancy, and pushed the spinning wheel a little way from her.

Heidi turned the leaves and read a line here and there.

"Here is something about the sun; I will read you that, grandmother"; and Heidi began, and became more and more eager and interested as she read:

"The sun o'erflowing
With splendor glowing,
From golden fountains
Pours o'er our mountains
A spirit-quickening glory of light.

"Below I wandered
And, mournful, pondered,
But now arising
With change surprising
I turn to the sky my raptured sight.

"Mine eye beholdeth
What God unfoldeth
To tell the story
Of boundless glory—
How vast the sum of His boundless might!

"Behind those portals
Henceforth immortals,
Our friends arisen
From fleshly prison
Have entered the realms of boundless delight.

"While all things falter,
God doth not alter:

No shade of turning
In His discerning:
His word and will are eternal right!

"His grace unbounded
In love is founded;
The humblest creature
May share His nature—
The lowest depth and the highest height.

"Today we languish
In grief and anguish,
But earthly sorrow
Shall fade tomorrow:
After the storm the sun shines bright.

"Sweet peace and pleasure
In boundless measure
We know is given
In the gardens of heaven;
And thither my hopes yearn day and night!"

The grandmother sat still with folded hands and an expression of indescribable joy on her face, such as Heidi had never seen there before, although the tears were running down her cheeks. When Heidi stopped reading she said entreatingly, "Oh, just once more, Heidi, let me hear it just once more:

"Today we languish
In grief and anguish."

And the child began again and read with eager delight:

"Today we languish

In grief and anguish,
But earthly sorrow
Shall fade tomorrow:
After the storm the sun shines bright.

"Sweet peace and pleasure
In boundless measure
We know is given
In the gardens of heaven;
And thither my hopes yearn day and night!"

"O Heidi, that gives me light! It gives me light in my heart. Oh, how much good you have done me, Heidi!"

The grandmother repeated the joyful words again and again; and Heidi beamed with pleasure, and had to keep looking at the grandmother, for she had never seen her so before. She no longer had the old expression on her face, but appeared happy and thankful, as if she already looked with new bright eyes into the beautiful heavenly garden.

Then someone knocked on the window, and Heidi saw her grandfather outside, beckoning to her to go home with him. She followed quickly, but not without assuring the grandmother that she would come again the next day, and that even if she went up to the pasture with Peter she would only stay there half the day, for to be able to make it light again for the grandmother was to her the very greatest pleasure she could enjoy, even much greater than to be in the sunny pasture among the flowers and goats.

Brigitte ran out the door after Heidi, with her dress and hat, that she might take them with her. She took the dress on her arm, for her grandfather knew her now, she thought; but the hat she obstinately refused. Brigitte must keep it for her, for she would never, never put it on her head again. Heidi was so full of her experiences that she had to tell her grandfather at once all that had delighted her heart: that they could get white bread for the grandmother down in Dörfli if they only had the money, and that it had suddenly become so light to the grandmother, and she looked so well; and when Heidi had described it all to the end she went back to the beginning and said very confidently, "Surely, grandfather, even if the grandmother is not willing, you will give me all my money, so that I can give Peter a piece for a roll every day and two on Sunday!"

"But the bed, Heidi?" said the grandfather. "A real bed would be a good thing for you, and then there would be enough left for many rolls."

But Heidi gave her grandfather no peace, and assured him that she slept much better on her bed of hay than she had ever done in her pillowed bed in Frankfurt, and begged so urgently and repeatedly that her grandfather finally said, "The money is yours, do whatever pleases you; you can get bread for the grandmother with it for many a long year."

Heidi shouted for joy, "Now the grandmother will never have to eat hard black bread anymore, and oh, grandfather, now everything is lovelier than it ever was before in our lives!"

Heidi took hold of her grandfather's hand and jumped into the air and shouted as merrily as the birds in the sky. But all of a sudden she grew quite serious and said, "Oh, if the dear Lord had done right away what I prayed for so hard, then everything would not be as it is now. I should only have come home again and brought the grandmother just a few rolls, and shouldn't have been able to read to her, which does her good; but the dear Lord had already thought it all out so much better than I knew; the grandmamma told me so, and now it has all come true. Oh, how glad I am that the dear Lord did not grant what I asked and longed for! Now I will always pray as the grandmamma told me, and always thank the dear Lord, and if He does not do what I ask, then I will surely think all the same, it will just be as it was in Frankfurt; the dear Lord is planning something much better. But we will pray every day, won't we, grandfather? And we will never forget Him, so that the dear Lord may never forget us."

"And if one should do so?" murmured the grandfather.

"Oh, it would not be well for him, for then the dear Lord would forget him, too, and let him go away, and if he should get into trouble and complain, nobody would pity him, but everybody would say: 'He first ran away from the dear Lord; now the dear Lord, who might have helped him, lets him go.'"

"That is true, Heidi; how did you know it?"

"From the grandmamma; she told me all about it."

The grandfather was silent for a while. Then he said to himself, following his own thoughts, "And if it is so, then it is so; no one can go back, and whomever God has forgotten, He has forgotten."

"Oh, no, grandfather; one can go back; that I know, too, from the grandmamma; and then it says so in the beautiful story in my book; but you don't know about that; we are almost home, and you shall see how beautiful the story is."

Heidi, in her eagerness to get home, hurried faster and faster the last part of the way, and they had scarcely reached the top when she let go her grandfather's hand and ran into the hut. Her grandfather had put half of the things from the trunk into a basket, for the entire trunk was too heavy for him to carry. He now took the basket from his back, sat down on the bench, and became absorbed in thought. Heidi came running out again, with her big book under her arm.

"Oh, this is good, grandfather, that you are already sitting down here"; and with one bound Heidi was by his side and had found her story, for she had read it so often over and over again that the book opened of itself at the place. Then Heidi read with great feeling about the son who was well off at home where the cows and lambs grazed in his father's fields and, in a beautiful cloak, leaning on his shepherd's staff, he could stand among them and watch the sunset.

"But suddenly he wanted to have his share of the property and be his own master, and he asked his father for it, and went away with it and wasted it in riotous living. And when he had nothing left he had to go and be a farmer's hired man, and he did not have such fine cattle as were in his father's fields, but only pigs; he had to take care of them and he had nothing but rags on him and had nothing to eat except a very little of the husks that had been thrown to the pigs.

"Then he thought how it had been at home in his father's house and how good his father had been to him and how ungratefully he had treated his father, and he wept from remorse and homesickness. And he thought, 'I will go to my father and ask him to forgive me and tell him I am no more worthy to be called his son, but ask him to let me be as one of his hired servants."

"And when he was a great way off from his father's house, his father saw him and came running out—

"What do you think now, grandfather?" Heidi broke off in the midst of her reading. "Do you think his father was cross and said to him, 'I told you so!'? Now just listen to what comes:

"And his father saw him and had compassion on him and ran and fell on his neck and kissed him, and the son said unto him, 'Father, I have sinned against heaven, and in thy sight, and am no more worthy to be called thy son.'

"But the father said to his servants, 'Bring forth the best robe and put it on him and put a ring on his hand and shoes on his feet and bring hither the fatted calf and kill it, and let us eat and be merry, for this my son was dead and is alive again; he was lost and is found.' And they began to be merry."

"Isn't that a beautiful story, grandfather?" asked Heidi, when he sat in silence and she had expected him to be delighted and surprised.

"Yes, Heidi, the story is beautiful," said her grandfather; but his face was so serious that Heidi became quite still and looked at her pictures. She quietly pushed her book in front of her grandfather and said, "See, how happy he is!" and pointed with her finger to the picture of the son's return home, where he stands in fresh garments beside his father, and once more belongs to him as his son.

A few hours later, when Heidi had long been in deep sleep, her grandfather climbed the little ladder; he put his lamp beside Heidi's bed so that the light fell on the sleeping child. She lay there with folded hands, for Heidi had not forgotten to pray. On her rosy face was an expression of peace and blessed trust that must have appealed to her grandfather, for he stood there a long, long time without moving or taking his eyes from the sleeping child. Then he too folded his hands and half aloud, with bowed head, said, "'Father, I have sinned against heaven, and before Thee, and am no more worthy to be called Thy son!'" and great tears rolled down his cheeks.

In the early daylight the Alm-Uncle stood in front of his hut, looking round with beaming eyes. The Sunday morning glistened and shone over mountain and valley. The sound of early bells came up from below, and the birds in the fir trees were beginning their morning songs.

The grandfather stepped back into the hut.

"Come, Heidi!" he called up to her. "The sun is up! Put on a good dress, and we will go to church together!"

It did not take Heidi long; this was an entirely new call from her grandfather, and she felt that she must follow quickly. In a short time she came running down in her fine Frankfurt dress, but she remained standing in front of her grandfather and looked at him in great surprise.

"O grandfather, I have never seen you look so before!" she exclaimed at last. "And you have never worn the coat I with the silver buttons. Oh, you are so splendid in your beautiful Sunday coat!"

The old man looked at the child with a contented smile and said, "And you in yours; now come!"

He took Heidi's hand in his, and thus they went together down the mountain.

The clear-toned bells were now sounding in every direction, and fuller and richer as they came nearer, and Heidi listened with delight and said, "Do you hear them, grandfather? It is like a great, great festival."

Down in Dörfli the people were already in the church and were just beginning to sing when the grandfather and Heidi entered and seated themselves far back in the last seat. But in the midst of the singing the person sitting next them nudged his neighbor with his elbow and said, "Have you noticed? The Alm-Uncle is in church!"

And the person nudged touched the next one and so on, and in a short time it was whispered in every corner, "The Alm-Uncle! The Alm-Uncle!" and almost all the women had to turn their heads for a moment, and most of them lagged in the singing, so that the leader had the greatest difficulty in keeping the time.

But when the pastor began to preach they became attentive, for there was such warm praise and thanksgiving in his words that all the listeners were affected by it, and it was as if a great joy had come to them all. When the service was over, the Alm-Uncle went out with the child's hand in his and walked to the parson's house. All those who went out with him, and those who were standing outside, gazed after him, and most followed to see whether he really went into the parson's house; he did so. Then they gathered in groups and discussed in great excitement this unheard-of thing—that the Alm-Uncle had been in church; and they all looked eagerly toward the parson's house to see how he would come out, whether in scorn and strife or in peace with the pastor, for they had no idea what had brought the old man down and what it really meant. But there was already a change of feeling experienced by many of them, and one said to another, "It may be that the Alm-Uncle is not so bad as they say; you can see how carefully he held the little one by the hand"; and another one said, "That is what I have always said; and he would not go to the pastor's house if he were so thoroughly bad, for he would be afraid; people think a great many things are worse than they are." And the baker said, "Didn't I tell you that the first of all? Do you suppose a little child that has all it wants to eat and drink, and everything else good besides, would run away from it all and go home to a grandfather if he was wicked and wild, and she was afraid of him?"

And a very friendly feeling for the Alm-Uncle arose and increased; the women also drew near. They had heard from Peter the goatherd and from the grandmother many things that represented the Alm-Uncle as quite different from the popular opinion, and now all at once it seemed as if they were waiting to welcome an old friend who had long been absent.

Meanwhile the Alm-Uncle had gone to the study door and knocked. The pastor opened it and met the visitor, not with surprise, as he might have done, but as if he were expecting him. The Alm-Uncle's unexpected appearance in the church could not have escaped him. He grasped the old man's hand and shook it heartily, and the Alm-Uncle stood in silence, and at first could not say a word, for he was not prepared for such a warm greeting. Then he collected himself and said, "I have come to ask the pastor to forget the words I said to him on the Alm, and that he will not bear me ill will for being stubborn toward his well-meant advice. The pastor was right in all that he said, and I was wrong; but I will now follow his advice, and next winter take up quarters in Dörfli, for the severe weather up yonder is not good for the child; she is too delicate. And even if the people down here look at me suspiciously, as one who is not to be trusted, I deserve nothing better, and certainly the pastor will not look at me in this way".

The pastor's friendly eyes beamed with delight. He took the old man's hand once more and pressed it in his, and said with feeling, "Neighbor, you went to the right church before you came down to mine; this delights me! You shall not be sorry for your willingness to come down and live among us again; you will always be welcome in my house as a dear friend and neighbor, and I expect to spend many a pleasant hour of a winter evening with you, for I find your company agreeable and worthwhile, and we shall find good friends also for the little girl."

And the pastor laid his hand very kindly on Heidi's curly head, and took her by the hand and led her out, as he accompanied the grandfather, and when they were outside the door he bade them farewell.

All the people standing round could see how the pastor shook hands with the Alm-Uncle, as if he were his best friend and he could hardly bear to part with him. Scarcely had the door closed behind the pastor, when the whole assembly pressed toward the Alm-Uncle, and each was eager to be the first, and so many hands were held out together to him that he did not know which he ought to grasp first.

One said to him, "I am glad! I am glad, uncle, that you are coming back to us again!" And another said, "I have long wanted to speak with you again, uncle!" Similar remarks were heard on every side, and when the uncle replied to all their friendly greetings that he intended to take up his quarters in Dörfli again and spend the winter with his old acquaintances, there was great rejoicing, and it seemed exactly as if the Alm-Uncle were the best-beloved person in all Dörfli, whom they had had great difficulty getting along without. Most of them accompanied the grandfather and the child far up the Alm, and when they left them each one wished the Alm-Uncle to promise to call on him when he came down again. And when the people turned to go down the mountain the old man stood for a long time gazing after them, and a warm light was spread over his face, as if the sun shone out from within him.

Heidi looked steadily at him and said with delight, "Grandfather, you never looked so handsome before as you have today!"

"Do you think so?" said her grandfather, smiling. "Well, you see, Heidi, I feel happy because I am on good terms with people and at peace with God and man; that does one good! The dear Lord was good to me when He sent you up on the Alm."

When they reached Peter the goatherd's hut the grandfather straightway opened the door and went in.

"Good day, grandmother," he called out. "I think we must do a little more mending, before the autumn wind comes."

"Dear me, that is the uncle!" exclaimed the grandmother, full of surprise and delight. "That I should live to see this! I can thank you for all you have done for us, uncle! May God reward you for it! May God reward you for it!"

Trembling with delight, the old grandmother held out her hand, and when the uncle shook it heartily she continued, still holding him fast, "I have one thing more at heart to ask of you, uncle: if I have ever done you any harm, do not punish me by letting Heidi go away again before I lie at rest in the churchyard. Oh, you do not know what the child is to me!" and she hugged Heidi fast, for she had already drawn close to the grandmother's side.

"Never fear, grandmother," said the uncle soothingly, "that I should punish either you or myself in that way. We shall all stay together, and, God willing, for a long time."

Then Brigitte drew the uncle somewhat mysteriously into a corner and showed him the lovely hat trimmed with feathers, and told him how the matter stood, and that she naturally did not like to take such a thing from a child.

But the grandfather looked well pleased at Heidi and said, "The hat is hers, and if she doesn't care to wear it any more it is all right, and if she gave it to you, why, take it."

Brigitte was highly delighted at this unexpected decision.

"It is really worth more than two dollars; only see!" and in her delight she held the hat high in the air. "What a blessing this Heidi has brought home with her from Frankfurt! I have often thought whether I would not send Peterli to Frankfurt for a little while; what do you think about it, uncle?"

The uncle's eyes twinkled merrily. He thought it could not do Peterli any harm, but he would wait for a good opportunity.

Just then the person in question came in the door, after he had first run against it and hit his head so hard that it made everything rattle; he must have been in haste. Panting and out of breath, he now stood in the middle of the room, holding out a letter. This was something that had never happened before—a letter addressed to Heidi, which had been given to him at the post office in Dörfli. They all sat down, full of expectation, round the table, and Heidi opened her letter and read it aloud without stumbling. The letter was from Klara Sesemann. She told Heidi that since she went away it had been so dreary in her house that she could no longer bear it, and she had begged her father so often that he had at last consented to take the journey to Ragatz the coming autumn; and the grandmamma would come with them, for she, too, would like to visit Heidi and her grandfather on the Alm. Moreover, the grandmamma sent word to Heidi that she had done right in wishing to buy the old grandmother some rolls, and in order that she might not have to eat them dry she had sent some coffee, which was already on the way, and if she should come to the Alm, Heidi must take her to see the grandmother.

Then there was such joy and wondering at this news, and so much to tell and ask about, for the great expectation concerned all alike, that even the grandfather had not noticed how late it was already getting; and they were all so happily content at the prospect of the days to come, and almost even more in the joy of being together at the present time, that the grandmother finally said, "The best of all is for an old friend to come and give us his hand again, as he used to do long ago; it gives one such a comforting feeling in the heart, to find everything that is dear to us once more. You will come again soon, uncle, and the child tomorrow?"

This was promised to the grandmother at once; now it was time to go, and the grandfather started up the Alm with Heidi; and as the clear bells from near and far in the morning had called them down, so now the peaceful sound of the evening bells rising from the valley accompanied them to the sunny Alm hut, which shone in the Sunday evening light.

PART TWO

Heidi Makes Use of What She Has Learned

Chapter 1

Preparations for a Journey

The kind doctor, who had decided that the child Heidi must be taken back to her mountain home, was just passing along the broad street toward the Sesemann house. It was a sunny September morning, so bright and lovely that it might be supposed that everyone must delight in it. But the doctor was gazing at the white stones at his feet, and did not notice the blue sky above him. In his face there was a sadness which had never appeared there before, and his hair had grown much grayer since the spring.

The doctor's only daughter, after his wife's death, had been very near to him, and the joy of his life. Some months before, the maiden had been taken away from him by death. Since then the doctor had never seemed so jolly as before.

In answer to the bell Sebastian opened the door with great politeness, and, when he saw who it was, gave every sign of being a most devoted servant; for not only was the doctor the best friend of his master and the little daughter, but by his kindness, here as everywhere, he had also won the goodwill of the entire household.

"Is everything as usual, Sebastian?" asked the doctor in his customary friendly voice, and went up the stairs, followed by Sebastian, who kept on making all sorts of signs of devotion, although the doctor could not see them.

"I am glad you have come, doctor," Herr Sesemann called out. "We must once more seriously consider the journey to Switzerland; I must hear from you whether you still abide by your decision even now that Klara seems to be better."

"My dear Sesemann, what is the matter with you?" replied the doctor, taking a seat beside his friend. "I really wish your mother was here; with her everything would be plain and simple. But there's no bringing you to reason. This is the third time you have sent for me today, although I keep telling you the same thing."

"Yes, you are right; the matter must make you impatient, but I want you to understand, my dear friend," and Herr Sesemann laid his hand entreatingly on the doctor's shoulder, "that it will be far too hard for me to deny the child what I promised her so faithfully, and what has made her so happy day and night for the past months. Besides, the child has borne all these last bad days so patiently, always hoping that the Swiss journey was near at hand, and that she would be able to visit her friend Heidi in the Alps; and now, after the child has had so much to bear, shall I with one blow crush the long-cherished hope? It is almost impossible for me to do so."

"Sesemann, it must be," said the doctor very decidedly; and as his friend was silent and sat looking very downcast, he went on after a time to say, "Think how the matter stands. Klara has not for years had so bad a summer as this last has been; there is no question about it; she could not take such a long journey without danger of the worst results. It is now September; it may still be fine up on the Alps, but it must be already very cool there. The days are growing short, and as Klara could not stay overnight on the mountain she would have hardly two hours there. The journey from Ragatz would take several hours, for she would most decidedly have to be carried up the mountain in a chair. In short, Sesemann, it cannot be! But I will go in with you and talk with Klara about it; she is a sensible girl, and I will tell her my plan. Next May she shall first go to Ragatz; there she shall take the baths for a long time, until it is warm and pleasant up on the mountains. Then she can be taken up there from time to time, and when she is refreshed and strengthened she will enjoy these mountain excursions far more than she would now. You understand also, Sesemann, that if we wish to cherish a slight hope for your child's recovery, we must use the greatest care and the most cautious treatment."

Herr Sesemann, who had listened silently and with an expression of sad submission, now sprang to his feet.

"Doctor, tell me honestly," he exclaimed, "have you really any hope for an improvement in her condition?"

The doctor shrugged his shoulders.

"Little," he said in a low voice. "But come, think for a moment of me, friend! Have you not a dear child who longs for you when you are away, and is delighted when you come home? You never have to return to a lonely house and sit down to a solitary table, and your child is well off at home. Although she has to go without much that others might enjoy, still she is, in some respects, more highly favored than a great many. No, Sesemann, you are not so much to be pitied; you are fortunate to be together; think of my lonely house!"

Herr Sesemann began to stride up and down the room, as he was in the habit of doing whenever he was deeply absorbed in any matter. Suddenly he stood still in front of his friend and clapped him on the shoulders.

"Doctor, I have an idea; I cannot see you like this; you are no longer the same. You must get out of yourself a little; and do you know how? You shall undertake the journey and visit the child Heidi in our place."

The doctor was very much surprised at this proposal and would have objected to it, but Herr Sesemann gave him no time. He was so delighted and filled with his new idea that he seized his friend by the arm and led him to his daughter's room. The doctor was always a delightful sight to sick Klarä, for he treated her with great friendliness, and every time he came he had something lively and entertaining to tell her. She knew well why he could do so no longer, and she wished she could make him happy again.

She held out her hand to him; and he sat down beside her. Herr Sesemann also moved up his chair, and, taking Klara's hand, began to talk about the journey to Switzerland, and how much pleasure he himself had taken in looking forward to it. He glided quickly over the most important fact, that it was now out of the question, for he was somewhat afraid of the tears that would be sure to come. He then passed on to the new plan and impressed Klara with the fact that her dear friend would be greatly benefited by taking this journey.

The tears indeed came and swam in Klara's blue eyes, although she tried her best to keep them back, for she knew how her papa disliked to see her cry. But it was hard to have it ended when all summer the prospect of this visit to Heidi had been her only joy and comfort during the long, lonely hours which she had endured. Klara was not in the habit of arguing, and she knew very well that her papa was denying her only what would lead to ill, and therefore ought not to be. She choked down her sobs and took refuge in the only hope remaining. She seized her good friend's hand, stroked it, and said entreatingly, "Oh, please, doctor, you will go to Heidi, won't you? And then come and tell me about everything up there, and what Heidi is doing, and her grandfather and Peter and the goats; I know them all so well. And then you must take what I want to send to Heidi; I have thought it all out; and something for the grandmother, too. Please, doctor, do go; and while you are gone I will truly take all the cod-liver oil you prescribe."

Whether this promise decided the matter or not we do not know, but suppose it must be so, for the doctor smiled and said, "Then I must certainly go, Klärchen, for you will grow round and strong as papa and I would like to have you. When must I start? Have you decided that, too?"

"Certainly; tomorrow early, doctor," replied Klara.

"Yes, she is right," said her father. "The sun is shining, the sky is blue, and no time is to be lost, for it is a shame not to be enjoying such a day in the Alps."

The doctor had to laugh.

"Next thing you will be reproaching me for not being there already, Sesemann, so I shall do well to get away."

But Klara held the doctor fast; she had first to give him all sorts of messages for Heidi and to remind him of so many things which he must notice and then tell her about. The things she wished to send to Heidi would be taken to him later, for Fräulein Rottenmeier would have to help pack them; she had just gone on one of her walks about the city, and was not likely to return very soon.

The doctor promised to carry out all her directions, to start on the journey as soon as possible, and to give her a faithful account of everything he should see and do.

Servants are often wonderfully clever at finding out, long before they have been told, what is going on in their master's house. Sebastian and Tinette must have been clever in a high degree, for just as the doctor, followed by Sebastian, was going down the stairs Tinette entered Klara's room.

"Bring me this box full of perfectly fresh, nice cakes, such as we have with our coffee, Tinette," said Klara, pointing to a box which had been standing ready for some time.

Tinette seized it by one corner and swung it scornfully in her hand; after she had closed the door she said pertly, "It's well worthwhile."

When, with his usual politeness, Sebastian had opened the front door he said with a bow, "If the doctor would be so kind as to give the little Mamselle Sebastian's regards."

"O Sebastian," said the doctor pleasantly, "do you know so soon that I am going away?"

Sebastian was obliged to cough.

"I am—I have—I don't know certainly—oh, yes, I remember, as I happened to be passing through the dining room just now I heard the little Mamselle's name mentioned; it often happens that we put one thought and another together, and stand in that way—"

"Yes, indeed! Yes, indeed!" said the doctor, laughing. "And the more thoughts one has, the more one knows. Good-bye, Sebastian, I will deliver your message."

The doctor was just about to pass through the open door when he met an obstruction; the strong wind had prevented Fräulein Rottenmeier from continuing her walk; she had returned and was just entering the door. The wind puffed out the big shawl in which she had wrapped herself; she looked exactly as if she were under full sail. The doctor started back instantly. Fräulein Rottenmeier had always shown a strange deference and politeness toward this man. She, too, started back with marked politeness, and for a time they both stood there, bowing and making room for each other. Then came such a strong gust of wind that Fräulein Rottenmeier was suddenly blown with full sail against the doctor. He was still able to turn aside, but the lady was driven a good way beyond him, so that she had to turn round again in order to speak courteously to the friend of the house. The absurd occurrence had put her somewhat out of sorts, but the doctor had a way which soon smoothed her ruffled temper and put her into good humor. He told her about his intended journey and begged her, in the most taking way, to pack the things for Heidi, as only she knew how to pack them. Then he took his departure.

Klara had expected to have a struggle with Fräulein Rottenmeier before she would give her consent to send away all the things that Klara intended for Heidi. But this time she was happily disappointed; Fräulein Rottenmeier was unusually good-natured. She immediately removed everything on the large table, in order to spread out on it all the articles that Klara had put together, and to pack them before her eyes. This was no easy task, the things to be done up together being of such different shapes. First came the thick cape with the hood, which Klara meant for Heidi, that she might be able to visit the grandmother the coming winter whenever she liked, and not have to wait for her grandfather and be wrapped in the sack to keep from freezing. Next came a thick, warm shawl for the old grandmother, to wrap round her when the cold wind shook the hut. Then came the big box of cakes, also intended for the grandmother, that she might have something different from rolls to eat with her coffee. A huge sausage followed; Klara had first intended this for Peter, because he never had anything but bread and cheese. But she changed her mind, fearing lest Peter in his delight should eat the whole sausage at once. So his mother Brigitte was to have it and first take a good share of it for herself and for the grandmother, and then give Peter his portion at different times. Then there was a little bag of tobacco; this was for the grandfather, who liked so well to smoke his pipe when he sat in front of the hut in the evening. Last came a number of mysterious little bags, packages, and boxes, which Klara had taken special delight in collecting, for Heidi was to find in them all sorts of surprises which would give her great pleasure. At last the work was finished, and an imposing package lay on the floor ready for the journey. Fräulein Rottenmeier, looking down on it, became absorbed in thought about the art of packing. Klara, for her part, cast looks of glad expectation toward it, for she saw Heidi before her as she would jump and shout with surprise when the huge bundle reached her.

Sebastian then came in, and swung the bundle up on his shoulder, in order to take it at once to the doctor's house.

Chapter 2

A Guest on the Alm

The mountains were glowing in the early dawn, and a fresh morning wind was blowing through the fir trees and rocking their old branches vigorously to and fro. Heidi opened her eyes; the sound had awakened her. This roaring of the wind always stirred the very depths of Heidi's soul and made her feel that she must run out under the great branches. She jumped from her bed and could hardly wait to dress herself properly; but it had to be done, for Heidi knew very well that one should always be clean and tidy.

She then came down the ladder; her grandfather's couch was already empty. She ran outdoors; there in front of the hut stood her grandfather, gazing up at the sky and all about, as he did every morning to see what the day was going to be.

Rosy clouds floated above, the sky grew bluer and bluer, and the heights and the pasture land seemed flooded with bright gold, for the sun was just rising above the lofty cliffs.

"Oh, how beautiful! Oh, how beautiful! Good morning, grandfather," Heidi called out as she came skipping along.

"Well, are your eyes already opened?" said the grandfather in reply, offering his hand to Heidi to give her a morning greeting.

Then Heidi ran under the fir trees and danced with delight under the swaying boughs, as she heard the rushing and roaring above, and with every new gust of wind and loud blustering in the treetops she shouted for joy and jumped a little higher.

Meanwhile the grandfather had gone to the shed and had milked Schwänli and Bärli; then he brushed and washed them for their journey up the mountain, and brought them outside. When Heidi saw her friends, she ran to them and threw her arms about the necks of both of them, greeting them affectionately, and they bleated gladly and trustfully. Each of the goats was anxious to give proof of affection, and pressed closer and closer to her shoulders, so that between them she was almost crushed. But Heidi was not afraid, and when the lively Bärli butted and pushed too hard with her head Heidi said, "No, Bärli, you push like the big Türk," and immediately Bärli drew back her head and retreated to a proper distance, and then Schwänli stretched up her head and bleated in a superior way, so that it was plain to be seen that she thought to herself, "No one shall say of me that I behave like Türk." For the snow-white Schwänli was rather more dignified than Bärli.

Peter's whistle from below was now heard, and soon all the lively goats came leaping up the mountain, the nimble Distelfinck bounding ahead of the others. Heidi was at once in the midst of the flock, which pushed her hither and thither with loud, stormy greetings; she shoved them aside a little, for she wished to make her way to the timid Schneehöpli, who was always pushed away by the larger goats, when struggling to reach Heidi.

Peter now came along and gave one last, startling whistle to frighten the goats and drive them on to the pasture, for he wished to have room to say something to Heidi. The goats sprang ahead a little at this whistle, so Peter was able to come forward and stand in front of Heidi.

"You can come with me again today," he said, somewhat peevishly.

"No, I cannot, Peter," replied Heidi. "They may come from Frankfurt at any moment now, and I must be at home."

"You have said that a good many times already," growled Peter.

"But it is still true, and it will be true until they come," replied Heidi. "Don't you know that I must be at home, when they are coming from Frankfurt to see me? Don't you know that, Peter?"

"They can come to the uncle," answered Peter with a snarl.

The grandfather's deep voice then sounded from the hut, "Why doesn't the army move forward? Is it the fault of the field marshal or the troops?"

In a twinkling Peter wheeled round, swung his rod in the air, making it whistle, and all the goats, knowing the sound well, started off, and, with Peter behind them, ran at full speed up the mountain.

Since Heidi had returned home to her grandfather, every now and then she would remember something which she had not thought of before. Every morning she tried hard to make her bed, smoothing it until it looked quite even. Then she ran about the hut, placing every chair in its place, and if anything was lying or hanging about, she put it tidily into the closet. Then she brought a cloth, climbed up on a stool, and rubbed the table until it was perfectly clean. When her grandfather came in again, he would look round him with satisfaction and say, "Now it is always like Sunday here; Heidi did not go away for nothing."

Today also, after Peter had gone, and Heidi had breakfasted with her grandfather, she set about her work; but it seemed as if she would never finish. It was such a lovely morning outdoors, and every moment something happened to interrupt her in her tasks. Now a sunbeam came in so gaily through the window, and it seemed exactly as if it said, "Come out, Heidi, come out!" So she could no longer stay in the house, and she ran out. The sparkling sunshine lay all round the hut and glistened on the mountains and far, far down in the valley, and the ground there on the cliff looked so golden and dry that she had to sit down and look round her for a little while. Then suddenly she remembered that the three-legged stool was still standing in the middle of the floor, and the table had not been cleared since breakfast.

She jumped up quickly and ran back into the hut. But it was not long before the wind roared so mightily through the fir trees that Heidi felt it in every limb, and she had to go out again and dance a little with them, when all the branches above her were rocking and swaying to and fro. Her grandfather, meanwhile, had all sorts of work to do in the shop; he came out to the door from time to time and looked smilingly at Heidi as she jumped about. He was just stepping back again when Heidi suddenly screamed at the top of her voice, "Grandfather, grandfather! Come, come!"

He hastened out again, almost afraid that something had happened to the child. Then he saw her running toward the cliff screaming, "They are coming, they are coming! And the doctor first of all!"

Heidi rushed to meet her old friend. He held out his hand to greet her. When the child reached him she grasped his outstretched arm affectionately and exclaimed with the greatest joy, "How do you do, doctor? I thank you many thousand times!"

"Good morning, Heidi! But what are you thanking me for?" asked the doctor with a pleasant smile.

"Because I could come home again to my grandfather," explained the child.

The doctor's face lighted up as with sunshine. He had not expected such a reception in the Alps. In his sense of loneliness, all the while he was climbing the mountain, he had been wrapped in thought and had not once noticed how beautiful it was round him, and that it was growing more and more beautiful. He had supposed that the child Heidi would hardly remember him, he had seen so little of her; and as he was coming to give them a disappointment he felt that he would be unwelcome because he had not brought the expected friends with him.

Instead of this, Heidi's eyes gleamed with pure joy, and, full of gratefulness and love, she continued to cling to her good friend's arm.

The doctor took the child by the hand with fatherly tenderness. "Come, Heidi," he said in a most friendly way, "now take me to your grandfather and show me where your home is."

But Heidi remained standing where she was and looked wonderingly down the mountain.

"But where are Klara and the grandmamma?" she then asked.

"Well, I shall have to tell you something that will pain you as well as myself," replied the doctor. "You see, Heidi, I have come alone. Klara has been very ill and was not able to take the journey, and so the grandmamma did not come either. But in the spring, when the days are warm and long again, then they will surely come."

Heidi was very much distressed; she could hardly realize that what she had been looking forward to as so certain suddenly had become impossible. She stood motionless for a time, as if bewildered by the disappointment. The doctor stood silently in front of her, and everything round was still, except the wind blowing through the fir trees high above them. Then it suddenly occurred to Heidi why she had run down the mountain, and that the doctor was there. She looked up at him.

There was something sad in the eyes looking down at her, such as she had never seen before; he had never looked at her so in Frankfurt. It went to Heidi's heart; she could not bear to see anyone look sad, and now least of all the good doctor. It certainly must be because Klara and the grandmamma could not come with him. She quickly sought some way to console him.

"Oh, it really won't be long before spring will be here again, and then they will surely come," said Heidi comfortingly. "With us it never is a great while; and then they can stay much longer; Klara will like that much better. Now we will go up to my grandfather."

Hand in hand with her good friend she climbed up to the hut. Heidi was so very anxious to make the doctor happy that she began to assure him again that on the Alm it was such a little while before the long summer days would come again, that it was hardly noticeable; and in this way she became comforted herself and called up to her grandfather quite cheerfully, "They did not come, but it won't be long before they will be here, too."

The doctor was no stranger to the grandfather, the child had told him so much about her friend. The old man held out his hand to his guest and gave him a hearty welcome. Then they both sat down on the bench beside the hut, made a little place for Heidi, and the doctor kindly motioned to her to sit beside him. Then he began to relate how Herr Sesemann had urged him to take the journey, and how he himself had felt that it would be good for him, since he had not been quite strong and well for some time. He then whispered in Heidi's ear that something which had come from Frankfurt with him would soon come up the mountain, and that it would give her much greater pleasure than the old doctor could. Heidi was very eager to know what it might be.

The grandfather urged the doctor to spend the beautiful autumn days on the Alm, or at least to come up every fine day, for he could not invite him to remain up there, because he had no way of making him comfortable at night. But he advised his guest not to go back as far as

Ragatz, but to take a room down in Dörfli, in a simple but well-kept inn which he would find there. In that way the doctor would be able to come up the Alm every morning, which the uncle thought would do him good. Moreover, he would be glad to take the gentleman farther up the mountain, whenever he liked. This plan very much pleased the doctor, and he decided to carry it out.

Meanwhile the sun announced that it was midday; the wind had long since ceased, and the fir trees were perfectly still. The air was still mild and delicious for such a height, and felt refreshingly cool round the sunny bench.

The Alm-Uncle rose and went into the hut, but immediately came out again, bringing a table, which he placed in front of the bench.

"There, Heidi, now bring out what we need to eat," he said. "The gentleman will have to make the best of it, for if our cooking is plain our dining room is all that could be desired."

"I think so, too," replied the doctor as he gazed down into the valley bathed in sunlight, "and I accept your invitation, for everything must taste good up here."

Heidi ran back and forth like a weasel and brought out everything she could find in the cupboard, for she found it an immense pleasure to be able to entertain the doctor. Meanwhile the grandfather prepared the meal and came out with the steaming jug of milk and the shining golden toasted cheese. Then he cut clear slices of delicious, rosy meat, which he had dried up there in the pure air. The whole year through the doctor had not eaten a single meal which tasted so good as this dinner did.

"Yes, indeed, our Klara must come here," he said. "She would gain new strength, and if she should have such an appetite as I have today, she would become plump and strong, as she never has been in all her life."

Then someone came climbing up from below with a big package on his back. When he reached the hut, he threw his burden down on the ground and drew in long breaths of the fresh mountain air.

"Ah, here is what came with me from Frankfurt," said the doctor, rising; and, drawing Heidi after him, he went to the package and began to undo it. After the first heavy wrapping was removed, he said, "There, child, now open it yourself and take out your treasures."

Heidi did so, and when everything rolled out together her eyes grew big with astonishment as she gazed at the things. When the doctor stepped back again and lifted the cover of the big box, saying to Heidi, "See what the grandmother has for her coffee," then she exclaimed with delight, "Oh! Oh! Now at last the grandmother can have some nice cakes to eat!"

She danced round the box, and was anxious to put everything together immediately, and hasten down to the grandmother's. But her grandfather promised her that toward evening they would go down with the doctor and take the things with them. Then Heidi found the nice bag of tobacco and brought it quickly to her grandfather. It pleased him very much; he immediately filled his pipe with it, and the two men then sat on the bench, talking about all sorts of things, and puffing out great clouds of smoke, while Heidi ran back and forth from one of her treasures to another.

Suddenly she came back to the bench, stood in front of her guest, and, as soon as there was a pause in the conversation, said very decidedly, "No, nothing has given me any more pleasure than the old doctor has."

The two men had to laugh a little, and the doctor said he wouldn't have thought it.

When the sun went down behind the mountains the guest rose to take his way back to Dörfli and to find lodgings there. The grandfather put the box of cakes, the big sausage, and the shawl under his arm; the doctor took Heidi by the hand, and they went down the mountain to goatherd Peter's hut. Here Heidi had to leave them; she was to wait inside with the grandmother until her grandfather should come for her, after going with his guest down to Dörfli.

When the doctor, as he said good night, offered his hand to Heidi, she asked, "Would you like to go up to the pasture with the goats tomorrow?"

That was the loveliest spot she knew.

"To be sure, Heidi," he replied, "we will go together."

Then the men continued their way, and Heidi went into the grandmother's hut. First she dragged in the box of cakes with difficulty; then she had to go out again to bring in the sausage, for her grandfather had laid everything down in front of the door; then she had to go out once more to get the big shawl. She brought them all as close to the grandmother as possible, so that she might touch them and know what they were. She laid the shawl in her lap.

"They are all from Frankfurt, from Klara and her grandmamma!" she exclaimed. The amazed Brigitte was so affected by her surprise that she stood motionless, watching Heidi as she, with the greatest difficulty, dragged in the heavy articles and spread out everything before her and the highly astonished grandmother.

"Surely, grandmother, you are terribly pleased with the cakes, aren't you? Just see how soft they are!" Heidi exclaimed again and again, and the grandmother replied, "Yes, yes, indeed, Heidi; what good people they are!" Then she would stroke the soft, warm shawl with her hand and say, "But this is something splendid for the cold winter! I never dreamed I should ever have anything so splendid in my life."

Heidi was very much surprised that the grandmother should be more delighted with the gray shawl than with the cakes. Brigitte continued standing before the sausage as it lay on the table, and gazed at it almost with reverence. In all her life she had never seen such a giant sausage, and she was going to possess it, and even cut it; she could not believe it possible. She shook her head and said timidly, "We must first ask the uncle what it is meant for."

But Heidi said very decidedly, "It is meant to eat, and for nothing else."

Then Peter came stumbling in.

"The Alm-Uncle is coming just behind me; Heidi must—" He could go no further. His eyes fell on the table where the sausage lay, and the sight of it so overcame him that he could not speak another word. But

Heidi had already noticed who was coming, and hastened to give her hand to the grandmother. The Alm-Uncle never went by the hut now without stepping in to speak to the grandmother, and she was always delighted to hear his step, for he was sure to have an encouraging word for her; but today it was late for Heidi, who was out every morning with the sun. Her grandfather said, "The child must have her sleep," and was firm. So he only called out a good night through the open door to the grandmother, took Heidi's hand as she ran to meet him, and the two made their way beneath the twinkling stars back to their peaceful hut.

Chapter 3

Heidi Consoles the Doctor

Early the next morning the doctor climbed the mountain from Dörfli in company with Peter and his goats. In a friendly spirit he tried several times to enter into conversation with the goat boy, but he did not succeed in getting more than the briefest answers to his leading questions. Peter was not so easily led into conversation. So the whole company traveled in silence up to the Alm hut, where Heidi already stood waiting with her two goats, all three as lively and glad as the early sunshine on the heights.

"Coming too?" asked Peter, for he said this every morning either as a question or a summons.

"To be sure, of course, if the doctor will come with us," replied Heidi.

Peter looked a little suspiciously at the gentleman.

Then the grandfather came out, bringing the dinner bag in his hand. He first greeted the doctor with great respect, then went to Peter and hung the bag over his shoulder.

It was heavier than usual, for the uncle had put in a good piece of the dried meat; he thought possibly the doctor might like it up in the pasture, and he would enjoy his dinner there at the same time with the children. Peter's mouth spread almost from one ear to the other with a grin of satisfaction, for he suspected that there was something unusual inside.

The journey up the mountain was now begun. Heidi was completely surrounded by the goats; each one wanted to be next her, and they kept pushing one another to one side. So she remained for some time in the midst of the flock, struggling with them. Then she stood still and said, "Now please run away and don't keep coming back and pushing and shoving me; I must go with the doctor a little while now."

Then she patted Schneehöpli gently on the back, for she still kept close to Heidi's side, and bade her especially to be very obedient. Then she made her way out of the flock and ran to the side of the doctor, who seized her hand at once and held it fast. He had no difficulty in getting Heidi to talk; she immediately began and had so much to tell him about the goats and their remarkable doings, and about the flowers up there and the rocks and the birds, that before they knew it they had reached the pasture.

As they climbed the mountain, Peter had frequently cast sidelong glances at the doctor, which might really have terrified him, but fortunately he did not see them.

When they reached the end of their journey, Heidi took her kind friend to the loveliest spot of all, where she always went, sat down on the ground, and looked round; this was her favorite place.

The doctor dropped down beside her on the sunny pasture ground. Round about, the golden autumn sun shone over the peaks and the distant green valley. Everywhere from the pastures below came the sound of the bells of the herd, so lovely and delightful, as if announcing sweet peace far and wide. The golden sunbeams flashed sparkling and glistening here and there on the great snow fields above, and the gray Falknis lifted its towers of rock in lofty majesty far up into the deep blue sky. The morning breeze blew gently and deliciously over the mountain and softly stirred the last bluebells, still remaining from the great numbers of the summer, and cheerfully nodding their little heads in the warm sunshine. The great robber-bird flew round in wide circles above, but today he did not scream; with outspread wings he floated peacefully through the blue and took his ease.

Heidi gazed first one way and then another. The gay nodding flowers, the blue sky, the merry sunshine, the happy bird in the air, all were so beautiful, so beautiful! Heidi's eyes sparkled with delight. She looked at her friend to see whether he, too, understood how beautiful it was. Until now the doctor had been looking round him silently and wrapped in thought. As he met the child's beaming eyes he said, "Yes, Heidi, it is beautiful here; but what do you think? If you brought a sad heart, how could you make it well, so that you could enjoy all this beauty?"

"Oh, oh!" exclaimed Heidi quite gaily. "Nobody ever has a sad heart here—only in Frankfurt."

A smile passed over the doctor's face, but it quickly vanished. Then he added, "And supposing someone should come and bring all his sorrow with him up here from Frankfurt, Heidi; do you know of anything that could help him then?"

"He must tell everything to the dear Lord, if he does not know what to do," said Heidi with perfect assurance.

"Yes, that is really a good thought, child," observed the doctor. "But if what makes you so very sad and miserable comes from Him, what can you say to the dear Lord?"

Heidi had to think what ought to be done in such a case; but she was very certain that one could obtain help from the dear Lord for every sorrow. She sought a reply from her own experience.

"Then you must wait," she said after a while with assurance, "and keep thinking: 'Surely now the dear Lord knows some joy which is to come out of this by and by, so I must be still for a little and not run away from Him.' Then all at once it will happen so that you will see quite clearly that the dear Lord had nothing but good in His mind all the time; but because you could not see it so at first, and only had the terrible sorrow all the time before you, you thought it would always remain so."

"That is a beautiful faith, and you must hold it fast, Heidi," said the doctor. For some time he gazed silently at the mighty mountains of rock and down into the green sunlit valley; then he continued, "You see, Heidi, you might sit here with a great shade over your eyes, so that you could not take in the beauty all about. Then indeed would your heart be sad, doubly sad, where it is so beautiful. Can you understand that?"

A pain shot through Heidi's happy heart. The great shade over the eyes reminded her of the grandmother, who could never again see the bright sun and all the beauty up there. To Heidi it was a grief that always wakened as often as the fact occurred to her. She remained perfectly silent for some time, for the pain had so broken into the midst of her joy. Then she said earnestly, "Yes, indeed, I can understand that. But I know something; then you must say the grandmother's hymns, and they will give you a little light, and perhaps so much light that you will become quite happy. The grandmother said so."

"What hymns, Heidi?" asked the doctor.

"I know only the one about the sun and the beautiful garden, and the verses the grandmother likes from the other long one, for I always have to read it three times," replied Heidi.

"Just tell me these verses; I should like very much to hear them." And the doctor sat up straight to listen attentively.

Heidi folded her hands and collected her thoughts for a little while.

"Shall I begin where the grandmother says that trust returns to one's heart?"

The doctor nodded assent.

Then Heidi began:

"Oh, trust His love to guide thee,
He is a Prince so wise
That what His hands provide thee
Is wondrous in thine eyes.
And He, if He be willing,
May bring the work about
And thus thy hopes fulfilling
Dispel thy fear and doubt.

"It may be for a season
He will no comfort show,
And for some hidden reason
His light will not bestow.
As if no more He heeded
What sorrow was thy share,
Or what relief thou needed
In all thy deep despair.

"But if thy sure faith stays thee
When thou art most perplex,
He will appear and raise thee
What time thou least expects.
He will remove the burden
That presses thy heart down,
And thou shalt have the guerdon
And thou shalt wear the crown. "*

Heidi stopped suddenly, for she was not sure that the doctor was still listening. He had laid his hand over his eyes and was sitting motionless. She thought perhaps he had fallen asleep; so if he should wake up and care to hear more verses she would repeat them to him. Everything was still. The doctor said nothing, but he was not asleep. He had been carried back to days of long ago. He stood as a little boy beside his dear mother's chair; she had placed her arm round his neck and was repeating the hymn which Heidi had just repeated, and which he had not heard for so long. Now he heard his mother's voice again and saw her gentle eyes resting on him lovingly, and when the words of the hymn had ceased, the kind voice seemed to be speaking still other words to him; he must have enjoyed listening to them and have gone far back in his thoughts, for he sat there for a long while, silent and motionless, with his face buried in his hands. When he finally rose he noticed that Heidi was looking at him in amazement. He took the child's hand in his.

"Heidi, your hymn was beautiful," he said; and his voice sounded more cheerful than it had been before. "We will come up here another day, and you shall repeat it to me once more."

During all this time Peter was having enough to do in giving expression to his vexation. Heidi had not been with him up to the pasture for several days, and now that she had finally come this old gentleman sat beside her the whole time, and Peter could not come near

* Translated by Nathan Haskell Dole

her at all. This greatly troubled him. He took his place at a distance higher up, where the unsuspecting gentleman could not see him, and here he first doubled up one fist and shook it, and after a while he doubled up both fists, and the longer Heidi remained sitting beside the doctor, the more madly Peter doubled up his fists and the higher and more threateningly he raised them in the air behind the gentleman's back.

Meanwhile the sun had reached the point where it stands when it is time for the midday meal; this Peter knew well enough. Suddenly he screamed down with all his might to the others, "We must have something to eat!"

Heidi rose and was going to get the bag, so that the doctor could have his dinner just where he was sitting. But he said he was not hungry; he wanted nothing but a bowl of milk to drink, and then he would like to go about a little more on the mountain and climb somewhat higher. Then Heidi discovered that she was not hungry either, and that she cared for only a bowl of milk, after which she would like to take the doctor to the big moss-covered rock, high up, where Distelfinck had almost jumped over and where all the spicy herbs grew. She ran to Peter and explained it all to him, how he must first take a bowl of milk from Schwänli for the doctor and another for herself. At first Peter looked at Heidi for some time in amazement, then he asked, "Who is to have what is in the bag?"

"You may have it, but you must get the milk first and be quick about it," was Heidi's reply.

Peter had never done anything in his life so quickly as he accomplished this task, for he saw the bag constantly before him, and he did not know how its contents looked, and yet it belonged to him. As soon as the two others had drunk their milk, Peter opened the bag and took a look into it. When he saw the wonderful piece of meat his whole body trembled with delight, and he looked into the bag again to make sure that it was really true. Then he put his hand in to take out the welcome gift and enjoy it. But suddenly he drew his hand back, as if he dared not take it. He recalled how he had stood there behind the doctor and shaken his fists at him, and now the same gentleman had given him all his splendid dinner. Then Peter was sorry for what he had done, for it seemed as if it hindered him from taking his fine present and enjoying it. Suddenly he jumped up and ran back to the place where he had been standing, stretched both his hands wide open up in the air, as a sign that his clenched fists had meant nothing, and so remained standing there for some time until he felt that his deed was atoned for. Then he took great leaps back to the bag; for now that his conscience was clear he could eat his unusually nice dinner with perfect enjoyment.

The doctor and Heidi wandered about together for a long while and enjoyed each other's company. Then the doctor found that it was time for him to go back, and thought that the child would like to stay a little longer with her goats. But Heidi had no such idea, for then the doctor would have to go alone down the whole length of the mountain. She would walk with him as far as her grandfather's hut, and even farther. She went hand in hand with her good friend, and had all the way a great deal to tell him and show him; she wanted him to see all the places where the goats liked best to feed, and where grew the greatest number of bright yellow wild roses and red centauries and other flowers to be found in the summertime. She knew them all, for her grandfather had taught her their names.

But at last the doctor said he must go. They bade each other good night, and as he went down the mountain he turned every little while to look back, and saw Heidi still standing in the same place, gazing after him and waving her hand to him. Just so had his own dear little daughter done when he went away from his house.

It was a clear sunny autumn month. Every morning the doctor came up on the mountain, and then there was a delightful excursion farther up. Often he went off with the Alm-Uncle far up into the rocky cliffs where the old weather-beaten fir trees were; the great robber-bird must have had his nest near, for he often whizzed past, whirring and croaking, close to the heads of the two men.

The doctor took great pleasure in his companion's society, and was more and more amazed to see how familiar the uncle was with all the plants round on his mountain, and how well he knew what they were good for, and how many valuable and good things he discovered everywhere up there, in the pitchy fir trees and the dark pines with their fragrant needles, in the crinkled moss, sprouting out between the roots of the old trees, and in all the delicate little plants and modest flowers, still growing quite high up in the nourishing mountain soil.

The old man was equally familiar with the life and habits of all the animals up there, both great and small, and he had very amusing things to tell the doctor about the ways of these little creatures living in holes in the rocks and caves, and even in the branches of the lofty fir trees.

The doctor did not know where the time went on these visits, and often at evening when he shook the uncle's hand heartily at parting, he would say, "My good friend, I never go away from you without having learned something new."

But on many days, and usually on the finest, the doctor chose to go with Heidi. Then the two would often sit together on the lovely cliff where they sat the first day, and Heidi had to repeat her hymns and tell the doctor what she knew. And Peter would often sit behind them in his place, but he was now quite peaceable and no longer shook his fists at them.

Thus the lovely month of September came to an end. Then one morning the doctor came, looking less happy than usual. He said it was his last day, and he must go back to Frankfurt; this grieved him very much, for he had become as fond of the mountain as if it were his own home. This news pained the Alm-Uncle also, for he had particularly enjoyed the doctor's company, and Heidi had become so accustomed to seeing her dear friend every day that she could not understand that the pleasure was now suddenly coming to an end. She looked up at him inquiringly and quite amazed. But it was really so. The doctor bade her grandfather farewell and then asked if Heidi would go with him a little way. With her hand in his she went down the mountain, but she could not fully realize that he was really going away.

After a while the doctor stood still and said that Heidi had come far enough, and she must turn back. He passed his hand tenderly over the child's curly hair two or three times and said, "Now I must go, Heidi! If only I could take you to Frankfurt and could keep you with me!"

All Frankfurt suddenly rose before Heidi's eyes, its many,—many houses and stony streets, as well as Fräulein Rottenmeier and Tinette, and she answered somewhat timidly, "I would rather have you come back to us again."

"Well, yes, perhaps it would be better, so good-bye, Heidi," said the doctor kindly, holding out his hand to her. Heidi laid hers in it and looked up at her departing friend. The kind eyes which looked down at her filled with tears. Then the doctor turned quickly and hastened down the mountain.

Heidi remained standing where she was and did not stir. The beloved eyes and the tears which she had seen in them went straight to her heart. Suddenly she burst into loud weeping and rushed with all her might after the fast-disappearing doctor and called between her sobs as loudly as she could, "Doctor! Doctor!"

He turned round and stood still.

The child had now reached him. The tears streamed down her cheeks while she sobbed out, "I will truly go with you to Frankfurt now, and I will stay with you as long as you like, but I must hurry back to tell my grandfather."

The doctor soothingly caressed the excited child.

"No, my dear Heidi," he said in the kindest tone, "not now; you must stay longer under the fir trees, for you might be sick again if you went with me. But come, I want to ask you something: if I am ever sick and alone, will you come to me then and stay with me? Can I think that then someone will care for me and love me?"

"Yes, yes; then I will surely come to you, the very same day; and I love you almost as well as my grandfather," said Heidi decidedly, still sobbing.

Then the doctor pressed her hand once more and hurried on his way. But Heidi remained standing in the same spot, waving her hand again and again, until the form of her friend, as he hastened away, was a mere speck in the distance. When he turned round for the last time and looked back at Heidi, waving her hand, and at the sunny mountain, he said softly to himself, "It is good to be on the mountain; body and soul get well there, and life becomes happy again."

Chapter 4

The Winter in Dörfli

Round the alm hut the snow lay so deep that it looked as if the windows were on a level with the ground, for not a bit of the wall was to be seen below them; moreover, the house door had completely disappeared. If the Alm-Uncle had been up there he would have had to do the same thing that Peter did every day. Every morning he had to jump out the window, and if everything was not frozen he sank so deep in the soft snow that had fallen during the night that he had to push and struggle and kick in every direction with his hands and feet and head, until he had worked his way out. Then his mother would hand him the big broom from the window, and with this Peter would push and shove the snow before him until he reached the door. Then he had great trouble, for there all the snow had to be dug away, or if it was still soft when the door opened, the whole great mass would fall into the kitchen, or else it froze up, and then they were completely walled in, for they could not make their way through these rocklike heaps of ice, and Peter was the only one who could slip through the little window.

Freezing weather brought many conveniences to Peter. If he was going down to Dörfli, all he had to do was to open the window, crawl through, and get out on the smooth surface of the firm snow field. Then his mother would push his sled through the window after him, and Peter had only to seat himself on it and slide wherever he liked; in any case he went down, for the whole Alm was one great unbroken slope.

The uncle was not on the Alm that winter; he had kept his word. As soon as the first snow fell he had shut up the hut and shed and had gone down to Dörfli with Heidi and the goats. Near the church and the parsonage stood a roomy building, which in old times had been a great mansion. This could still be seen in many places, although now the building was more or less in ruins. A brave warrior had once lived in it; he had gone to the Spanish wars and had performed many brave deeds and gained great wealth. Then he had come home to Dörfli, and with his gains built a splendid house in which he intended to live. But he did not stay long; it was so tiresome to him, for he had lived too much in the noisy world to be able to bear the quiet Dörfli. He went away again and never came back. After many, many years, when it was known that he was really dead, a distant relative down in the valley took the house, but it was already tumbling to pieces, and the new owner did not care to build it up again. So poor people who had to pay little for it came into the house, and if a part of the building fell, they let it lie.

Since that time many years had passed. When the uncle came back with the young boy Tobias, he took the ruined house and lived in it. Since then it had stood empty most of the time, for no one without skill to stop the work of destruction to some extent and to fill up and mend the holes and gaps could stay there. The winter in Dörfli was long and cold. The wind blew in from every side through the rooms, so that the lights were blown out and the poor people shook with the cold. But the uncle knew how to manage. As soon as he had made up his mind to spend the winter in Dörfli, he took the old house again, and often during the autumn came down to mend and repair it as he liked. About the middle of October he brought Heidi down.

Entering the house from the rear, one came at once into an open room, of which the entire wall on one side, and half on the other, had fallen in. Above this an arched window was still to be seen, but the glass had long been out of it, and thick ivy crept round it and high up on the roof, which was, for the most part, still solid. It was beautifully arched, and one could easily see that the room had been a chapel. There being no door, one came directly into a large hall, and here in places in the floor were still handsome tiles between which the grass grew thick. The walls were half gone, and great pieces of the roof had given way; had it not been for two heavy pillars, the whole roof would have been gone; as it was, it looked as if it might at any moment fall on the heads of those standing underneath.

Here the uncle had put up a partition of boards and had covered the floor thickly with hay, for in this old hall the goats were to be housed.

Then there were all sorts of passageways, all half uncovered, so that the sky could be seen through, and sometimes meadows and the road outside. But in the front, where the heavy oaken door still hung firmly on its hinges, one came to a large spacious room which was still in good condition. The four walls were all standing, the dark wood panels showed not a break, and in one corner stood a huge stove, reaching almost to the ceiling, and on the white tiles were big blue pictures. Some showed old castles, with tall trees all round, and underneath a huntsman passing with his dogs. Another picture showed a peaceful lake, under wide-spreading oaks, with a fisherman standing by it and holding his rod far out over the water. There was a seat all round the stove so that one could sit down and study the pictures. This at once took Heidi's fancy. As soon as she came into the room with her grandfather, she ran to the stove, sat down on the bench, and began to look at the pictures. But as she moved along on the seat and came behind the stove, something new occupied her whole attention; in the quite large space between the stove and the wall four boards were placed, like a bin for apples. But there were no apples in it; there actually lay Heidi's bed exactly as it had been upon the Alm; a thick bed of hay, with the linen sheet and a bag for a coverlet. Heidi shouted, "O grandfather, here is my bedroom! Oh, how lovely! But where will you sleep?"

"Your bedroom must be near the stove, so that you won't freeze," said her grandfather. "You may see mine too."

Heidi skipped across the big room after her grandfather, who opened a door on the other side; and this led into a little room where he had arranged his bed. Then came another door. Heidi quickly opened it and stood still in amazement, for it looked into a sort of kitchen more enormous than any she had ever seen in her life. It had given her grandfather a great deal of work, and there was still much to do; for in the walls on all sides there were holes and wide cracks, where the wind blew in, although so many had been nailed up with boards that it looked as if little cupboards had been made all round in the wall. The grandfather had also succeeded in repairing the big ancient door with wires and nails, so that it could be shut; and this was a good thing, for it opened into the most ruined part of the building, overgrown with thick briars, where many lizards and beetles had their abode.

The new dwelling place pleased Heidi well, and on the very next day, when Peter came to see how they were getting along there, she had spied out every nook and corner so thoroughly that she was quite at home and could take Peter everywhere. She gave him no rest until he had thoroughly seen all the wonderful things which their new house contained.

Heidi slept excellently in the nook behind the great stove, but in the morning she thought she had wakened on the mountain, and that she must open the door of the hut at once to see if the reason the fir trees were not roaring was because the deep, heavy snow was lying on them and bending down their branches. So at first every morning she had to look round her for a long while until she remembered where she was, and every time when she saw that she was not at home on the mountain, she felt something stifling and pressing her heart. But when she heard her grandfather talking outside with Schwänli and Bärli, and the goats bleating so loud and merrily, as if they were calling to her, "Hurry and come out, Heidi," then she felt that she was at home after all, and jumped gaily out of bed and hurried to the big goat barn. On the fourth day Heidi said, "Today I must really go up to see the grandmother; she can't be alone so long."

But her grandfather did not agree to this. "Not today, nor tomorrow either," he said. "The Alm is six feet deep with snow, and it keeps on snowing; stout Peter can hardly get through it. A little thing like you, Heidi, would be snowed in and covered up the first thing, and you never could be found again. Wait a little, until it freezes, then you can easily walk over the crust."

At first it was a grief to Heidi to have to wait. But now the days were so full of work that one passed away and another came before she knew it.

Every morning and every afternoon now Heidi went to school and was quick in learning all her lessons. She hardly ever saw Peter in school, for he seldom came. The teacher was a meek man and only occasionally said, "It seems to me Peter is absent again; school would do him good; but there is a great deal of snow up there, perhaps he can't get through."

But toward evening, when school was out, Peter usually got through and paid a visit to Heidi.

After a few days the sun came out again and threw its rays over the white earth; but it went down behind the mountains again very early, as if it were not so well pleased to look down as in summer, when everything was green and in bloom. In the evening the moon rose very bright and big, and all night long shone over the vast snow fields, and the next morning the whole mountain from top to bottom glistened and glittered like a crystal. When Peter jumped out the window into the deep snow, as he had done the day before, something happened which he had not expected. Instead of coming down into the soft snow, he struck on a surprisingly hard surface, and, before he knew it, had slipped a good piece down the mountain, like an empty sled. In great surprise he finally succeeded in getting on his feet again, and then stamped with all his might on the crust, to assure himself that what had just happened was really possible. It was actually so; as he stamped and beat with his heels, he could scarcely break off the least bit of ice; the whole Alm was frozen as hard as a rock. Peter liked this; for he knew that this state of things was necessary for Heidi to be able to come up there again. He promptly turned back, swallowed the milk which his mother had just put on the table, tucked his piece of bread into his pocket, and said hastily, "I must go to school."

"Yes, do go and study hard," said his mother.

Peter crawled through the window, for now they were shut in again on account of the heaps of ice before the door, pulled his little sled after him, sat down on it, and shot down the mountain.

It went like lightning, and when he came near to Dörfli, where it goes farther down toward Maienfeld, Peter kept on, for it occurred to him that he might injure himself and his sled if he should stop suddenly. So he went on until he was down on level ground and the sled stopped of itself. Then he got up and looked round. The force of the descent had carried him somewhat beyond Maienfeld. Then he considered that he should be too late for school, as it had begun some time before, and it would take him almost an hour to climb back there again. So he had plenty of time to go back to Dörfli. This he did, and arrived just as Heidi had returned from school and was sitting down to dinner with her grandfather. Peter went in, and as this time he had a definite idea to express, it was uppermost in his mind, and he had to say it at once.

"We've got it," said Peter, standing still in the middle of the room.

"Got what, general? That sounds rather warlike," said the uncle.

"The crust," replied Peter.

"Oh! Oh! Now I can go up to see the grandmother!" shouted Heidi joyfully, for she had at once understood Peter's manner of expressing himself. "But why didn't you come to school, then? You could slide down well enough," she suddenly added in reproach; for it occurred to Heidi that it was not right to remain away from school if one could go as well as not.

"Went too far on my sled; 'twas too late," replied Peter.

"That is called 'running away,'" said the uncle, "and people who do that are taken by the ears! Do you hear?"

Peter pulled his cap in alarm, for there was nobody in the world for whom he had so great respect as for the Alm-Uncle.

"And, besides, a leader such as you are ought to be doubly ashamed of running away so," continued the uncle.

"What would you think if your goats should run one this way and another that, and refuse to follow you and do what was good for them? What would you do then?"

"Beat them," replied Peter knowingly.

"And if a boy behaves like an unruly goat and is beaten a little, what would you say to that?"

"Served him right," was the answer.

"Well, now understand, goat-colonel, if you go past the school on your sled a single time when you ought to be in it, come here to me and get what you deserve."

Then Peter understood what the Alm-Uncle meant: that he considered any boy who played truant an unruly goat. He was quite impressed by this likeness and looked a little anxiously into the corner to see whether he could discover what the uncle used at such times for the goats.

The uncle then said cheerfully, "Come to the table now and sit down with us, then Heidi may go with you. If you bring her back home at evening, you will find your supper here."

This unexpected turn of affairs was highly delightful to Peter; his face was twisted in every way with delight. He obeyed instantly and sat down beside Heidi. But the child had already had enough and could swallow no more; she was so delighted that she could go to see the grandmother. She pushed the big potato and the toasted cheese, still left on her plate, toward Peter, who had already had his plate filled from the other side by the uncle, so that he had a regular wall before him; but courage to attack it was not lacking. Heidi ran to the cupboard and brought out the little cape Klara had given her; now she could take the journey, warmly wrapped up, with the hood over her head. She placed herself beside Peter, and as soon as he had shoved in his last mouthful she said, "Now come!"

Then they started along. Heidi had a great deal to tell Peter about Schwänli and Bärli: that neither of them would eat anything the first day in their new barn, and that they had hung their heads the whole day and not made a sound. She had asked her grandfather why they did so, and he said that they felt just as she did in Frankfurt, for they had never been down from the Alm in all their lives. And Heidi added, "You just ought to know once what that is, Peter."

The two had almost reached the end of their journey before Peter said a word, and it seemed as if he were so deep in thought that he could not hear right, as usual. When they reached the hut, Peter stood still and said somewhat crossly, "There! I would rather go to school than take from the uncle what he said."

Heidi was of the same opinion and encouraged him eagerly in his decision.

In the room inside, Peter's mother was sitting alone with her mending; she said the grandmother had to spend the day in bed, as it was too cold for her, and besides she was not quite well. This was something new to Heidi; the grandmother always before had been sitting in her place in the corner. Heidi ran straight to her in her room. She was lying entirely wrapped up in the gray shawl in her narrow bed with the thin covering.

"God be praised and thanked!" said the grandmother as soon as she heard Heidi running in. All the autumn long she had had a secret worry in her heart, and it still followed her, especially if Heidi did not come to see her for a long time. Peter had reported how a strange gentleman from Frankfurt had been there and always went up to the pasture with them and talked with Heidi, and the grandmother believed nothing else than that the gentleman had come to take Heidi away again. After he finally went off alone, her anxiety returned lest some person should be sent from Frankfurt to take the child back. Heidi ran to her bedside and asked anxiously, "Are you very ill, grandmother?"

"No, no, child," said the old dame to console her, while she stroked the child's face affectionately, "the cold weather has got into my limbs a little."

"Will you be well right away, as soon as it is warm again?" asked Heidi eagerly.

"Yes, yes, God willing, even before that, so that I can get to my spinning wheel. I even thought today that I would try it; tomorrow it will surely be going again," said the grandmother; for she had already noticed that the child was alarmed.

Her words soothed Heidi, who was very much troubled, for she had never found the grandmother sick in bed before. She looked at her a little while in surprise, and then said, "In Frankfurt they put on a shawl to go outdoors in. Did you think you ought to put it on when you go to bed, grandmother?"

"Do you know, Heidi," she replied, "I wrap the shawl round me so in bed in order not to freeze. I am so glad to have it, for the bed covering is rather thin."

"But, grandmother," Heidi began again, "your head goes downhill, where it ought to go up; a bed ought not to be like that."

"I know it, child, I realize it well enough"; and the grandmother tried to find a better place for the pillow that lay like a thin board under her head. "You see the pillow was never thick, and now I have slept so many years on it that I have made it rather flat."

"Oh, if only I had asked Klara when I was in Frankfurt to let me take my bed home with me!" exclaimed Heidi. "It had three big, thick pillows, one on top of another, so that I couldn't sleep, and always slipped down where it was flat, and then I had to move up again because I oughtn't to sleep so. Could you sleep so, grandmother?"

"Yes, indeed; it would make me warm, and I could breathe so easily if I could lie with my head high," said the grandmother, lifting her head rather wearily, as if to find a higher place for it. "But we won't talk about that, for I have to thank the dear Lord for so much that other sick old people do not have: the nice rolls that I have all the time, and the nice warm shawl here, and your coming to see me, Heidi. Will you read something to me again today, Heidi?"

Heidi ran out and brought back the old hymn book. Then she found one beautiful song after another, for she knew them well now, and enjoyed them herself, and it was many days since she had heard all the verses she was so fond of.

The grandmother lay with folded hands, and on her face, which at first had looked so troubled, now rested a happy smile, as if a great good fortune had come to her.

Suddenly Heidi stopped.

"Grandmother, are you well again already?"

"I'm feeling much better, Heidi. What you have read to me has done me good. Finish it, will you?"

The child read the hymn to the end, and when she came to the last words—

When mine eyes grow dimmer, sadder,
Pour Thy light into my heart,
That I may pass over gladder
Than men to their homes depart—

the grandmother repeated them over and over, and an expression of very joyful trust came over her face. Heidi felt very happy to see it. All the sunny day of her journey home rose before her, and she exclaimed with delight, "Grandmother, I know very well how it feels to be traveling home!"

The grandmother did not answer, but she had heard the words perfectly, and the expression which had pleased Heidi remained on her face.

After a while the child said, "It is growing dark now, grandmother; I must go back; but I am so glad that you are happy again."

The grandmother took the child's hand in hers and held it fast; then she said, "Yes, I am so happy again; if I must stay lying here, I am content. You see, nobody who has not been through it knows what it is to have to lie for days and days all alone, and not hear a word from another human being, and not be able to see—not see even a single sunbeam. Then such gloomy thoughts come to one that it often seems as if it never could be bright again and one could not bear it any longer. But when I hear the words which you have read to me, it is as if a light arose in my heart, and that makes me happy again."

Then the grandmother let go Heidi's hand, and after she had said good night, Heidi ran back into the other room and hurriedly drew Peter out, for it had already grown late. However, outside the moon was in the sky and shone as brightly on the white snow as if the daylight had come back. Peter arranged his sled, sat down on it in front, with Heidi behind, and away they shot down the Alm, exactly as if they were two birds rushing through the air.

Later, when Heidi was lying in her lovely, deep bed of hay, she began to think about the grandmother again, and how uncomfortably her head lay; and then she remembered all that she had said, and the light the words kindled in her heart. And she thought if the grandmother only could hear the words every day, then she would feel well all the time. But she knew that now a whole week, or perhaps even two, must pass before she could go up to her again. This seemed so sad to Heidi that she kept thinking harder and harder what she could do to have the grandmother hear the words every day. Suddenly help came to her, and she was so glad about it that it seemed to her she could hardly wait for the morning to come so that she might carry out her plan. All at once Heidi sat straight up in bed, for she had been so deep in thought that she had not sent up her evening prayer to the dear Lord, and she would never forget that again.

When she had prayed straight from her heart for herself and her grandfather and the grandmother, she fell back at once into her soft hay and slept very soundly and peacefully until the bright morning.

Chapter 5

The Winter Still Continues

After this, Peter came down to school at exactly the right time. He brought his dinner with him in his bag, for this was the custom there. When all the children in Dörfli had gone home at noon, the other scholars, who lived at a distance, sat on the long desks, braced their feet firmly against the seats, and spread in their laps the luncheon they had brought for their midday meal. They could enjoy themselves until one o'clock, when school began again. When Peter had spent the day in school, he went after it was over to the uncle's, to pay a visit to Heidi.

When he entered the big room, Heidi ran to meet him for she had been expecting him.

"Peter, I know something," she called to him.

"Say it," he replied.

"You must learn to read," was the news she had for him.

"It's no use," was the reply.

"O Peter! I don't agree with you," said Heidi eagerly. "I think that you can after a little while."

"Cannot," remarked Peter.

"Nobody believes such a thing as that, and I don't either," said Heidi very decidedly. "The grandmamma in Frankfurt knew that it wasn't true, and she told me that I ought not to believe it either."

Peter was astonished at this news.

"I will teach you to read; I know how very well," Heidi continued. "You must learn now once for all, and then you must read one or two hymns every day to your grandmother."

"Don't want to," grumbled Peter.

This stubborn objection to something which was good and right and which Heidi had set her heart on made her angry. With flashing eyes she placed herself in front of the boy and said threateningly, "Then I will tell you what will happen, if you will never learn anything; your mother has already said twice that you would have to go to Frankfurt to learn something, and I know very well where the boys go to school there; Klara showed me the frightfully big house when we were out driving. There they don't go merely when they are boys, but just the same when they get to be great, big men; I saw that myself; and then you mustn't suppose that there is only one teacher there, as we have here, and such a kind one. Whole rows, ever so many together, are always going into the house, and all of them are dressed in black, as if they were going to church, and have such high black hats on their heads"; and Heidi measured the size of the hats from the floor up.

The shivers ran down Peter's back.

"And then you would have to go in among all the masters," continued Heidi eagerly, "and if it came your turn, you couldn't read at all and would make mistakes even in the alphabet. Then you would see how the masters would laugh at you, and that is much worse than Tinette, and you ought to know how it is when she laughs at you."

"Then I will learn," said Peter half fretfully, half whiningly.

In a moment Heidi was calmed.

"Well, that is right, and we will begin at once," she cried in her delight; and pulling Peter in a businesslike way to the table, she brought out the articles needed for work.

In Klara's big package there was a little book which had pleased Heidi very much, and it had occurred to her the night before that it would be a good thing to use for teaching Peter. It was an A-B-C book in rhyme.

They both sat down at the table, their heads bent over the little book, and the lesson began.

Peter had to spell the first sentence over and over again, for Heidi insisted on having it done nicely and without hesitation.

Finally she said, "You don't know it yet, but I will read it over and over to you; if you know what it means, you can spell it out better"; and Heidi read:

"If A, B, C you do not know,
Before the school board you will go."

"I will not go," said Peter angrily.

"Where?" asked Heidi.

"Before the school board," was the reply.

"Then try to learn the three letters, and you won't have to go," explained Heidi.

Then Peter began again and repeated the three letters over and over until Heidi said, "Now you know these three."

But as she noticed what an effect the words had made on Peter, she wanted to prepare a little for the following lessons.

"Wait—I will read you the other sentences," she continued, "then you will see all that is coming."

And she began to read very clearly and distinctly:

"D, E, F, G must smoothly fly,
Or else misfortune will be nigh.

"If H, I, J, K are forgot,
Misfortune is upon the spot.

"Whoe'er on L, M still will stumble
Must pay a fine and then feel humble.

"There's something bad, and if you knew
You'd quickly learn N, O, P, Q.

"If still on R, S, T you halt,
The harm that comes will be your fault."

Here Heidi stopped, for Peter was as still as a mouse, and she had to see what he was doing. All these threats and mysterious horrors had so overcome him that he could not move a muscle, and was staring at Heidi in terror.

This immediately touched Heidi's tender heart, and she said comfortingly, "You mustn't be frightened, Peter; just come to me every afternoon, and if you learn as well as you have today, you will know all the letters after a while, and then nothing will happen to you. But you must come every day, and not the way you go to school. If it snows it won't do you any harm."

Peter promised to do so, for fear had made him quite meek and obedient. Then he started home.

Peter followed Heidi's orders strictly, and every afternoon studied the other letters eagerly and learned the rhymes by heart.

The grandfather often sat in the room and listened to the exercise, while he smoked his pipe contentedly, and every little while the corners of his mouth twitched, as if he could hardly keep from laughing.

After the great struggle Peter was usually invited to remain and take supper with them; and this at once richly rewarded him for the suffering that day's verse had caused him.

Thus the winter days passed away. Peter came regularly and really made progress with his letters.

But he had to wrestle every day with the verses.

They had gone as far as U. When Heidi read the couplet,

"If ever you mix U and V,
You'll go where you'll not like to be,"

Peter growled, "Yes, see if I will!"

But he learned them thoroughly, as if he were under the impression that someone might take him secretly by the throat and carry him where he would not care to go.

On the following afternoon Heidi read:

"If now you fail to know the W,
There hangs a stick and it will trouble you."

Then Peter looked round and said scornfully, "There isn't any."

"Yes, there is; don't you know what grandfather has in the chest?" asked Heidi. "A stick as big round as my arm, and when he takes it out he can say, 'Behold the stick, and it will trouble you.'"

Peter knew the big hazel stick. He bent over his W at once and tried to grasp it.

The next day the verse read:

"If you the letter X forget,
For you no supper will be set."

Then Peter looked inquiringly toward the cupboard where the bread and cheese were kept, and said snappishly, "I have never said that I should forget X."

"That is right, if you don't forget it; then we can learn one letter more," suggested Heidi, "and tomorrow you will have only one left."

Peter was not agreed, but Heidi read:

"If you on Y today delay,
With scorn and shame you'll go away."

Then there rose before Peter's eyes all the masters in Frankfurt with their tall, black hats on their heads and scorn and laughter in their faces. He immediately attacked the letter Y, and did not let it go again until he knew it so well that he could close his eyes and still see how it looked.

On the next day Peter was feeling rather proud when he came to Heidi, for there was only one letter left for him to study, and when Heidi read the verse to him,

"Who hesitates upon the Z,
With the Hottentots shall be,"

he said sneeringly, "Yes, when nobody knows where they are!"

"Indeed, Peter, my grandfather knows," asserted Heidi. "Just wait and I will ask him right away where they are; he is over at the pastor's house"; and Heidi jumped up and was going out the door.

"Wait!" screamed Peter in great alarm, for he already saw in his imagination the Alm-Uncle coming in with the pastor, and the two seizing him at once and sending him off to the Hottentots, for he really did not know the letter Z. His troubled cry made Heidi stand still.

"What is the matter with you?" she asked in surprise.

"Nothing! Come back! I will learn it," stammered Peter. But Heidi wanted to know where the Hottentots were, and she was going to ask her grandfather anyway. But Peter screamed so anxiously after her that she gave it up and came back. He had to do something to make up for it, however. Not only did Heidi make him repeat the letter Z so many times that it remained fast in his memory forever, but she went on at once to syllables, and Peter learned so much that afternoon that he made great progress.

Thus it went on day after day.

The crust had become soft again, and every day there was a fresh fall of snow, so that for three long weeks together Heidi could not go up to see the grandmother. All the more eager was she, in her work with Peter, to have him able to read the hymns. One evening Peter came home from Heidi's and ran into the room, saying, "I can do it!"

"What can you do, Peter?" asked his mother, full of hope.

"Reading," he answered.

"Is it possible! Did you hear, grandmother?" exclaimed Brigitte.

The grandmother had heard it and also wondered how it had happened.

"Now I must read a hymn, for Heidi said so," Peter went on to say. His mother at once took down the book, and the grandmother was delighted, it was so long since she had heard any good words. Peter sat down at the table and began to read.

His mother sat down beside him to listen; after each verse she said in amazement, "Who could have thought it?"

His grandmother followed one verse after another attentively, but said nothing about it.

The day after this occurrence it happened that Peter's class had a reading lesson. When Peter's turn came the teacher said, "Peter, must I pass by you again, as usual, or will you once more—I will not say read, I will say try to stammer through a line?"

Peter began and read three lines one after another with out stopping.

The teacher laid his book aside. He looked at Peter in dumb surprise, as if he had never seen anything like it before. At last he said, "Peter, a wonder has happened to you! Long as I have worked over you with the greatest patience you have never been able to grasp even the alphabet. Now that I have, although unwillingly, given up working over you as a useless task, it happens that you come out and have learned, not only the alphabet, but also to read properly, as well as quite clearly. Who has been able to work such a wonder in our time, Peter?"

"Heidi," was the reply.

In the greatest surprise the teacher looked toward Heidi, who was sitting quite innocently in her seat, so that there was nothing extraordinary in her appearance. He continued, "I have noticed a change in you in many ways, Peter. While you used to be absent from school often the whole week—yes, several weeks together—lately you have not stayed away a day. Who can have caused such a change for the better in you?"

"The uncle," was the reply.

With increasing astonishment the teacher looked from Peter to Heidi, and from her back again to Peter.

"We will try it once more," he then said cautiously; and Peter had to prove his knowledge with three lines more. It was a fact, he had learned to read.

As soon as school was over, the teacher hastened to the pastor's house to tell him what had happened, and what a good influence the uncle and Heidi were having in the village.

Every evening now Peter read a hymn at home. So far he obeyed Heidi, but no further, for he never undertook a second one; nor did the grandmother ever ask him to do so.

His mother Brigitte wondered every day that Peter had succeeded in learning to read, and many an evening when the reading was over and the reader lay in his bed, she would say again to the grandmother, "We can't be pleased enough that Peter has learned to read so beautifully; now there's no knowing what he may become."

Then the grandmother would answer, "Yes, it is a good thing for him that he has learned something; but I shall be heartily glad if the dear Lord sends the spring soon, so that Heidi can come up again. It is as if she read entirely different hymns. Something is so often left out in the verses when Peter reads them, and I have to try to remember it, and then I can't follow the thought, and it doesn't impress my heart as it does when Heidi reads the words."

This happened because Peter arranged the reading a little so that it would not be too difficult for him. If a word came that was too long or looked hard, he chose to leave it out, for he thought it would be all the same to the grandmother whether there were three or four words in a line.

So it came about that there were hardly any nouns left in the hymns Peter read.

Chapter 6

Distant Friends Are Heard From

Day had come. From every height the overflowing brooks were rushing down into the valley. Warm, bright sunshine lay on the mountain. It had grown green again; the last traces of snow had melted away and the first little flowers, awakened by the inviting sunbeams, were peeping up with their bright eyes out of the fresh grass. The joyous spring wind blew through the fir trees and shook off the old, dark needles, so that the young, bright green ones could come out and dress the trees in splendor. High above, the old robber-bird was swinging his wings in the blue air, and round the Alm hut the golden sunshine lay warm on the ground, drying up the last damp places so that one could sit down wherever one liked.

Heidi was on the mountain again. She ran here and there and could not tell which spot was the loveliest. Now she had to listen to the wind as it blew down deep and mysterious from the cliffs above, coming nearer and growing mightier, and then leaping into the fir trees, bending and shaking them until it seemed as if it were shouting with delight; and Heidi had to shout too, while she was blown hither and thither like a little leaf. Then she would run back to the sunny spot in front of the house, sit down on the ground and peep into the short grass to see how many flower cups were going to open or were open already. So many gay gnats and little beetles were hopping and crawling and dancing about in the sun and enjoying themselves that Heidi was happy with them, and drew in long breaths of the spring fragrance, which came up out of the fresh earth. It seemed even more beautiful on the mountain than ever before. The thousand little creatures must have liked it as well as she did, for it seemed exactly as if they were all humming and singing for sheer delight, "On the Alm! On the Alm! On the Alm!"

From the workshop behind the house, every now and then, came the sound of busy hammering and sawing; and Heidi listened, for it was the old familiar sound she knew so well, and which she had heard ever since she came to live on the Alm. She had to jump up and run at once to the shop, for she wished to know what her grandfather was doing. In front of the workshop door there was standing a fine new stool already finished, and her grandfather was working skillfully on another.

"Oh, I know what that is for!" exclaimed Heidi with delight. "That will be needed when they come from Frankfurt. It is for the grandmamma, and the one you are making now is for Klara, and then—then there will have to be one more," continued Heidi hesitatingly. "Or do you think, grandfather, that Fräulein Rottenmeier will not come with them?"

"That I can't say now," said her grandfather, "but it will be safer to have one ready, so that we can invite her to sit down if she comes."

Heidi looked questioningly at the little wooden stool and quietly considered how it would suit Fräulein Rottenmeier. After a while she said doubtfully, shaking her head, "Grandfather, I don't believe she would sit on it."

"Then we will invite her to the sofa with the beautiful green grass covering," replied the grandfather quietly.

As Heidi was thinking where the beautiful sofa with the green grass covering could be, suddenly there sounded from above a whistling and calling and rod swinging through the air, so that Heidi knew at once what it was. She ran out and was surrounded in a twinkling by the leaping goats. They must have been as glad as Heidi to be up on the mountain again, for they jumped higher and bleated more merrily than they had ever done before, and Heidi was pushed back and forth by them, for each one was anxious to get next to her and express its delight. But Peter pushed them all away, some to the right and others to the left, for he had a message to give to Heidi. When he had made his way to her, he held out a letter toward her.

"There!" he said, leaving Heidi to find out the rest for herself. She was very much surprised.

"Did you find a letter for me up in the pasture?" she asked in great astonishment.

"No," was the answer.

"Well, where did you get it, then, Peter?"

"Out of the lunch bag."

That was so. The evening before, the postmaster in Dörfli had given him the letter for Heidi. Peter had put it in the empty bag. In the morning he had put his cheese and his piece of bread on top of it and had started off. He had seen the uncle and Heidi when he went to get their goats; noon, when he had finished his bread and cheese and was going to shake the crumbs out of the bag, the letter fell into his hand.

Heidi read the address carefully; then she ran back to her grandfather in the shop and held out the letter to him in high glee.

"From Frankfurt! From Klara! Will you hear it now, grandfather?"

He was very ready to hear it, and so was Peter, who had followed Heidi. He leaned his back against the doorpost in order to have a firm support while she read her letter, as it was easier to follow Heidi so.

"Dear Heidi,

"Everything is already packed, and in two or three days we shall start on our journey as soon as papa is ready, but he cannot go with us, for he has to go to Paris first. The doctor comes every day and calls out at the door: 'Away! Away! To the mountains!' He is impatient for us to get off. You ought to know how much he liked it himself on the Alm! He has come to see us almost every day all winter long; whenever he came to see me he always said he must tell me all about it again! Then he would sit down by me and tell me about all the days he spent with you and your grandfather on the Alm, about the mountains and the flowers, and the stillness so high up above all the villages and roads, and about the fine fresh air; and he often said, 'Everybody ought to get well up there.' He himself is so different from what he had been for a long time, and looks quite young and happy again. Oh, how glad I shall be to see it all and be with you on the mountain, and learn to know

Peter and the goats! But first I have to take the cure in Ragatz for about six weeks; the doctor has ordered it. Afterward we shall stay in Dörfli, and I shall be carried up on the mountain in my chair, in fine weather, to spend the day with you.

"Grandmamma is coming too and will stay with me; she also will enjoy going up to see you. But think of it, Fräulein Rottenmeier will! not come with us. Almost every day grandmamma says to her, 'How is it about the journey to Switzerland, worthy Rottenmeier? If you would like to come with us, you may do so.'

"But she always thanks her very politely and says she wouldn't be so presuming. But l know what she is thinking about: Sebastian gave such a frightful description of the mountains, when he came back from going with you—what terrible overhanging rocks there were, and what danger there was everywhere of falling down into the chasms and ravines; that it was so steep climbing up that there was risk at every step of falling down backwards, and that goats might be able to climb up there, but no human being could do so without peril to his life—that she shuddered at it, and since then has not been enthusiastic about traveling in Switzerland, as she was before. Tinette too has become frightened and will not come with us. So we are coming alone, grandmamma and I; Sebastian will come with us as far as Ragatz, then he can go back home.

"I can hardly wait to come to you.

"Good-bye, dear Heidi. Grandmamma sends you a thousand greetings.

Your true friend, Klara"

When Peter heard these words he ran away from the doorpost and struck out right and left so recklessly and furiously with his rod that the goats, in the greatest terror, all took to flight and ran down the mountain, making such enormous leaps as they had seldom done before. Peter rushed after them beating the air with his rod, as if he had to express his great spite toward some invisible enemy. This enemy was the prospect of guests coming from Frankfurt, and this was what had so enraged him.

Heidi was so full of happiness and joy that she really had to go to visit the grandmother the next day and tell her all about it—who were coming from Frankfurt, and also who were not coming. This was of the greatest importance to the grandmother, for she knew all the people well and always felt the greatest interest in everything that had to do with Heidi's life. So early on the following afternoon Heidi started; for now she could go alone once more to make her visits, as the sun was shining brightly again and remained longer in the sky, and there was a fine mountain path over the dry ground; the joyous May wind blew behind her and pushed her along faster and faster.

The grandmother was no longer in bed. She was sitting once more in the corner spinning. But there was an expression on her face as if she had troublesome thoughts. It had been there since the evening before; and the whole night long these thoughts had followed her and kept her from sleeping. Peter had come home in the midst of his great anger, and she had understood from his broken outcries that a crowd of people from Frankfurt was coming up to the Alm hut. What would happen afterward he did not know; but the grandmother could not help thinking about it, and it was just these thoughts that had troubled her and kept her from sleeping.

Heidi ran in, went straight to the grandmother, sat down on the little footstool which always stood there, and told her all that she knew with such eagerness that she herself began to realize it even more. But all of a sudden she stopped in the middle of a sentence and asked anxiously, "What is the matter, grandmother? Don't you like all this a single bit?"

"Yes, Heidi, I am glad for you, because it will give you so much pleasure," she replied, trying to look a little happier.

"But, grandmother, I can see very well that it troubles you. Do you think Fräulein Rottenmeier will come with them?" asked Heidi, feeling somewhat anxious herself.

"No, no! It is nothing, it is nothing!" said the grandmother soothingly. "Let me take your hand for a little, Heidi, so I can feel that you are still here. It will be a good thing for you, even if I don't live to see that day."

"I don't care for what is best for me, if you are not going to live to see it, grandmother," said Heidi, so decidedly that suddenly a new fear arose in the old dame's mind; she must take it for granted that the people from Frankfurt were coming to take Heidi away; for now that she was well once more they would surely want to take Heidi back with them. This was a great grief to the grandmother. But she felt that she ought not to say anything about it before Heidi; she would be so sorry for her that she would perhaps object to going, and that must not be. She sought for some remedy, but not long, for she knew but one.

"I know something, Heidi," she then said, "that will make me feel better and bring me good thoughts again. Read me the hymn where it begins, 'God will bring.'"

Heidi had now become so familiar with the old hymn book that she at once found the place the grandmother desired and read in a clear voice:

"God will bring
Everything
Into order as is wholesome for thy soul;
Thou shalt be
Safe at sea,
Though the foaming billows wildly round thee roll."

"Yes, yes, that is exactly what I want to hear," said the grandmother, relieved, and the expression of distress disappeared from her face.

Heidi looked at her thoughtfully and then said, "Grandmother, does 'wholesome' mean when everything is cured so that one is entirely well again?"

"Yes, yes, that is what it will be," said the grandmother, nodding in assent. "And because the dear Lord will make it so, we can be sure how it will come out. Read it once more, Heidi, so that we can fix it in our minds and not forget it."

Heidi read the lines over again, and then twice more, for the thought of safety pleased her very much.

When evening came and Heidi was climbing up the mountain again, one little star after another came out and sparkled and twinkled down at her, and it seemed exactly as if each one wanted to send a new beam of great delight into her heart, and Heidi had to stand still every moment and look up, and when they all in every part of the sky looked down, with still greater delight she had to exclaim quite loudly, "I know now; because the dear Lord knows so well what is best, we can have such joy and be perfectly safe!"

And the little stars all twinkled and sparkled and winked at Heidi, until she reached the hut, where her grandfather was standing, and also gazing up at the stars, for they had not shone so beautifully for a long time.

Not only the nights but also the days in this month of May were brighter and clearer than they had been for many years, and the grandfather often looked out in the morning in surprise to see how the sun was coming up again in a cloudless sky, so that the sunrise was as glorious as the sunset, and he would repeat, "It is a remarkably sunny year; it will make the pasturage very rich. Take care, leader, that your leapers don't get too wild from the good feed!"

Then Peter would swing his rod boldly in the air, and the answer was plainly written on his face, "I'll be a match for them."

So the green-growing May soon passed and June came with its still warmer sun and long, long, light days, inviting all the flowers on the whole mountain to come out, so that they shone and glowed everywhere, and filled the air all about with their sweet fragrance. This month too was drawing to an end when one morning Heidi, having already finished her morning tasks, came running out of the hut. She hurried out under the fir trees and then a little higher up to see if the big centaury bush was in bloom, for the little flowers were enchant-ingly lovely with the sun shining through them. But as Heidi was running round the hut she suddenly screamed with all her might so loud that the grandfather came out of his shop, for it was something unusual.

"Grandfather! Grandfather!" cried the child as if beside herself. "Come here! Come here! See! See!"

The grandfather came at her call, and his eyes followed the excited child's outstretched arm.

A strange procession, such as had never been seen there before, was winding up the Alm. First came two men with a sedan chair in which sat a young girl wrapped up in ever so many shawls. Then came a horse on which sat a stately lady, who was looking with great interest in every direction and talking eagerly with the young guide walking by her side. Then came an empty wheelchair, pushed by another young fellow, for the invalid to whom it belonged could be carried more securely up the steep mountain in the sedan chair. Last of all walked a porter, who had so many wraps, shawls, and furs piled up in the basket on his back that they reached high above his head.

"There they are! There they are!" screamed Heidi, jumping up in the air with delight. They really were coming. They came nearer and nearer and at last they were there. The porters put the chair down on the ground. Heidi ran to it and the two children greeted each other with immense delight. Then the grandmamma arrived and dismounted from the horse. Heidi ran to her and was embraced with great tenderness. Then the grandmamma turned toward the Alm-Uncle, who had come to welcome her. There was no stiffness in their greeting, for she knew him and he knew her as well as if they had been acquainted for a long time.

As soon as the first words of greeting had been said, the grandmamma exclaimed with great enthusiasm, "My dear uncle, what a splendid situation you have! Who would have believed it! Many a king might envy you! How well my Heidi looks! Like a little June rose!" she continued, drawing the child to her and stroking her fresh cheeks. "How glorious it is everywhere all about! What do you say, Klärchen, my child; what do you say?"

Klara was looking round her perfectly enchanted; she had never seen anything, never imagined anything like it in all her life.

"Oh, how beautiful it is here! Oh, how beautiful it is here!" she exclaimed again and again. "I never imagined it. O grandmamma, I should like to stay here!"

Meanwhile the uncle had pushed along the wheelchair, taken some shawls out of the basket, and arranged them in it. Then he stepped up to the sedan chair.

"If we should put the little daughter in her accustomed chair now, it would be better for her; the traveling chair is a little hard," he said; and, without waiting for anyone to assist him, at once lifted the little invalid gently in his strong arms out of the straw chair and placed her with the greatest care in the soft seat. Then he laid the shawls over her knees and wrapped her feet as comfortably on the cushion as if he had done nothing else all his life but care for invalids who could not use their limbs. The grandmamma looked at him in the greatest astonishment.

Then she exclaimed, "My dear uncle, if I knew where you learned to care for the sick, I would send all the nurses I know there to take lessons. How is it possible?"

The uncle smiled a little. "It comes more from experience than from study," he replied; but in spite of the smile a look of sadness came over his face. Out of the dim past before his eyes rose the suffering face of a man who used to sit wrapped up in a chair just like this, and was so crippled that he could hardly use a limb. It was his captain, whom he had found lying on the ground after a fierce battle in Sicily, and had carried off the field; and from that time the captain would allow no other nurse round him, and would never let him out of his sight, until his great sufferings came to an end. The uncle saw his sick friend before him again; his only thought now was that it would be his duty to care for sick Klara and show her all those comforting attentions he understood so well.

The sky spread deep blue and cloudless above the hut and the fir trees, and high above the lofty cliffs which towered up so gray and sparkling. Klara could not look round enough; she was perfectly charmed with all that she saw.

"O Heidi, if I could only go round with you, about the hut and under the fir trees!" she exclaimed longingly. "If I could go with you to look at all the things I have heard so much about and haven't as yet seen!"

Then Heidi made a great effort and succeeded in rolling the chair smoothly over the dry, grassy ground under the fir trees. Here she paused. Klara had never seen anything in her life like the tall old fir trees whose long, wide-spreading branches grew down to the ground and became larger and thicker there. The grandmamma, who had followed the children, also stood still in great wonder. She could not tell which was the more beautiful, the full roaring tops of the ancient trees, high up in the blue sky, or their straight, strong trunks, which with their mighty branches could tell of so many, many years that they had been standing there and looking down into the valley where men came and went and everything else was constantly changing, while they always remained the same.

Meanwhile, Heidi pushed the wheelchair in front of the goat shed and opened the little door wide, so that Klara could see everything inside. There was really not much to see now, for the goats were not at home. Klara called back quite regretfully, "O grandmamma, if I could just wait for Schwänli and Bärli and all the other goats, and Peter! I can never see them all if we always have to go away as early as you said; it is such a shame!"

"Dear child, we will enjoy all the beautiful things that are here, and not think about those that are wanting," was the grandmamma's advice, as she followed the chair, which Heidi was now pushing back.

"Oh, the flowers!" exclaimed Klara. "Whole bushes of fine red flowers, and all the nodding bluebells! Oh, if I could only go and get some!"

Heidi immediately ran and brought back to her a great bunch of them.

"But this is nothing, Klara," she said, laying the flowers in her lap. "If you could come up to the pasture with us once, then you would see something! In one place there are so many, many bushes of red centauries and ever so many more bluebells than here, and so many thousand bright yellow wild roses that it looks as if the ground were shining with pure gold. And then there are some with large leaves, which my grandfather says are called heliopsis, and, besides, the brown ones, you know, with little round heads, which smell so good—and it is so beautiful! If you once sit down there, you can never get up again, it is so lovely!"

Heidi's eyes sparkled with longing to see what she was describing, and Klara was so excited by it that out of her gentle blue eyes there shone a complete reflection of Heidi's fiery enthusiasm.

"O grandmamma, can I go up there? Do you think I could go so high?" she asked eagerly. "Oh, if I could only go, Heidi, and climb round everywhere on the mountain with you!"

"I will push you," said Heidi soothingly; and to show how easily it went she took such a run round the corner that the chair almost ran away from her down the mountain. But her grandfather was standing near and stopped its course just in time.

During their visit to the fir trees the grandfather had not been idle. The table and necessary chairs were standing by the bench in front of the hut and everything was ready; the good dinner was still steaming in the kettle and roasting on the big fork over the fire inside the hut. It was not long before the grandfather had everything on the table and the whole company sat down gladly to the meal.

The grandmamma was perfectly enchanted with this dining room, from which one could see far, far down into the valley and above all the mountains into the blue sky. A cool, mild breeze gently fanned the faces of the guests and rustled as pleasantly in the fir trees as if it had been music especially ordered for the feast.

"Nothing like this has ever happened to me. It is really glorious!" exclaimed the grandmamma again and again. "But what do I see?" she added in the greatest surprise. "I believe you are taking a second piece of toasted cheese, Klärchen!"

Sure enough, a second golden shining piece of cheese lay on Klara's slice of bread.

"Oh, it tasted so good, grandmamma—better than everything on the table at Ragatz," asserted Klara, taking the appetizing food with great relish.

"Eat away! Eat away!" said the Alm-Uncle, well pleased. "It is our mountain air, which succeeds when the cook fails."

So the happy meal went on. The grandmamma and the Alm-Uncle took a great liking to each other, and their conversation became more and more lively. They agreed in all their opinions about men and things and the progress of the world as well as if they had been friends for years. Thus the time passed until the grandmamma suddenly looked toward the west and said, "We must soon be getting ready, Klärchen; the sun is already going down; the people will be back with the horse and the chair."

Immediately an expression of sadness came over Klara's happy face and she begged, "O grandmamma, just one hour more, or two! We haven't seen the hut yet, or Heidi's bed, and all their other arrangements. Oh, if the day were only ten hours longer!"

"That is not possible," said the grandmamma; but she too wanted to see the hut. So they rose at once from the table, and the uncle directed the chair with steady hands to the door. But here it would go no farther; the chair was much too wide to go through the opening. The uncle did not stop long to consider. He lifted Klara out and carried her in his strong arms into the hut.

The grandmamma went back and forth looking carefully at all the furnishings, and was greatly amused at the household inventions which were so prettily arranged and well ordered.

"That is surely your bed up above there, Heidi, is it not?" she then asked, and straightway, without any timidity, climbed the little ladder leading to the hayloft.

"Oh, how sweet it smells! It must be a healthful sleeping room!" and the grandmamma went to the window and peeped through.

The grandfather followed with Klara in his arms, and Heidi came on behind.

They then all stood round Heidi's beautifully made hay bed, and the grandmamma looked at it quite critically, every now and then drawing in with delight deep breaths of the spicy fragrance of the new hay. Klara was perfectly charmed with Heidi's sleeping place.

"Oh, Heidi, what a jolly place you have here! From your bed you can see straight out into the sky, and you have such a lovely odor round you, and you can hear the fir trees roar outside. Oh, I have never seen such a jolly, pleasant sleeping room before!"

The uncle then looked over at the grandmamma.

"I have an idea," he said, "if the grandmamma could have enough confidence in me to let me try out my plan. I think if we could keep the daughter up here a little while she would gain new strength. You have brought shawls and wraps out of which we could arrange an entirely separate soft bed, and the grandmamma need have no anxiety about the care of the little daughter; that I will undertake myself."

Klara and Heidi both shouted with joy like two escaped birds, and the grandmamma's face lighted up with sunshine.

"My dear uncle, you are a wonderful man!" she exclaimed. "How did you know what I was just thinking about? I was saying to myself: 'Wouldn't a stay up here give the child especial strength? But the nursing! The care! The inconvenience to the host!' And here you speak of it as if it would be nothing at all. I must thank you, my dear uncle, I must thank you with my whole heart!" and the grandmamma shook the uncle's hand again and again, and the uncle also shook hers with great delight.

The uncle immediately began to carry out his plan. He carried Klara back to her chair in front of the hut; Heidi followed, not knowing how high she wanted to jump in her delight. Then he piled up all the shawls and fur robes in his arms and said, smiling with satisfaction, "It is a good thing that grandmamma brought enough things for a winter's campaign; we can use them."

"My dear uncle," she replied, approaching briskly, "foresight is an excellent virtue, and protection from many an evil. If one escapes storm and wind and violent rains in traveling over your mountains, one may be thankful; and so we are, and my wraps may be useful yet; about that we are agreed."

During this little conversation the two climbed up to the hayloft and began to spread the shawls, one after another, over the bed. There were so many that the bed finally looked like a little fortress.

"Now let a single wisp of hay stick through if it can," said the grandmamma, and she pressed with her hand on all sides; but the soft wall was so thick that nothing really could stick through. Then she climbed down the ladder quite satisfied and went out to the children, who were sitting close together with beaming faces, and planning what they would do from morning till night, as long as Klara stayed on the mountain. But how long would that be? That was now the great question, which was at once laid before the grandmamma. She said the grandfather knew best about that; they must ask him. As he happened along just then, the question was put to him, and he said he thought that in about four weeks it would be safe to judge whether the mountain air would do its duty by the little daughter or not. Then the children shouted aloud, for the prospect of being together so long surpassed everything they had expected.

The porters with the chair and the guide with the horse were now seen coming up the mountain. The first were allowed to turn round again immediately.

When the grandmamma was preparing to mount the horse, Klara exclaimed cheerfully, "O grandmamma, we won't say farewell, if you are going away, for you will come back every little while to visit us on the mountain, to see what we are doing; and that will be so delightful, won't it, Heidi?"

Heidi, who had had one pleasure after another that day, could only express her assent by jumping high with delight.

Then the grandmamma mounted the steady beast, and the uncle took the bridle and led the horse safely down the steep mountain. Although the grandmamma tried not to have him go so far, it was of no use; the uncle explained that he was anxious to accompany her as far as Dörfli, for the mountain was steep and the ride not free from danger.

The grandmamma thought that now she was by herself she would not stay in Dörfli, where it was lonely. She would return to Ragatz and take the journey up the mountain occasionally from there.

Before the uncle returned, Peter came along with his goats. When they noticed Heidi they all rushed toward her; in a moment Klara in her chair, together with Heidi, was in the midst of the flock, and some one goat was always crowding and pushing to see over another, and each was immediately called and presented by Heidi to Klara.

So it happened that in a very short time Klara had made the long-wished-for acquaintance with Schneehöpli, the jolly Distelfinck, the grandfather's clean goats, and all the rest, up to the big Türk. But Peter meanwhile stood aside and threw occasional threatening glances at happy Klara.

When the children both called out pleasantly to him, "Good night, Peter!" he made no reply, but raised his rod angrily in the air, as if he would like to beat them to pieces. Then he ran away, with his followers after him.

Now came an end to all the lovely things Klara had seen that day on the mountain.

When she lay on her great soft bed in the hayloft, to which Heidi had also climbed, she looked through the round, open window, out at the twinkling stars, and, completely charmed, exclaimed, "O Heidi, see, it is just as if we were riding in the sky in a high carriage!"

"Yes, and do you know why the stars are so full of joy, and wink at us so with their eyes?" asked Heidi.

"No, I don't know; what do you think about it?" asked Klara.

"Because they see up in heaven how well the dear Lord directs everything for people, so that they need have no worry and can be safe, because everything will happen for the best. That delights them so; see how they wink, that we may be happy too! But do you know, Klara, we must not forget our prayers; we must ask the dear Lord to think of us, when He is directing everything so well, that we may always be safe and never be afraid of anything."

So the children sat up in bed and said their evening prayers. Then Heidi laid her head on her round arm and was asleep in a moment. But Klara stayed awake for a long time, for she had never seen anything so wonderful in her life as this sleeping room in the starlight.

Moreover, she had hardly ever seen the stars, for she never went outside the house at night, and indoors the thick curtains were drawn long before the stars came out. Now whenever she closed her eyes she had to open them again once more to see if the two big bright stars were still shining in and winking as remarkably as Heidi had said. And it was always so, and Klara could not look enough at their twinkling and sparkling, until at last her eyes closed of themselves, and in her dreams she still saw the two big shining stars.

Chapter 7

What Further Happened on the Mountain

The sun was just coming up behind the mountains and casting its golden beams over the hut and down across the valley. The Alm-Uncle had been silently and attentively watching, as he did every morning, how all round on the heights and in the valley the light mists were lifting, and the landscape appeared out of the twilight shadows and awoke to the new day.

Brighter and brighter grew the morning clouds until the sun came out in all its glory, and rocks and woods and hilltops were bathed in golden light.

Then the uncle went back into his hut and climbed softly up the little ladder. Klara had just awakened, and was gazing in the greatest amazement at the bright sunbeams, which came in through the round window and glanced and danced on her bed. She did not know what she was looking at or where she was. Then she looked at Heidi, sleeping beside her, and the grandfather's friendly voice sounded, asking, "Did you sleep well? Are you tired?"

Klara assured him that she was not tired, and that after she was once asleep she did not wake up again all night. This pleased the grandfather, and he immediately set to work and cared for Klara as well and as understandingly as if it had always been his profession to care for sick children and make them comfortable.

By this time Heidi had opened her eyes and was surprised to see that her grandfather had already finished Klara's toilet and was carrying her away in his arms. She felt that she must be with them. She dressed as quick as lightning; then went down the ladder and was out the door and stood looking in the greatest surprise at what her grandfather had been doing further. The evening before, when the children had gone to bed in the loft, he had planned how to bring the wide rolling chair under cover. The door of the hut was much too small to allow it to enter. Then a thought had come to him. Behind the shop he loosened two large boards and thus formed a wide opening. The chair was pushed in, and then the planks were put back in their places, though they were not fastened.

Heidi came along just as her grandfather was putting Klara in her chair, for he had taken away the boards and was coming out of the shop with her into the morning sunshine. He left the chair standing in a safe place and went to the goat shed. Heidi ran to Klara's side.

The cool morning breeze blew round the children's faces, and the spicy fragrance from the fir trees came down with every new gust of wind. Klara drew in deep breaths and leaned back in her chair with a feeling of health such as she had never known before.

Never in her life had she breathed in the fresh morning air outdoors under the open sky, and now the pure mountain breeze blew round her so cool and refreshing that every breath was a pleasure. And then there was the bright, sweet sunshine, which was not at all hot up here and which lay lovely and warm on her hands and on the dry, grassy earth at her feet. Klara had never imagined that it could be like this on the mountain.

"O Heidi, if only I could always, always stay up here with you!" she said, turning with delight first one way and then another in her chair, to take in the air and sunshine from every side.

"Now you see it is just as I told you," replied Heidi, much pleased, "that here at my grandfather's on the Alm is the loveliest spot in the whole world."

Just then the grandfather came out of the shed to the children. He brought two bowls full of foaming, snow-white milk, and handed one to Klara and the other to Heidi.

"This will do the little daughter good," he said, nodding to Klara. "It is from Schwänli and will make you strong. To your good health! Drink away!"

Klara had never tasted goat's milk; so she had to smell it a little first, to see what it was like. But when she saw how eagerly Heidi drank down her milk without stopping once —it tasted so wonderfully good to her—then Klara began and drank and drank, and really it was as sweet and nourishing as if there were sugar and cinnamon in it, and Klara drank until there was nothing left in the bowl.

"Tomorrow we will take two," said the grandfather, who was well satisfied to see how Klara followed Heidi's example.

Peter now appeared with his flock, and while Heidi was surrounded by the goats, giving their morning greeting on every hand, the uncle took Peter aside that the boy might hear what he had to say to him, for the goats kept up a great bleating, each one trying to outdo the other in expressing its delight and affection, as soon as Heidi was with them.

"Now listen and mind," said the uncle. "From today on let Schwänli do as she likes. She knows where the best feed is; so if she wants to go up, follow her. It will be good for the others too; and if she wants to go higher than you usually go with her, follow on and don't keep her back—do you hear? If you have to climb a little, it won't do any harm; go wherever she likes, for in this respect she has more sense than you, and she must have the very best feed, so that she will give splendid milk. Why are you looking over there as if you would like to swallow somebody? No one is in your way. There, now, go on, and remember what I have told you!"

Peter was accustomed to follow the uncle's orders. He immediately started along; but it was plain to be seen that something disturbed him, for he kept turning his head and rolling his eyes. The goats followed and pushed Heidi along with them for a little distance. Peter approved of this.

"You must come too," he called out threateningly. "You must come too, if I have to go after Schwänli."

"No, I cannot," Heidi called back, "and I cannot come with you for a long, long time, as long as Klara is with us. But grandfather has promised that someday we may come up together."

With these words Heidi had torn herself away from the goats and now ran back to Klara. Then Peter shook both fists so threateningly toward the wheelchair that the goats sprang to one side; but he at once sprang after them and, without stopping, went on up a long distance until he was out of sight, for he thought the uncle might have seen him, and he preferred not to know what sort of impression his actions had made on the uncle.

Klara and Heidi had planned so much for that day that they did not know where to begin. Heidi proposed to write a letter to the grandmamma, for the good lady for her part was not perfectly sure that it would please Klara up there for any length of time, or indeed be good for her health; so she had made the children promise to write her a letter every day, and to tell her everything that happened. In this way the grandmamma would know when she was needed on the Alm, and until then could stay quietly where she was.

"Must we go into the house to write?" asked Klara, who was willing to send a report to her grandmamma, but it was so pleasant outdoors that she did not want to go in.

Heidi knew how to manage. In a twinkling she ran into the hut and came back laden with all her school materials and a three-legged stool. She laid her reader and writing book in Klara's lap, so that she could write on them, and seated herself on the little stool by the bench, and then they began to tell the grandmamma what had happened. But, after every sentence she wrote, Klara had to lay her pencil down and look round her. It was quite too lovely! The wind was no longer so cool as it had been; it hovered round their faces, gently fanning them, and whispered softly up in the fir trees. Merry little insects danced and hummed in the clear air, and a great stillness lay over all the sunny landscape. The lofty, rocky peaks looked down big and still, and the whole wide valley below lay wrapped in quiet peacefulness. Only now and then the merry shouts of some shepherd boy sounded through the air, and the echo gave back the tones softly from the cliffs.

The morning passed, the children knew not how, and the grandfather came with the steaming bowls, for he said they must stay outdoors with the little daughter as long as there was a ray of light in the sky. So the dinner, as on the previous day, was placed before the hut and was eaten with enjoyment. Then Heidi rolled Klara in her chair out under the fir trees, for the children had decided that they would spend the afternoon sitting in the lovely shade and tell each other what had happened since Heidi left Frankfurt. Although everything had gone on in the usual way, still Klara had all sorts of things to tell about the people whom Heidi knew well, living in the Sesemann house.

So the children sat together under the old fir trees, and the more eagerly they talked the louder whistled the birds up in the branches, for the chatting below pleased them and they were anxious to take part in it. Thus the time passed and before they knew it evening had come, and the army of goats came rushing down, their leader behind them, with wrinkled brow and with anger in his manner.

"Good night, Peter!" Heidi called out to him, when she saw that he had no idea of stopping.

"Good night, Peter!" called out Klara pleasantly.

He gave no reply and, angrily snorting, drove the goats ahead of him.

When Klara saw the grandfather lead pretty Schwänli to the stall to be milked, she was all at once seized with such a longing for the spicy milk that she could hardly wait until he came out with it. She was surprised at herself.

"It is very strange, Heidi," she said. "As long as I can remember, I have eaten only because I had to, and everything I took tasted like cod-liver oil, and I have thought a thousand times, 'If only I never had to eat!' and now I can hardly wait until your grandfather comes with the milk."

"Yes, I know what that is," replied Heidi quite understandingly, for she thought of the day in Frankfurt when everything stuck in her throat and would not go down. But Klara could not see how it was. In all her life long she had never eaten outdoors in the fresh air, as she had done today, and never in this high, bracing mountain air.

When the grandfather came with his little bowls, Klara seized hers quickly, thanking him for it, drank it eagerly, and this time finished before Heidi.

"May I have a little more?" she asked, holding out her bowl to the grandfather.

He nodded, much pleased, took Heidi's bowl, also, and went back to the hut. When he came out again, he brought with each bowl a cover, made of a different material from what covers are usually made of.

In the afternoon the grandfather had taken a walk to the green Maiensäss to the cowkeeper's hut where they made sweet, bright, yellow butter. He had brought home from there a lovely round ball. Now he had taken two nice slices of bread and spread them thick with the sweet butter. These the children were going to have for their supper. Both immediately took such deep bites of the appetizing slices that the grandfather stood still to see them continue, for it pleased him.

Later, when from her bed Klara was again gazing at the sparkling stars, she followed Heidi's example; her eyes closed immediately, and such a sound, healthful sleep came over her as she had never known before.

The following day passed in the same delightful way, and also the next, and then came a great surprise for the children. Two strong porters came climbing up the mountain, each one carrying on his back a high bed, all arranged in the bedstead, both covered exactly alike with a white coverlet, clean and brand-new. The men also brought a letter from the grandmamma. It said that these beds were for Klara and Heidi, that the hay beds were to be taken away, and that from this time on Heidi must sleep in a regular bed. In the winter one of them must be sent down to Dörfli, but the other was to remain up there, so that Klara would always find it, if she came back. Then the grandmamma praised the children on account of their long letters and urged them to continue writing every day, so that she might always know everything about them as if, well—as if she were with them.

The grandfather went into the hut, threw the contents of Heidi's bed on the big heap of hay, and laid away the covers. Then he came back to help the men carry the two beds up into the loft. He pushed them close together so that the view through the window might be the same from both pillows, for he knew what delight the children took in the morning and evening light as it came in there.

Meanwhile the grandmamma stayed down in Ragatz and was highly delighted with the excellent reports which reached her every day from the Alm.

Klara became more and more charmed with her new life and she could not say enough about the grandfather's kindness and thoughtful care of her, and how merry and amusing Heidi was—much more so than in Frankfurt—and how every morning her first thought when she awoke was: "Oh, praise the Lord; I am still on the Alm!"

This remarkably delightful news was a fresh joy to the grandmamma every day. She found also that as things were she could put off her visit to the Alm a little longer, for which she was not sorry, since the ride up the steep mountain and down again was rather difficult for her.

The grandfather must have felt a remarkable interest in his little charge, for not a day passed when he did not think of something new to strengthen her. Every afternoon now he took a walk up among the rocks, higher and higher, and every time he brought back a little bundle which scented the air for a long distance like spicy pinks and thyme, and attracted the goats at evening, so that they all began to bleat and leap and tried to push all together into the shed where the plants lay, for they knew the odor well. But the uncle had made the door fast, because he had not climbed high up on the rocks after the rare plants, that the whole crowd of goats might get a good meal without any trouble. The herbs were all intended for Schwänli, that she might give still richer milk. It was plain to see how this unusual care affected her, for she tossed her head in the air more and more vigorously, and, besides, her eyes flashed fire. It was now the third week since Klara had come up on the mountain. For several days when the grandfather had brought her down in the morning to place her in her chair, he had said to her, "Will the little daughter not try just once to stand on the ground a moment?"

Klara had tried to do as he wished, but had always said immediately, "Oh, it hurts me so!" and had clung fast to him; but each day he had let her try a little longer.

Such a beautiful summer had not been seen on the Alm for many years. Every day the beaming sun shone in a cloudless sky, and all the little flowers opened their cups wide, and gleamed, and sent their fragrance up to it; and at evening it threw its purple and rosy light over the rocky peaks and across the snow fields and then disappeared in a blazing sea of gold.

Heidi told her friend Klara about it all again and again, for it could only be seen properly up in the pasture, and she was especially enthusiastic about the place up on the slope where there were great quantities of shining, golden wild roses, and so many bluebells that one would think the grass was blue, and close by great bushes full of little brown flowers which smell so lovely that one has to sit down on the ground among them and never wants to leave them. Sitting under the fir trees, Heidi had just been telling again about the flowers up there and the sunset and the fiery rocks, and then such a longing seized her to go up there again that she suddenly jumped up and ran to her grandfather, who was sitting in his shop carving.

"O grandfather," she called out before she was at all near him, "will you come with us up to the pasture tomorrow? It is so lovely up there now!"

"I will agree to it," said the grandfather in assent, "but the little daughter must also do me a favor: she must try hard again this evening to stand."

Heidi came back, shouting for joy, with her news to Klara; and Klara promised to try to stand on her feet as many times as the grandfather wished, for she was immensely delighted to take this journey up to the beautiful goat pasture. Heidi was so full of joy that she called out to Peter as soon as she saw him coming down that evening, "Peter! Peter! We are coming up with you tomorrow, to stay all day."

In reply Peter growled like an angry bear and struck out furiously at the innocent Distelfinck, trotting along beside him. But the alert Distelfinck had noticed the movement at the right time. He made a leap high over Schneehöpli and the blow whizzed in the air.

Klara and Heidi went up to their two beautiful beds with great expectations, and they were so full of their plans for the next day that they decided to stay awake all night and to talk about them until they could get up again. But scarcely had they lain down on their soft pillows when their talk suddenly ceased and Klara saw before her in a dream a great big field, which looked as blue as the sky, it was so thickly studded with bright bluebells; and Heidi heard the robber-bird up in the air screaming down, "Come! Come! Come!"

Chapter 8

Something Unexpected Happens

Very early the next morning the uncle came out of the hut and looked round to see what the day was going to be.

On the lofty mountain peaks lay a reddish-golden light; a cool breeze was beginning to rock the branches of the fir trees to and fro; the sun was coming up.

For a while the old man stood earnestly watching how, after the high mountaintops, the green hills began to shine golden, and then the dark shadows gently faded away from the valley and a rosy light flowed in, and both heights and depths gleamed in the morning gold. The sun was up.

Then the uncle brought the wheelchair out of the shop, placed it in front of the hut ready for the journey, and afterward went in to tell the children how beautiful the morning had dawned, and to bring them out.

Just then Peter came climbing up the mountain. His goats did not come so trustfully as usual by his side, and close in front of him and behind, up the mountain, they sprang timidly round here and there, for Peter kept striking about him without any occasion like a madman; and wherever he hit he hurt. Peter had reached the highest point of anger and bitterness. For weeks he had not had Heidi to himself as usual. When he came up in the morning, the strange child had always been brought out in her chair, and Heidi was busy with her. When he came down at evening, the wheelchair with its occupant was still standing under the fir trees, and Heidi was busy doing something for her. She had not been up to the pasture all summer long, and now today she was coming, but with the chair and the stranger in it, and would devote herself to her the whole time. Peter saw how it would be, and it had brought his secret anger to the highest point. He noticed the chair standing there so proudly on its wheels, and looked at it as if it were an enemy which had done him all sorts of harm, and today was going to do still more.

Peter looked round him; everything was still, not a person was to be seen. Then, as if he were crazy, he rushed at the chair, seized it and pushed it with such force, in his anger, toward the slope of the mountain that it actually started away and in a moment had disappeared.

Then Peter rushed up the Alm as if he had wings, and did not once stop until he had reached a great blackberry bush, behind which he could hide, for he was not anxious to have the uncle catch sight of him. But he wanted to see what became of the chair, and the bush was favorably situated on a mountain ledge. Partly concealed, Peter could look down the Alm, and if the uncle appeared hc could quickly hide himself. This he did, and what a sight met his eyes! His enemy had already gone rushing far below, driven on faster and faster; then it turned over again and again; then it bounded up in the air and fell down on the ground again, and went rolling over and over to its destruction.

Pieces were flying away from it in every direction—feet, cushions, back, all thrown high in the air. Peter took such furious delight in the sight that he jumped high with both feet together; he laughed aloud, he stamped with joy, he leaped round in circles, he kept coming back to the same spot and looking down the mountain. He burst out into fresh laughter and danced anew for joy. He was completely beside himself with delight at the ruin of his enemy, for he saw good things in prospect for him. Now the strange child would have to go away, for she had no means of moving about. Heidi would be alone again and come up to the pasture with him, and in the morning and at evening she would be there when he came, and everything would be as it was before. But Peter did not consider what it meant when one has begun to do a wicked deed, or what the consequences may be.

Heidi came jumping out of the hut and ran to the shop. Her grandfather followed her with Klara in his arms. The shop door stood wide open; both boards had been taken away, so that it was as light as day in the farthest corner. Heidi looked all about, ran round the corner, and came back again with the greatest surprise in her face. Just then her grandfather came along.

"What is it? Have you rolled the chair away, Heidi?" he asked.

"I have looked for it everywhere, grandfather, and you said it was standing by the shop door," said the child.

Meanwhile the wind had grown stronger; it rattled round the shop door and suddenly threw it with a crash back against the wall.

"Grandfather, the wind has done it!" exclaimed Heidi; and her eyes flashed at the suggestion. "Oh, if it has blown the chair down to Dörfli, it will be too late before we can get it back, and we can't go at all."

"If it has rolled down there, it will never come back, for it is in a hundred pieces," said her grandfather, stepping round the corner and looking down the mountain. "It is strange how it happened," he added as he looked back at the distance, for the chair had to go round the corner of the hut first.

"Oh, what a shame! We can't go now, and perhaps never," mourned Klara. "Now I shall really have to go home, for I haven't any chair. Oh, what a shame!"

But Heidi looked quite trustfully up at her grandfather and said, "Surely, grandfather, you can find a way, so that Klara won't have to go home right off?"

"We will go up to the pasture this time; then we will see what will happen next," said the grandfather.

The children shouted for joy.

He went back into the hut, brought out a good number of wraps, laid them in the sunniest place near the hut, and set Klara down on them. Then he brought the children their morning milk and led Schwänli and Bärli out of the shed.

"Why is he so long coming up this morning?" said the uncle to himself, for Peter's whistle had not yet sounded.

The grandfather then took Klara up in his arms.

"There, now, forward!" he said, starting along. "The goats may come with us."

This greatly pleased Heidi. With one arm round Schwänli's neck and the other round Bärli's, Heidi followed after her grandfather; and the goats were so delighted to go again with Heidi that out of pure affection they almost squeezed her to death between them.

When they reached the pasture, they saw the goats standing in groups, peacefully grazing here and there on the slopes, and Peter lying at full length in the midst of them.

"Another time I will cure you of passing us by, sleepyhead; what did you mean?" the uncle called out to him.

Peter jumped up at the sound of the well-known voice.

"Nobody was up," he replied.

"Did you see anything of the chair?" asked the uncle.

"Of what?" said Peter crossly, in reply.

The uncle said nothing more. He spread the shawls out on the sunny slope, placed Klara on them, and asked if she was comfortable.

"As comfortable as in my chair," she said, thanking him. "And I am in the most beautiful place. It is so beautiful here, Heidi, so beautiful!" she exclaimed, looking all about her.

The grandfather started to go back. He said they ought to enjoy themselves together now, and when it was time Heidi must bring out the dinner, which he had left packed in the bag, over in the shade. Then Peter would give them as much milk as they wanted to drink, but Heidi must take good care that it came from Schwänli. Toward evening the grandfather would return; now he wanted above all to go after the chair and see what had become of it.

The sky was deep blue, and not a single cloud was to be seen anywhere. The great snow field beyond them sparkled like thousands and thousands of gold and silver stars. The gray rocky peaks stood high and steadfast in their places, as they had done for ages, looking down solemnly into the valley below. The great bird rocked himself up in the blue, and the mountain wind passed over the heights and blew cool round the sunny Alm. The children were wonderfully happy. Now and then a little goat would come and lie down by them for a while; the affectionate Schneehöpli came most frequently and laid her little head against Heidi, and would not have gone away at all if another one of the flock had not driven her off. Thus Klara learned to know the goats so well that she never mistook one for another, for each had a quite different face and manner.

They now felt so familiar with Klara that they came quite near and rubbed their heads against her shoulder; this was always a sign of friendship and affection.

Several hours had passed in this way, when it occurred to Heidi that she would like to go over to the place where there were so many flowers, and see if they were all open and as beautiful as they were the year before.

When her grandfather came back at evening they might go there with Klara, but perhaps the flowers would already have their eyes closed then. Heidi's longing kept increasing until she could resist it no longer. So she asked timidly, "Would you be angry, Klara, if I should run away very fast and leave you alone? I should so much like to see how the flowers are; but wait"—a thought came to Heidi. She jumped aside and pulled up some beautiful bunches of green plants; Schneehöpli immediately came running toward her and she took her round the neck and led her to Klara.

"There, you must not be left alone," said Heidi, pushing Schneehöpli to a place a little nearer Klara. This the goat understood very well and lay down. Then Heidi threw the leaves into Klara's lap, and she said, much delighted, that Heidi must go now and take a good look at the flowers; she was perfectly willing to stay alone with the goat; it was something she had never done before.

Heidi ran away and Klara began to hold out one leaf after another for Schneehöpli; and the goat was so tame that she nestled up to her new friend and ate the leaves slowly out of her fingers. One could easily see how contented she was that she dared to lie so quietly and peacefully in this place of refuge; for outside with the flock she always had to endure a great deal of chasing by the big, strong goats. How delightful it seemed to Klara to sit in this way, all alone on a mountain, with only a little trusting goat looking up at her so helplessly. A great desire arose in her to become her own master and be able to help someone else and not always be obliged to take help from others. And so many thoughts which she had never had before came to Klara, and a strange desire to live on in the beautiful sunshine and do something to give pleasure to someone as she was now pleasing Schneehöpli. An entirely new joy came into her heart, and it seemed as if everything she knew might be much more beautiful and different from what she had ever seen before; and she felt so contented and happy that she had to throw her arms round the goat's neck and exclaim, "Oh, Schneehöpli, how beautiful it is up here; if I only could stay here always with you!"

Meanwhile Heidi had reached the place where the flowers were. She screamed with delight. The whole slope lay covered with shining gold. They were the bright rockroses. Thick, deep clusters of bluebells nodded above them, and a strong spicy odor filled the air about the sunny spot, as if cups of the most precious balsam were poured out up there. All the fragrance, however, came from the little brown blossoms which stretched up their round heads modestly here and there between the golden flower cups. Heidi stood and looked and drew in long breaths of the sweet air. Suddenly she turned round and came panting with excitement back to Klara.

"Oh, you really must come," she called out before she had reached her. "They are so beautiful, and everything is so beautiful, and perhaps by evening it won't be so any longer. Perhaps I can carry you; don't you think I could?"

Klara looked at the excited Heidi in surprise; she shook her head.

"No, no; what are you thinking of, Heidi? You are ever so much smaller than I. Oh, if I only could walk!"

Then Heidi looked all round her trying to think of some new plan. Up where he had been lying on the ground Peter still sat staring down at the children. He had been sitting thus for hours, always gazing down, as if he could not realize what he saw. He had destroyed the hated chair that he might make an end of it all, and so that the stranger might not be able to move; and a short time afterward she had appeared up here and was sitting before him on the ground next to Heidi. It could not be possible, and yet it was true, and whenever he chose he could see that it was so.

Heidi looked up at him.

"Come down here, Peter!" she called very decidedly.

"Shan't come," he called back.

"But you must! Come, I can't do it alone, and you must help me; come quick!" urged Heidi.

"Shan't come," he replied again.

Then Heidi ran a little way up the mountain toward him.

She stood there with flashing eyes and called out, "Peter, if you don't come here at once, I will do something to you that you won't like at all; you can believe what I say!"

These words stabbed Peter, and he was seized with great fear. He had done something wicked which no one must know. Until now it had delighted him; but Heidi spoke as if she knew all about it, and would tell her grandfather everything she knew, and Peter was more afraid of him than of anyone else. If he should hear what had become of the chair! Peter's distress choked him worse and worse. He rose and came toward Heidi, who was waiting for him.

"I am coming, but then you mustn't do it," he said, so meek with fright that Heidi was quite touched.

"No, no, I will not do it now," she promised reassuringly, "only come with me; there is nothing to be afraid of in what I want you to do."

When they reached Klara, Heidi began to give orders. Peter was to take Klara firmly under one arm and Heidi to take her under the other, and then they would lift her up.

This went quite well, but then came the real difficulty. Klara could not stand; how could they hold her and get her along? Heidi was much too small to support her with her arm.

"You must put your arm round my neck now very firmly —so. And you must take Peter's arm and lean on it hard; then we can carry you.

But Peter had never given anyone his arm before. Klara took it all right, but he held it stiffly down by his side like a long stick.

"That is not the way to do, Peter," said Heidi very decidedly. "You must make a ring with your arm, and then Klara must put hers through it, and she must lean on it very hard, and you mustn't let go at any price; then we can move along."

This was done, but they did not make much progress. Klara was not so light, and the others were too unlike in size; one side went up and the other down, making the support uncertain.

Klara tried to bear weight on her feet a little, but she could not move them forward.

"Just stamp right down," suggested Heidi, "then it will hurt you less afterwards."

"Do you think so?" said Klara timidly.

But she obeyed and ventured to take one firm step on the ground and then another; but it made her give a little scream. Then she lifted one foot again and put it down more carefully.

"Oh, that didn't hurt nearly so much," she said, full of delight.

"Do it once more," urged Heidi eagerly.

Klara did so, and then again and again, and suddenly she cried out, "I can, Heidi! Oh, I can! See! See! I can take steps, one after another."

Then Heidi shouted still louder.

"Oh, oh! Can you really step yourself? Can you walk now? Can you really walk yourself? Oh, if only grandfather would come! Now you can walk, now you can walk!" she exclaimed again and again in triumphant delight.

Klara leaned on both of them, but with each step she gained a little more confidence, as all three could see. Heidi was quite beside herself with delight.

"Oh, now we can come up to the pasture together every day and go wherever we please on the mountain!" she exclaimed again. "And you can go about as I do all the rest of your life, and never be pushed in a chair, and be well. Oh, this is the greatest joy we could have!"

Klara agreed with all her heart. Surely she could have no greater fortune in the world than to be well and be able to go about like other people, and not be miserably condemned to sit all day long in an invalid chair.

It was not far to the slope where the flowers grew. They could already see the gleam of the golden roses in the sun. Then they came to the clusters of bluebells where the sunny ground showed through so invitingly between the flowers.

"Can't we sit down here?" asked Klara.

This was just what Heidi wished to do, and the children sat down in the midst of the flowers, Klara for the first time on the dry mountain ground; this pleased her more than she could tell. All round them the nodding bluebells, the shining golden roses, the red centauries, and everywhere the sweet fragrance of the brown blossoms and the spicy wild plum. Everything was so lovely—so lovely!

Heidi, too, as she sat next her, thought it had never been so beautiful up there before, and she did not know why she felt such joy in her heart, so that she had to keep shouting aloud. But suddenly it occurred to her that Klara had been made well; this was a far greater joy than all the beauty round them. Klara was perfectly silent; she was so delighted and fascinated with everything she saw, and with the prospect which the experience she had just had presented to her. There was hardly any room in her heart for the great fortune; and, besides, the sunshine and fragrance of the flowers overpowered her with a feeling of joy which made her quite speechless.

Peter lay silent also and motionless in the midst of this field of flowers, for he was almost asleep. The wind blew down softly and caressingly behind the protecting rocks and whispered up in the bushes. Now and then Heidi had to get up and run about, for there was always some place even more beautiful, where the flowers were thicker, the fragrance stronger, because the wind blew it here and there; she had to sit down everywhere.

Thus the hours fled away.

The sun was long past midday when a troop of goats came walking quite gravely up to the flower field. It was not their pasturage; they had never been brought there before; they did not like to graze among the flowers. They looked like an embassy with Distelfinck ahead. The goats had evidently come to look for their companions who had left them so long behind and stayed away beyond all rules, for the goats knew the time well. When Distelfinck spied the three missing ones in the flower field he began to bleat loudly, and immediately all the others joined in a chorus and came along making a great noise. Then Peter woke up. But he had to rub his eyes hard, for he had been dreaming that the wheelchair was standing again, all cushioned in red and unharmed, in front of the hut, and now that he was awake he still saw the gold nails in the cushions shine in the sun; but quickly he discovered that they were only the yellow, glistening flowers on the ground. Then Peter's distress, which had entirely disappeared at sight of the uninjured chair, came back to him. Although Heidi had promised not to do anything, yet Peter grew very much afraid that what he had done might be found out. He was very meek and willing to be the guide and do everything exactly as Heidi wished.

When they had all three come back to the pasture, Heidi quickly brought out her well-filled dinner bag and set about keeping her promise, for her threat had had reference to the contents of the bag. She had especially noticed in the morning what good things her grandfather put in, and had been pleased to think that a good part of it would fall to Peter's share. But when Peter was so disagreeable, she wanted to make him understand that he would not have what otherwise had been intended for him. Heidi took piece after piece out of the bag and made three little heaps of them, so high that she said to herself with satisfaction, "Besides, he will have all that we leave."

Then she gave a little pile to each one and sat down beside Klara with her own, and the children thoroughly enjoyed their dinner after their great exertion.

It happened just as Heidi expected; when they both were satisfied, there was still so much left that they gave Peter another pile as large as the first. He ate it all silently without stopping, even to the crumbs, but he finished without the usual satisfaction. Something lay in Peter's stomach which gnawed and choked him and squeezed him at every mouthful.

The children had returned so late to their dinner that immediately afterward the grandfather was seen coming up the Alm to get them. Heidi rushed to meet him; she had to tell him first of all what had happened. She was so excited over her good news that she could hardly find words to tell her grandfather; but he understood at once what the child meant, and his face lighted up with joy. He hastened his steps, and when he reached Klara, he said, smiling gladly, "Well, and did we dare? Now we have really succeeded!"

Then he lifted Klara from the ground, put his left arm round her, and held out his right as a strong support for her hand, and Klara walked, in this way, even more surely and less timidly than before.

Heidi shouted and danced round, and her grandfather looked as if some great good fortune had come to him. But he suddenly took Klara in his arms and said, "We will not overdo it; it is time now to go home." And he started on the way at once, for he knew that Klara had had enough exertion for that day and that she needed rest.

When Peter with his goats came down late that evening to Dörfli, a crowd of people were standing together, pushing each other this way and that to get a better view of what lay in their midst. Peter had to see too; he pushed and squeezed right and left and made his way through.

Then he saw what it was.

On the grass lay the middle part of the wheelchair with a portion of the back still hanging to it. The red cushions and the bright nails still showed how splendid it had looked when it was perfect.

"I was here when it came down," said the baker, who was standing next to Peter. "It was worth at least a hundred dollars. I'll wager that with anyone. But it's a wonder to me how it happened."

"The wind must have brought it down; the uncle said so himself," remarked Barbel, who could not admire the handsome red material enough.

"It is a good thing that it wasn't anyone else who did it," said the baker again. "He would be in a fine fix. If the gentleman in Frankfurt hears of it, he will try to find out how it happened. As for me, I am glad that I haven't been up on the Alm for two years; suspicion may fall on anyone who was seen up there at that time."

A good many other opinions were expressed, but Peter had heard enough. He crept quite meekly and softly out of the crowd and ran with all his might up the mountain, as if someone were after him to catch him. The baker's words had given him a terrible scare. He felt sure that at any moment an officer from Frankfurt might come to look into the matter, and might find out that he had done it, and would seize him and take him to the house of correction in Frankfurt. Peter saw this before him and his hair stood on end from fear.

He came home very much distressed. He would make no reply to any remark and would not eat his potatoes; he crept hurriedly into bed and groaned.

"Peter has been eating sorrel again; he has some in his stomach, and that makes him groan so," said his mother Brigitte.

"You must give him a little more bread to take with him; give him a piece of mine tomorrow," said the grandmother kindly.

When the two little girls that night looked up from their beds at the starlight, Heidi said, "Haven't you been thinking all day long today how good it is that the dear Lord doesn't give us what we pray so terribly hard for, when He knows of something much better?"

"Why do you say that now, Heidi?" asked Klara.

"Don't you know, because I prayed so hard in Frankfurt that I might go home right away, and because I couldn't go, I thought the dear Lord had not heard me. But, do you know, if I had gone right away, you would never have come up on the mountain, and you wouldn't have got well."

Klara became quite thoughtful.

"But, Heidi," she began again, "then we ought not to pray for anything, because the dear Lord certainly has always something better in mind than we know and ask Him for."

"O Klara, you really do not think so?" Heidi hastened to say. "We ought to pray to the dear Lord every day, and about every single thing; for then He will know that we do not forget that we receive everything from Him. And if we forget the dear Lord, He will forget us too; your grandmamma told me that. But, you know, if we do not receive what we would like, we must not think the dear Lord has not listened, and stop praying, but we must pray like this, 'Now I know, dear Lord, that You have something better in store, and I will be glad that You will be so good to me.'"

"How did you find out all this, Heidi?" asked Klara.

"Your grandmamma explained it to me first, and then it happened exactly so, and then I knew it. But I think, Klara," Heidi continued, sitting up, "that tonight we ought really to thank the dear Lord heartily, because He has sent us the great good fortune that you are able to walk now."

"Yes, indeed, Heidi; you are right, and I am glad that you remind me. I was so delighted I almost forgot it."

Then the children prayed, and each thanked the dear Lord in her own way for sending such a wonderful blessing to Klara, who had been ill so long.

The next morning the grandfather thought they could write the grandmamma that if she would come up on the Alm there would be something new for her to see. But the children had another plan. They wanted to give the grandmamma a great surprise. First, Klara was to learn to walk better, so that she could go a little way with only Heidi's support; but the grandmamma must not have the least suspicion of it. The grandfather must decide how long it would take, and as he thought that it would not take more than a week, in the next letter they would give her a pressing invitation to come up on the mountain at the end of that time; but not a word must be said to her about anything new.

The days which followed were by far the most beautiful which Klara had passed on the Alm. Every morning she awoke with these delightful words in her mind: "I am well! I am well! I do not need to sit in a wheelchair any longer; I can go about by myself like other people!"

Then followed the walking; and every day she went more easily and better, and was able to take longer walks. The exercise caused such an appetite that the grandfather made her thick slices of bread and butter larger and was well pleased to see them disappear. He always brought with them a large pot of foaming milk and filled bowl after bowl with it. The end of the week came and with it the day that was to bring the grandmamma!

Chapter 9

Parting to Meet Again

A day before her arrival the grandmamma had written a letter and sent it up to the Alm that they might know there exactly when she was coming. Peter brought this letter with him early the next day, as he was going up to the pasture. The grandfather had already come out of the hut with the children, and Schwänli and Bärli were both standing outside, gaily shaking their heads in the cool morning air, while the children stroked them and wished them a pleasant journey up the mountain. The uncle stood by and looked first at the children's fresh faces, and then at his clean, sleek goats. Both must have pleased him, for he smiled with satisfaction.

Then Peter came along. When he saw the group he approached slowly, handed the letter to the uncle, and, as soon as he had taken it, ran timidly back as if something had frightened him; then the boy looked quickly behind him, exactly as if something else were going to frighten him; then he gave a leap and ran up the mountain.

"Grandfather," said Heidi, who had been watching Peter in surprise, "why does Peter act like the big Türk when he feels the rod behind him; he ducks his head and shakes himself all over and makes sudden leaps in the air."

"Perhaps Peter feels that there is a rod behind him too, and knows he deserves it," answered her grandfather.

It was only the first slope that Peter ran up without stopping; as soon as he could no longer be seen from below, it was different. Then he stood still and turned his head timidly in every direction; suddenly he leaped into the air and looked behind him, as frightened as if someone had just seized him by the nape of the neck. From behind every bush and out of every thicket Peter thought he saw a policeman from Frankfurt rushing out at him. The longer this anxious expectation lasted, the more terrible it became to Peter, so that now he had not a moment's peace.

Heidi had the hut to put in order, for the grandmamma must find everything tidy when she came. Klara always found this busy cleaning in every corner of the hut so interesting that she was very glad to watch Heidi at work.

So the early morning hours passed before the children were aware of it, and the grandmamma was expected to arrive at any moment.

Then the children came out again, all ready to welcome her, and sat down together on the bench in front of the hut, full of expectation.

The grandfather also joined them; he had taken a walk and had brought home a great bunch of deep-blue gentians, which looked so lovely in the bright morning sun that the children shouted for joy when they saw them. The grandfather took the flowers into the hut. Every little while Heidi jumped up from the bench to see whether she could catch sight of the grandmamma's party.

At last Heidi saw exactly what she had been expecting coming up from below. First came the guide, then the white horse with the grandmamma on it, and last the porter with the deep basket on his back, for the grandmamma would never think of coming up on the mountain without plenty of wraps.

Nearer and nearer they came. Then the top was reached; the grandmamma looked down at the children from her horse.

"What is that? What do I see, Klärchen? You are not sitting in your chair! How is that possible?" she exclaimed in alarm and dismounted hastily. But before she had reached the children she clapped her hands and exclaimed in the greatest excitement, "Klärchen, is it you or is it not? You really have red cheeks, as round as an apple! Child! I don't know you any longer!"

Then the grandmamma was going to rush at Klara; but Heidi had slipped unnoticed from the bench, and Klara quickly leaned on her shoulders, and the children started away quite calmly to take a little walk. The grandmamma suddenly stood still, first from fear, for her only thought was that Heidi was trying to do something rash.

But what did she see before her!

Klara was walking upright and safely beside Heidi; then they came back again, both with beaming faces, both with rosy cheeks.

Then the grandmamma rushed toward them. Laughing and crying, she embraced Klara, then Heidi and then Klara again. In her delight she could find no words.

Suddenly she caught sight of the uncle, who was standing by the bench and smiling with satisfaction as he watched the three. Then she seized Klara's arm and with continual cries of delight that it was really true that she could walk round with the child, went to the bench. Here she let Klara go and grasped both of the old man's hands.

"My dear uncle! My dear uncle! How much we have to thank you for! It is your work! It is your care and nursing—"

"And our Lord's sunshine and mountain air," interrupted the uncle, smiling.

"Yes, and Schwänli's lovely, good milk, too," added Klara. "Grandmamma, you ought to see how I can drink the goat's milk, and how good it is!"

"I can see that by your cheeks, Klärchen," said her grandmamma, laughing. "No, no one would ever know you; you have grown round and broad, as I never dreamed you could be, and you are tall, Klärchen! Is it really true? I cannot look at you enough! I must send a telegram at once to my son in Paris; he must come immediately. I will not tell him why; it will be the greatest joy of his life. My dear uncle, how can it be done? Have you sent the men away already?"

"They have gone," he replied. "But if the grandmamma is in haste, we can send down the goatherd, who has time."

The grandmamma insisted upon sending a message at once to her son, for this good fortune must not be kept from him a single day.

So the uncle went a little way aside and gave such a shrill whistle through his fingers that it whistled back from the rocks above, so far away had it wakened the echo. It was not long before Peter came running down, for he knew the whistle well. Peter was white as chalk, for he thought the Alm-Uncle was calling him to judgment. A paper which the grandmamma had written meanwhile was then given to him, and the uncle explained that he was to carry it immediately down into Dörfli and give it to the postmaster; the uncle would pay for it later himself, for Peter could not be entrusted with so many things at once.

He went along with the paper in his hand, much relieved for this time, as the uncle had not whistled to call him to account, and no policeman had come.

At last they were able to sit down quietly together round the table in front of the hut, and then the grandmamma had to be told from the beginning how it had all happened; how at first the grandfather had tried to have Klara stand and then take steps, then how they had taken the journey up to the pasture and the wind had rolled away the chair; how Klara's eagerness to see the flowers had brought about her first walk, and so one thing grew out of another. But it was a long time before the children finished their story, for every little while the grandmamma had to break forth in amazement and in praise and thankfulness, and exclaimed again and again, "Is it really possible? Is it then really no dream? Are we all awake and sitting here in front of the Alm hut, and is the little girl before me, with the round, fresh face, my old, pale, weak Klärchen?"

Klara and Heidi were in a constant state of delight because their beautifully planned surprise had succeeded so well with the grandmamma.

Meanwhile Herr Sesemann had finished his business in Paris and had also been preparing a surprise. Without writing a word to his mother, he took the train one sunny summer morning and went directly through to Basle, leaving there early the following day, for he was seized with a great longing to see his little daughter again, having been separated from her the whole summer long. He reached Ragatz a few hours after his mother had left there.

He found that she had that very day started to go up the mountain. So he immediately took a carriage and drove to Maienfeld. When he learned there that he could drive on to Dörfli he did so, for he thought it would be far enough to have to walk up the mountain.

Herr Sesemann had not been mistaken; the constant climbing up the mountain was very tiresome and hard for him. No hut appeared in sight, and he knew that he ought to come to goatherd Peter's dwelling halfway up, for he had often heard about this journey.

There were footpaths leading in all directions. Herr Sesemann was not sure that he was on the right path or whether the hut might not perhaps lie on the other side of the mountain. He looked round him, to see if he could discover any human being whom he could ask about the way. But it was silent all round; far and wide there was nothing to be seen, nothing to be heard. Only the mountain wind blew now and then through the air, and the little flies buzzed in the sunshine, and a merry bird piped here and there on a lonely larch tree. Herr Sesemann stood still for a while and let the mountain breeze cool his heated brow.

Just then someone came running down from above; it was Peter with the message in his hand. He was running straight ahead, down the steep places, paying no attention to the footpath where Herr Sesemann stood. As soon as the boy came near enough, Herr Sesemann beckoned for him to come to him. Peter came trembling and frightened, sideways, not straight forward, and as if he could only advance properly with one foot and had to drag the other after him.

"Here, youngster, brace up!" said Herr Sesemann encouragingly.

"Now tell me if this path will bring me up to the hut, where the old man lives with the child Heidi, where the people from Frankfurt are."

A dull sound of the greatest terror was the answer, and Peter darted away with such swift bounds that he rushed heels over head down the steep mountainside, and rolled away, turning somersaults farther and farther, very nearly as the wheelchair had done, except that fortunately Peter did not go to pieces, like the chair.

Only the telegram was badly treated and torn to shreds. "A remarkably bashful mountaineer," said Herr Sesemann to himself, for he supposed that the appearance of a stranger had produced this strong impression on the simple son of the Alps.

After watching Peter's violent descent for a little while, Herr Sesemann continued his way.

In spite of all his efforts Peter could not reach a place of safety; he kept rolling on, and from time to time turned somersaults in the strangest fashion.

But this was not the most frightful side of his misfortune at this moment; far more frightful were the fear and the terror that filled him, for he was sure now that the policeman from Frankfurt had really come. He had no doubt that the stranger who had asked for the people from Frankfurt at the Alm-Uncle's was the very one. Finally, on the last high slope above Dörfli, Peter rolled against a bush to which he could cling fast. He lay still there for a moment, for he had first to think what had happened to him.

"Very good, here's another one," said a voice close by Peter. "And who is going to catch it tomorrow for sending you down like a badly sewed potato sack?"

It was the baker, who was making fun of him. To amuse himself a little up there after his hot day's work, he had been quietly watching Peter as he came down the mountain very much as the wheelchair had done.

Peter jumped to his feet. New fear had seized him. Now the baker must know that the chair had been pushed. Without looking back once, Peter ran up the mountain again.

He would have preferred to go home now and creep into his bed, so that no one could find him, for he felt safest there. But he had left the goats up in the pasture, and the uncle had impressed it upon him to come back soon, that the flock might not be alone too long. He feared the uncle more than anyone else, and had such respect for him that he had never dared to disobey him. Peter groaned aloud and limped on, for it had to be; he was obliged to go back up the mountain again. But he could not run any longer; his fear and the many knocks that he had received had made him almost ill. So he went slowly, limping and groaning, up the Alm.

Herr Sesemann had reached the first hut shortly after meeting Peter, and knew then that he was on the right path. He climbed on with renewed zeal and at last, after long, tiresome exertion, he saw his goal before him. There stood the Alm hut with the dark branches of the old fir trees swaying above it.

Herr Sesemann climbed the last part of the way with delight, for he was soon to surprise his child. But the father had already been seen and recognized by the company in front of the hut, and something was in store for him which he had never suspected.

When he had taken the last step up the mountain, two forms came toward him from the hut. A tall young girl, with light-yellow hair and rosy face, was leaning on little Heidi, whose dark eyes sparkled with the keenest delight. Herr Sesemann stopped short; he stood still and gazed at the approaching children. Suddenly big tears rushed from his eyes. What memories arose in his heart! Exactly so had Klara's mother looked, a blonde maiden with cheeks slightly tinged with red. Herr Sesemann did not know whether he was awake or dreaming.

"Papa, don't you know me any longer?" called out Klara to him, while her face beamed with delight. "Am I so changed?"

Herr Sesemann rushed toward his little daughter and folded her in his arms.

"Yes, you are changed! Is it possible? Is it really so?"

And the overjoyed father stepped back again to see whether the picture would not disappear before his eyes.

"Is it you, Klärchen, is it really you?" he had to exclaim again and again. He folded his child in his arms once more, and then he had to look again to see whether it really was Klara standing erect before him.

Then the grandmamma came out, for she could not wait any longer to see her son's happy face.

"Well, my dear son, what do you say now?" she called out to him. "The surprise which you have given us is very lovely, but the one prepared for you is still lovelier, is it not?" And the delighted mother greeted her dear son with great affection.

"But now, my dear," she then said, "come with me over there to see the uncle, who is our greatest benefactor."

"Certainly, and our little companion, our little Heidi, I must greet also," said Herr Sesemann as he shook Heidi's hand. "Well? Always fresh and well on the mountain? But I don't need to ask; no Alpine rose could be more blooming. This is a joy to me, child; this is a great joy to me!"

Heidi looked with beaming eyes at the kind Herr Sesemann. How good he had always been to her! And that now he should find such a joy here on the mountain made Heidi's heart beat loud with delight.

Then the grandmamma took her son to the Alm-Uncle, and while the two men were shaking hands very heartily, and Herr Sesemann was beginning to express his deep-felt thanks and his boundless astonishment that such a wonderful thing could happen, the grandmamma turned and went a little way in the other direction, for she had already talked the matter over. She wanted to look at the old fir trees again.

Here there was another surprise awaiting her. Under the fir trees, where the long branches had left a free space, stood a great bunch of wonderful deep-blue gentians, as fresh and shining as if they had grown there. The grandmamma clapped her hands with delight.

"How exquisite! How wonderful! What a sight!" she exclaimed again and again. "Heidi, my dear child, come here! Did you bring these here to please me? They are perfectly wonderful!"

The children were already there.

"No, no, I really did not," said Heidi, "but I know who did."

"It is like that up in the pasture, grandmamma, and even more beautiful," said Klara. "But just guess who brought the flowers down from the pasture for you early this morning!" and Klara smiled with so much satisfaction at what she had said that for a moment it occurred to her grandmamma that the child herself had perhaps been up there that day. But that was almost impossible.

A gentle rustling was then heard behind the fir trees; it came from Peter, who had come back in the meantime. When he saw who was standing in front of the hut with the uncle, he went a long way round and was going to slip very stealthily behind the fir trees. But the grandmamma caught sight of him, and a new thought suddenly came to her. Had Peter brought down the flowers, and was he creeping away now so stealthily from sheer timidity and shyness? No, that must not be; he should have a little reward.

"Come, my lad, come here quickly, and don't be afraid!" the grandmamma called loudly, putting her head a little way between the trees.

Speechless with fear, Peter stood still. He had not the strength to resist anything more that might happen. This was what he felt: "Now it is all up!" His hair stood on end, and with a pale face, twisted by great distress, Peter came slowly out from behind the fir trees.

"Come right straight here," said the grandmamma encouragingly. "There, now tell me, my boy, if you did this."

Peter did not lift his eyes, and did not see where the grandmamma's finger was pointing. He had noticed that the uncle was standing by the corner of the hut, and that his keen eyes were fastened on him, and that next the uncle stood the most terrible person Peter knew, the policeman from Frankfurt. Trembling in every limb, Peter stammered forth one single sound; it was a "Yes."

"There now," said the grandmamma, "what is there to be frightened about?"

"Because—because—because it is broken to pieces and can never be made whole again." Peter brought these words out with difficulty; and his knees shook so that he could hardly stand. The grandmamma went along to the corner of the hut.

"My dear uncle, is the poor boy really out of his mind?" she asked sympathetically.

"Not in the least, not in the least," asserted the uncle. "The boy is the wind that blew away the wheelchair, and now he is expecting the punishment which he well deserves."

The grandmamma could not believe this, for she did not think Peter looked wicked in the least, and besides he had no reason to destroy the wheelchair, which was so much needed. But his confession only had confirmed the uncle in a suspicion which had been aroused in him immediately after the occurrence.

The dark looks which Peter had cast at Klara from the very first, and other signs of a bitter feeling toward the newcomer on the mountain had not escaped the uncle. He had added one thought to another, and so he had felt sure enough of the way things had gone and explained it all very clearly now to the grandmamma. When he had finished, the lady burst out in great excitement, "No, no, my dear uncle; no, no, we will not punish the poor fellow any further. One must be just. Strange people came here from Frankfurt and for long weeks together took away Heidi, his only good, and really a great good for him, and he sits alone there day after day, looking for her. No, one must be just; anger overpowered him and drove him to revenge, which was rather foolish; but in our anger we are all foolish."

Whereupon the grandmamma went back to Peter, who was still trembling and shaking.

She sat down on the bench under the fir trees and said kindly, "There, now come here, my boy, to me; I have something to say to you. Stop trembling and shaking and listen to me; this you must do. You sent the wheelchair down the mountain, in order to smash it. That was a wicked deed, and you knew it very well, and you also knew that you deserved a punishment, and in order not to receive one, you have had to try very hard not to let anyone know what you have done. But you see, whoever does a wicked thing and thinks no one knows about it is always mistaken. The dear Lord sees and hears everything, and as soon as He notices that a person wants to conceal his wicked deed, He quickly awakens a little watchman that was placed in him at his birth, and that sleeps in him until the person does something wrong. And the little watchman has a little goad in his hand with which he continually pricks the person so that he has no rest for a moment. And with his voice he also torments him further, by constantly calling to him in a torturing way: 'It will all come out! You are going to be punished!' So he lives in continual fear and trembling, and is no longer happy, not a bit. Have you not had such an experience as this just now, Peter?"

Peter nodded, quite crushed, and as one who knew, for it had happened to him exactly so.

"And in one way you were disappointed," continued the grandmamma. "See how the wrong that you did turned out for the best for the one you wished to harm! Because Klara no longer had a chair to be carried in, and yet wanted to see the beautiful flowers, she made a very great effort to walk, and so learned how and now keeps improving; and if she stays here she will at last be able to go up to the pasture every day, much oftener than if she were taken in her chair. Do you understand, Peter? So when one wishes to do a wicked thing, the dear Lord can take it quickly into His own hands and turn it into good for the one who was to be harmed; and the scoundrel has his trouble for nothing and injures himself.

"Have you understood everything well, Peter? Then think of it; and every time you desire to do something wicked, think of the little watchman within you, with his goad and his disagreeable voice. Will you do that?"

"Yes, I will," answered Peter, very much impressed; for he did not yet know how everything would end, since the policeman was still standing over there by the uncle.

"That is good; then the matter is settled," said the grandmamma. "But now you ought to have something you like, to remember the people from Frankfurt by. Tell me, my boy, is there something you have wished to have? What was it? What should you like to have best?"

Peter then lifted his head and stared at the grandmamma with round, astonished eyes. He was still expecting something frightful, and now he was suddenly to have whatever he liked best. Peter's thoughts were all in confusion.

"Yes, yes, I am in earnest," said the grandmamma. "You shall have something which you will like, as a remembrance of the people from Frankfurt, and as a token that they will think no more about the wrong that you did. Do you understand now, boy?"

It began to dawn on Peter that he had no punishment to fear now, and that the good lady sitting before him had rescued him from the power of the policeman. Then he felt as relieved as if a mountain which was almost crushing him had been taken away from him. He also understood now that it is better to confess one's faults, and he at once said, "And I lost the paper, too."

The grandmamma had to reflect a little, but she soon remembered and said kindly, "There, that is right to tell me about it! Always confess what is wrong, then it will be settled. Now what should you like to have?"

Now Peter could choose anything in the world that he would like to have. It almost made him dizzy. The whole fair at Maienfeld came before his eyes, with all the beautiful things which he had often looked at for hours and had thought he could never have, for Peter's possessions had never gone beyond one penny, and such attractive objects always cost double that amount. There were the lovely red whistles, which he could use so well for his goats. Then there were the fascinating round-handled knives with which he could do a thriving business on all the neighboring hazel-rod hedges.

Peter stood deep in thought, for he was considering which of the two was the more desirable, and he could not decide. Then a bright idea came to him; by this means he could think it over until the next fair.

"Two cents," replied Peter decidedly.

The grandmamma laughed a little.

"That is not too much. So come here!" She then opened her purse and took out a great, round dollar; on it she laid four pennies.

"There, we will count it out exactly," she continued. "I will explain it to you. Here you have twice as many pennies as there are weeks in the year! So you can take two out to use every Sunday the whole year through."

"All my life long?" asked Peter quite innocently.

Then the grandmamma had such a fit of laughter that the gentlemen yonder had to stop talking to hear what was going on.

The grandmamma kept on laughing.

"You shall have it, my boy; I will put it in my will—do you hear, my son? And then it will be handed over to you; thus: To goatherd Peter two pennies weekly, as long as he lives."

Herr Sesemann nodded in assent and laughed too at the idea.

Peter looked again at the present in his hand, to see if it was really true. Then he said, "God bless you!"

And he ran away, making extraordinary leaps; but this time he stayed on his feet, for now he was not driven by fear but by a delight such as he had never known before in all his life. All his suffering and fear had disappeared, and he could expect two pennies every week all his life long.

Later when the company in front of the Alm hut had ended their happy midday meal and were still sitting together talking about all sorts of things, Klara took her father's hand, and while his face beamed with delight, said with an enthusiasm which had never been known in the old-time feeble Klara, "O papa, if you only knew all that the grandfather has done for me! So much every day that I can't tell you about it, but I shall never forget it in my life. I am always thinking, if I could only do something for the dear grandfather or give him something to make him as happy or even half as happy as he has made me."

"That is my greatest desire also, my dear child," said her father. "I am continually thinking how we can prove our gratitude in some measure to our kind friend."

Herr Sesemann then rose and went to the uncle, who was sitting beside the grandmamma, and was having an unusually pleasant talk with her. He also rose. Herr Sesemann grasped his hand and said in the most friendly way, "My dear friend, let us have a word together! You will understand me when I tell you that for many long years I have had no real happiness. What were all my money and wealth to me when I looked at my poor child whom I could not make well and happy with all my riches? Next to our God in heaven, you have made the child well for me and given new life to me also. Now tell me how I can show my gratitude to you. I can never repay you for what you have done for us, but whatever is in my power I place at your disposal. Tell me, my friend, what I can do."

The uncle had listened in silence, and watched the happy father with a smile of contentment.

"Herr Sesemann, believe me, I also have my share in the great joy at the recovery on our Alm; my work has been well rewarded," said the uncle in his decided way. "I thank you, Herr Sesemann, for your kind offer, but there is nothing that I need; as long as I live I have enough for the child and myself. But I have one wish; if I could have that granted, I should have no more worry during my life."

"Name it, name it, my dear friend!" urged Herr Sesemann.

"I am old," continued the uncle, "and cannot live here much longer. When I go, I cannot leave the child anything, and she has no relatives, only one single person, and that person would take advantage of her. If Herr Sesemann would give me the assurance that Heidi would never in her life have to go out among strangers to seek her bread, then he would have richly rewarded me for what I have done for him and his child."

"But, my dear friend, that goes without saying," Herr Sesemann burst forth. "The child belongs to us. Ask my mother, my daughter, the child Heidi will never be left to other people! But if it will be any comfort to you, my friend, here is my hand on it. I promise you; never in her life shall this child go out to earn her bread among strangers; I will see to that as long as I live. I will say even more. This child is not made for life in a strange land, whatever might happen; we have seen that. But she has made friends. I know one who is in Frankfurt; he is settling up his business there, in order to go later on wherever he likes and take a rest. It is my friend the doctor, and he is coming up here again this autumn, and, taking your advice, will settle in this region; for he found more pleasure in your company and the child's than anywhere else. So you see the child Heidi will have two protectors near her. May they both be preserved to her for a long, long time!"

"The dear Lord grant it may be so!" the grandmamma added; and, confirming her son's wish, she shook the uncle's hand heartily for a long while. Then she suddenly threw her arms round Heidi's neck, as she was standing beside her, and drew her toward her.

"And you, my dear Heidi, we must also ask you a question. Come, tell me if you have a wish which you would like to have granted."

"Yes, indeed, I have," answered Heidi, looking very much delighted at the grandmamma.

"Well, that is right, speak it out," she said encouragingly. "What should you like to have, my child?"

"I should like to have my bed in Frankfurt, with the three thick pillows and the thick quilt, for then the grandmother would not have to lie with her head downhill so that she can hardly breathe, and she would be warm enough under the quilt, and wouldn't always have to go to bed with a shawl on, because she is terribly cold."

Heidi said this all in one breath in her eagerness to obtain what she so much desired.

"Oh, my dear Heidi, what are you telling me?" exclaimed the grandmamma in excitement. "It is a good thing that you remind me. In our joy we easily forget what we ought to think of most. When the dear Lord sends us something good, we ought at once to think of those who are in need! We will telegraph immediately to Frankfurt! Rottenmeier shall have the bed packed up this very day; in two days more it will be here. God willing, the grandmother shall sleep well in it!"

Heidi danced merrily round the grandmamma. But all at once she stood still and said hurriedly, "I must really go as fast as I can down to the grandmother's; she will be troubled because I haven't been there for so long."

For Heidi could not wait any longer to carry the joyful message to the grandmother, and it also came to her mind again how troubled she had been when Heidi was there last.

"No, no, Heidi; what are you thinking about?" said her grandfather reprovingly. "When one has visitors, one doesn't run away from them all of a sudden."

But the grandmamma took Heidi's part.

"My dear uncle, the child is not wrong, ' she said. "The poor grandmother has been a loser for a long time in my opinion. Now we will all go together to see her, and I think I will wait for my horse there, and then we will continue our way, and we can send the telegram at once to Frankfurt from Dörfli. My son, what do you think of it?"

Herr Sesemann had not had time before to speak about his plans.

So he had to ask his mother not to start away at once, but to sit still a moment longer until he had told her what he intended to do.

Herr Sesemann had proposed to take a little journey through Switzerland with his mother, and first to see whether his little Klara was in a condition to travel a short distance with them. Now it had so happened that he saw he could take the enjoyable journey in company with his little daughter, and he was anxious to take advantage at once of these lovely late summer days. He had in mind to spend the night in Dörfli and on the following morning to take Klara away from the Alm, to go with her to meet her grandmamma down in Ragatz, and from there to travel on farther.

Klara was a little disturbed to hear of this sudden departure from the Alm; but there were many other things to be happy about, and besides there was no time to give way to grief.

The grandmamma had already risen and had grasped Heidi's hand to lead the way. Then all of a sudden she turned round.

"But what in the world will you do with Klärchen?" she exclaimed in alarm, for it had occurred to her that the walk would be much too long for one who had been ill.

But the uncle had already taken his little charge in his usual way in his arms, and was following the grandmamma with firm steps, and she nodded back to him with satisfaction. Last came Herr Sesemann, and so the procession went on down the mountain.

Heidi could not help dancing with delight as she went along by the side of the grandmamma, who wanted to know everything about the grandmother, how she lived, and how the family got along, especially in winter, during the severely cold weather up there.

Heidi told her about everything, for she knew how they managed, and how the grandmother sat bowed over in her corner and trembled with the cold. She also knew very well what they had to eat and what they did not have.

The grandmamma listened with the liveliest interest to all that Heidi had to tell her until they reached the hut.

Brigitte was just hanging out Peter's second shirt in the sun, so that when his other one had been worn long enough he could change it. She noticed the people and rushed into the house.

"They are all going away now, mother," she said. "There is a whole procession of them; the uncle is with them; he is carrying the sick child."

"Oh, must it really be?" sighed the grandmother. "Did you see whether they were taking Heidi with them? Oh, if she would only give me her hand once more! If I could only hear her voice once again!"

Now the door was suddenly flung open as if by a whirlwind, and Heidi came springing into the corner where the grandmother was, and threw her arms round her neck.

"Grandmother! Grandmother! My bed is coming from Frankfurt, and all three pillows, and the thick quilt, too; in two days it will be here, the grandmamma said so."

Heidi could hardly bring out her message fast enough, for she could scarcely wait to see the grandmother's great delight. She smiled, but there was sadness in her voice as she said, "Oh, what a good lady she is! I ought to be glad that she is going to take you with her, Heidi; but I shall not live long after it."

"What? What? Who says such a thing to the good old grandmother?" asked a friendly voice here; and the old dame's hand was grasped and heartily pressed, for the grandmamma had come in and heard everything. "No, no, it is no such thing! Heidi will stay with the grandmother and make her happy. We shall want to see the child again, but we will come to her. We shall come up to the Alm every year, for we have reason to offer our especial thanks to the dear Lord annually in this place where such a miracle has been done to our child."

Then the true light of joy came into the grandmother's face, and with speechless thanks she pressed the good Frau Sesemann's hand again and again, while great tears of joy glided down her aged cheeks. Heidi at once noticed the joyful light in the grandmother's face and was quite happy.

"Truly, grandmother," she said, pressing close to her, "it has come just as I read to you the last time! Really, the bed from Frankfurt is wholesome, isn't it?"

"Oh, yes, Heidi, and so much more, so much good the dear Lord has done for me!" said the grandmother, deeply moved. "How is it possible that there are such good people who trouble themselves about a poor old woman and do so much for her? There is nothing that can so strengthen one's belief in a good Father in heaven who will not forget even the lowliest, as to learn that there are such people, full of goodness and pity for a poor, worthless woman such as I am."

"My good grandmother," broke in Frau Sesemann, "before our Father in heaven we all are equally poor, and it is equally necessary to all of us that He should not forget us. And now we must leave you, but we hope to see you again, for as soon as we come back again next year to the Alm, we shall try to find the grandmother once more; she will never be forgotten!"

Whereupon Frau Sesemann grasped the old grandmother's hand again and shook it.

But she did not get away so quickly as she intended, for the grandmother could not stop thanking her and wishing all the good that the dear Lord had it in His power to give for the kind friend and all her household.

Then Herr Sesemann went down toward the valley with his mother, while the uncle carried Klara back home once more; and Heidi, without pausing, jumped high as she went beside her, for she was so pleased with what the grandmother could look forward to that she had to jump at every step.

But the following morning Klara shed hot tears because she had to go away from the beautiful Alm, where she had been better than she had ever been before in all her life. But Heidi comforted her and said, "It will be summer again in no time, and then you will come back, and then it will be more beautiful than ever. Then you can walk all the time, and we can go up to the pasture with the goats every day and see the flowers, and everything will be jolly from the very first."

Herr Sesemann came according to agreement to get his little daughter. He was standing with the grandfather, for the men had all sorts of things to talk over. Klara was wiping away her tears. Heidi's words had comforted her a little.

"I will leave a greeting for Peter," she said, "and for all the goats, especially Schwänli. Oh, if only I could make Schwänli a present; she has helped so much to make me well."

"You can do that very easily," asserted Heidi. "Only send her a little salt. You know how gladly she licks the salt from grandfather's hand at night."

This advice pleased Klara very much.

"Oh, then, I will certainly send her a hundred pounds of salt from Frankfurt!" she exclaimed with delight. "She, too, must have a remembrance from me."

Herr Sesemann then beckoned to the children, for he wished to start. This time the grandmamma's white horse came for Klara, and she was now able to ride down; she no longer needed a sedan chair. Heidi stationed herself at the extreme edge of the slope and waved her hand to Klara until the last speck of horse and rider had disappeared.

The bed came, and the grandmother still sleeps so well in it that she is really gaining new strength. The kind grandmamma did not forget the hard winter on the mountain. She had a great case sent to goatherd Peter's house; there were many warm things packed in it in which the grandmother could wrap herself up, and now she never has to sit anymore shivering with the cold in the corner.

There is a large building in progress in Dörfli. The doctor has come and has taken up his old quarters. Through the advice of his friend he purchased the old building where the uncle lived with Heidi in the winter, and which had been once a great mansion, as could still be seen from the lofty room with the handsome stove and the artistic paneling. This part of the house the doctor is having rebuilt for his own dwelling. The other side is being restored as winter quarters for the uncle and Heidi, for the doctor knew the old man was independent and would want to have his own house. Back of it is a firmly built, warm goat shed where Schwänli and Bärli can spend their winter days most comfortably.

The doctor and the Alm-Uncle are becoming better friends every day, and when they climb together about the building to look after the progress of the work, their thoughts turn mostly to Heidi, for to both of them the chief joy in the house is that they will be together with their happy child.

"My dear uncle," said the doctor the other day, as he was standing upon the wall with the old man, "you must look at the matter as I do. I share all joy in the child with you, as if next to you I were the one to whom the child belongs; I will share all expenses and care for the child as well as I know how. So I have also my right in our Heidi, and can hope that she will care for me in my old age and stay with me; this is my greatest desire. Heidi shall share in my property as my own child; so we can leave her without any worry when we have to go away from her—you and I."

The uncle pressed the doctor's hand for a long time; he spoke not a word, but his good friend could read in the old man's eyes the emotion and great delight which his words had aroused.

Meanwhile Heidi and Peter were sitting with the grandmother, and the first had so much to relate, and the other so much to listen to, that they could hardly get their breath, and in their eagerness kept getting nearer and nearer to the happy grandmother.

There was a great deal to talk about regarding the events of the summer, for they had been together very little all this time.

And each of the three looked happier than the other at being together again, and because of the wonderful things that had taken place. But the face of mother Brigitte looked almost the happiest, for with Heidi's help she now for the first time understood clearly the story of the continual pennies. Finally the grandmother said, "Heidi, read me a song of praise and thanksgiving! I feel like praising and glorifying our Lord in heaven and giving Him thanks for all that He has done for us."